Written in the Sand

R.J. Groves

Copyright © 2019 by R.J. Groves
Edited by Graham Toseland.
ISBN: 978 0 6452675 7 0
Groves Publishing
Formats available: eBook, Paperback

About the author

Australian author R.J. Groves has been passionate about writing since she could put pen to paper and can usually be found jotting plots and stories down on anything she can get her hands on. Describing herself as a mum, wife, author, and coffee lover, her other passions include music, cooking, books, adventures, and searching for plot bunnies in even the most mundane activities.

Facebook: facebook.com/rjgauthor
Instagram: instagram.com/r.j.groves_author
Twitter: twitter.com/rjg_author
Website: www.rjgrovesauthor.com

Books by R. J. Groves

The Bridal Shop series
Save the Date
Be My Valentine
Say You'll Be Mine

Jilted Brides series
Finding a Bride
Written in the Sand

Cities of the World series
In Paris
The Irish Maiden

Set Ups series
The Set Up

Mail Order Brides series
The Calm in the Storm

The Warmth in the Winter
The Song in the Silence

Standalones
Writing You
Two Babies Too Many
Second Chance
The Boyfriend Application
Sweeter Things
Home Bound
Stay With Me
Her First Noel
When Dreams Come True
To Fall For You

To my forever, for never giving up on me.

Written in the Sand

R.J. Groves

Chapter 1

There was a word for it. A word to describe something like this—when you're not sure if you're heartbroken, devastated, relieved, or just don't know how the hell you feel. When you're yet to shed a tear and feel like a fool for not seeing it coming.

Empty.

That's what she felt. It's also what her glass was. *Empty*.

Wren waved her hand to catch the bartender's attention, not taking her eyes off the bench. Her left hand still had the imprint of where her ring used to sit—a tan line determined to remind her of this day for the rest of her life.

'Another one, sweetheart?'

'Do you have to ask?'

She nudged her glass closer to the bartender and watched as he poured a shot of the amber liquid into her glass. He reached under the bench and pulled out a small bowl of mixed nuts, placing it in front of her.

'Eat something.'

He moved to the other end of the bar to serve another lonely soul, leaving her to think in peace. Just her, her drink, and a bowl of nuts. She scrunched her nose up at the bowl of nuts and pushed it to the side. She wasn't one to eat food with the same name as inappropriate body parts or anything that resembled them in any way. Nuts were out. And kiwi fruit was out just for looking like one.

She took a sip of her scotch, the smooth woody texture rolling around in her mouth before leaving a trail of fire down her throat and into her stomach. Already, she felt the mellowing effect. She swallowed the lump in her throat. She would *not* cry. She would *not* shed a tear for that asshole. She wouldn't give him the satisfaction. But to be honest, he probably didn't care. He'd played her like a fool and tossed her to the curb.

But she should have seen it coming. She was good at predicting outcomes. She was a social media marketer, with six years of experience in her marketing career. She was good at seeing what would come out of a situation. But this? She hadn't seen *this* coming. Maybe if she hadn't been so caught up on the whole plan of being married by the time she was thirty, she might have seen the signs.

And maybe that's why she wasn't so hung up on him. Sure, she was disappointed—disappointed that she would be thirty next year and no prospective husband in sight, that is—but she wasn't devastated. She wasn't heartbroken over him. Looking back on it, there really wasn't anything there. There couldn't have been. Not when she wasn't what he was interested in.

At least the rest of her life was on track. She had a nice nest egg of savings, a car that ran, a nice apartment with semi-affordable rent, and a good job. Well, the job was only going to get better. She'd been working her ass off for three years to line herself up for the marketing manager position. And now, there was actually a position available and her boss, Hans Durgan, knew that she wanted it. If anything, he'd made more hoops for her to jump through to prove her worthiness for the job. It was only a matter of time before he announced who the next marketing manager would be. But God, she was not a patient woman.

She downed the remainder of her scotch, shutting her eyes tightly as it burned down her throat. She wasn't one to drink those fruity or sweet drinks. Scotch was sophisticated. It was sharp and smooth at the same time. It didn't need to be mixed with anything to taste good. It practically represented her—sophisticated, sharp, independent. Her eyes still closed, she placed the empty glass back on the bar, and rested on her elbows. She heard a stirring in the pub behind her—a heated dispute of some kind—and she heard the bartender's raised voice moving towards the ruckus to break it up. But she wasn't bothered. In a few moments, they would calm down or at least take it outside where it wouldn't disturb her.

'You know, a scotch drinker would know that scotch should be savoured, not downed in one go.'

Her eyes shot open and she stared into eyes the colour of grey marble that flashed with amusement. She examined the features sporting the eyes—tussled ash brown hair that was a couple inches long, slightly tanned skin, a defined square jaw with the best damn three-day growth she'd ever seen, and lips curved into a mischievous grin that made her heart skip a beat. He was resting on his elbows on the bar, so he was level with her, his broad shoulders and biceps bulging underneath his black tight-fitting shirt.

'Ahh,' she said, regaining her composure. 'But a *true* scotch drinker knows that the first drink is to be savoured, and the rest to get drunk.'

'And who said that?'

'I did.' She pushed her glass towards him. 'Hit me.'

His grin widened as he pushed off the bench with his hands and grabbed the bottle from behind him. She took a moment while he wasn't looking to appreciate his masculine back and very defined ass and legs that his jeans fit snugly. Hey, she was back on the market now, right? She could look at whoever the hell she pleased. He placed a fresh glass next to hers and poured a shot into each of them. He nudged hers back towards her and raised the other one in a toast.

'To getting drunk,' he said.

She clinked her glass against his and they both downed the liquid. He poured another shot into their glasses and put the bottle back on the shelf.

'So, tell me what we're celebrating,' he said.

***

Nate had just finished his last shift at the pub when he saw her take a seat at the bar. Wavy chin-length hair the colour of champagne, a body that made any man take a second glance at her, and dressed in a black knee-length skirt, white buttoned shirt, and a navy-blue jacket that was long enough to cover her ass—it near on pulled him towards her. From the other end of the bar, he'd watched her drink her first drink slowly—twelve-year-old single malt scotch whisky—and watched as she downed the second drink. He liked a woman who could handle her whisky. But he hadn't expected her to drink it like it was a shot. When he saw Russ—his best friend and now ex-colleague—move towards the ruckus at the back of the room, he took his chance to meet this intriguing woman who caught his eye.

She was even better up close.

Beautiful couldn't even begin to describe what she was. The way her long eyelashes had rested against her cheeks when he'd come over to her, her striking eyes that were like looking into the deep blue of the ocean, the soothing tone of her voice as she countered his remark, the look she gave him when she wanted another drink. She was something. She was enough to make a man's mind run in circles and have him at her mercy. She was the most incredible creature he'd ever laid eyes on.

'I'm supposed to be getting married tomorrow,' she replied, her eyebrow raised into a perfect arc, examining the glass between her hands.

Her answer felt like a knife being pushed through his chest. He'd been selective with women—always had been. He wanted to be the kind of guy who'd treat a woman right. Sure, he'd had a couple of one-night stands in the past and been on a few bad first dates. But he always had one rule: he would never get involved with someone who was already in a relationship. That was guaranteed to get messy. But something about this woman made him want to forget any rule he ever had.

His eyes dropped to her left hand. There was a faint line where a ring used to sit, but no ring. Then, he realised that she hadn't said that she *was* getting married tomorrow.

'What happened?' he urged.

She sighed. 'He decided it would be a good idea to elope, instead.'

'I take it you didn't?'

Her other eyebrow joined the one that was already raised. 'Oh, I didn't. He did.'

Nate shook his head slowly, squinting,

questioning. Was this going to be one of those cliché he-ran-off-with-my-best-friend stories he'd heard so many times in his years of working at the bar?

'With a man,' she finished, taking a sip of her scotch while it sunk in.

'Oh.'

Oh. So, a bit of a different twist to the cliché story he'd heard. But God, wouldn't the guy have worked it out before getting engaged and planning a wedding with someone he's not even interested in?

She let out a breath. 'Yeah,' she said, twirling the glass between her hands again. 'I really should have seen it coming though. I mean, he used to fix up my outfits and my hair and makeup. He had a real knack for anything design.' She shook her head. 'I should have suspected it when I realised he knew more colours than I did.'

'Why didn't you?'

She shrugged. 'I guess I was just caught up in the whole plan to be married by the time I'm thirty.' She leaned back spreading her arms to the side, her top few buttons that were undone granting him a glimpse of her cleavage. 'But here I am—almost thirty and I got stood up by a gay guy.' She dropped her gaze into her lap. 'Show's how good my taste in men is.'

'Well, he's a bastard for leading you on. But I'm sorry it didn't work out,' he said, though he knew he was lying. If anything, he was grateful it didn't work out. It gave him a chance to meet her. That wasn't selfish, right?

'It's not your fault,' she said, fluttering her eyelashes at him. 'At least my career is more promising than my love life. I'm due for a promotion, so that should keep my mind busy.'

'What do you do?'

'I'm a social media marketing manager for now,' she said, her eyes flashing. 'But I'm hoping that will change soon enough. I've waited too long for it.'

'I'm sure you'll get it,' he said. 'You do drink scotch, after all. My bets are you'd have it over any other person you're up against.'

'Just because I drink scotch?' Her eyes were questioning, challenging.

He nodded. 'What you drink says a lot about you.'

'And what *does* it say about me?' She was leaning on her elbows, her hands propped under her chin. He had a better view of her cleavage, and he struggled to hold onto his train of thought.

'Well, scotch is a sophisticated drink,' he started, leaning on his own elbows, and trying to keep his gaze from dropping away from her eyes. 'It has a certain distinction to it and would often be thought as a manly drink. But a woman who drinks it—she's strong, independent, always up for a challenge, gets the job done, and doesn't let anything get her down.'

Her mouth dropped open slightly, and he could see her jaw moving slightly as if trying to say something but not quite getting it out. Her head tilted to the side, examining him. Then, her lips curved into a smile.

'It says all that?' she said. He was sure he caught

a flirty tone in her voice.

He nodded, a smile of his own spreading across his face. Who was this woman? And why the hell was he so drawn to her that he was doing stupid things? Like standing behind the bar he no longer worked at, serving drinks to a pretty woman sitting by herself. He heard a throat clear and turned to see Russ standing next to him, his arms crossed over his chest.

'Have you forgotten you don't work here anymore, Nate?'

He slapped his hand on Russ's shoulder. 'Just filling in for you while you dealt with'—he waved his hand in the direction of where the fight was—'that. I couldn't let this lovely lady wait for her drink, could I?'

'You know the rules. Staff only behind the bar.' Russ pointed across the bar. 'Move it.'

'Aww, don't be like that, Russ,' Nate said. He spread his arms out to the side. 'What if my life depended on it?'

'It doesn't. But my *job* depends on it.'

'Wait, you don't work here?' She was staring straight at him, the flash in her eyes somewhere between surprise and amusement.

'Oh, no, I did. I just finished my last shift,' he said. 'Russ is just sad because I'm leaving him.'

'You've already been replaced, Nate, by someone much prettier than you.' Wow, they moved quick. He liked to think he was a little more … irreplaceable. 'Now, before every man and his dog wants to come behind the bar.' He shook his hand to emphasise that he was still pointing across the bar.

He glanced at the woman at the bar, still very much amused with the interaction, plucked the half-empty bottle of scotch from the shelf, and slid across the bar, somehow landing himself next to the woman.

'I hope you're going to pay for that,' Russ said, his arms crossed again, his head shaking slowly.

'Take it out of my last paycheck,' he said, winking. He reached his hand out towards the woman who'd caught his eye. 'Shall we?'

He wasn't sure if he'd been expecting her to take his hand or not, but when he felt the warmth of her hand in his and the shock it sent through his body, he was glad that she did.

***

'I have to admit, that was some stunt you pulled,' Wren said, walking along the street next to Nate. 'I think you genuinely pissed him off.'

His side grin brought a blush to her cheeks. She didn't even know why she left with this guy. Sure, he took the scotch that she was drinking, so there wasn't much point in her staying behind. But she didn't have to leave *with* him. What were they to do now? There was just something about his overly flirtatious manner and in the way he looked at her that made her feel something with him—connected. Granted, she was most likely drunk. But she didn't think that clouded her judgement. Besides, she was sober when she met Griffin, and look how that turned out.

'I don't think so,' he said, his shoulder bumping against hers as they walked. 'Russ is my best friend—I know not to push him too far.'

She laughed, staring at the pavement in front of them. 'I guess that explains it then,' she teased. 'So, tell me, what are you planning on doing now that you don't work there?'

'Actually, I'm in marketing, too,' he said. 'I start a new job on Monday. I worked at the bar while I worked on my Masters. Wasn't really in the field, but it paid the bills.'

'Nate from Marketing,' Wren said. 'It's got a good ring to it.'

'I don't think I caught your name,' he said, stopping, his eyes on her.

'Wren.'

Another smile tugged at his lips. 'Wren,' he repeated as if rolling the name around in his mouth. 'I like it. Are your parents birdwatchers?'

'If you count watching them from their breakfast spot on the porch,' she said. 'The superb fairywren was my mother's favourite. She died while giving birth to me, and Dad wanted to give me a name that she would be proud of. So, why not name me after her favourite bird?'

His eyes sobered, his brow furrowed. 'I'm sorry to hear it.'

'Dad and I have done just fine,' she said.

Though, if she were being honest, not having her

mother around was the hardest thing she'd ever had to deal with. Sure, she never knew her, but maybe that was worse than knowing her for a while before losing her. She had no memories of her to fall back on. And the thought that she'd caused her mother's death had crossed her mind on more than one occasion.

'Well, Wren from Marketing,' he said, nodding towards the door behind her. 'This is me.' Wait, *what?* Had she just walked him home? How very gentlemanly of her. He held the bottle of scotch up between them. 'And I've got half a bottle of scotch that I have plans for.'

He took a step closer towards her, their faces inches apart. She felt her back press against the cold hard timber of the door and heard the jingle of his keys as he pulled them out of his pocket and placed one in the lock. She could feel her breath quicken and a tingle radiate from her core to the rest of her body.

'Am I drinking it alone, or will you be joining me?'

She could smell the scotch lingering in his breath, mixing with a hint of mint and something totally irresistible that she couldn't quite place her finger on. A breeze picked up, blowing her hair across her face, but his hand beat hers. His fingertips brushed against her cheek as he tucked her hair behind her ear and followed the trail down her neck and back up to gently lift her chin towards him.

He wasn't talking about the whisky.

But judging from the quiver she felt in her legs

just from his touch and the overwhelming desire of need and want pulsing through her, her mind was already made up—even if she couldn't form a single coherent thought.

'I could go for another drink,' she whispered.

She saw the flash in his eyes and the quick smile cross his face right before his lips were on hers. The satisfyingly smooth taste of the scotch lingered on his lips, mixed with a hint of copper and something authentically him—something sweet, tender. Pure. She could blame it on the fact she hadn't really been with a man for a long time—things with Griffin were never *that* advanced—but she wanted more of him. She parted her lips, letting him inside. He didn't hesitate, his tongue teasing hers with smooth deliberate movements. She felt his hand leave her chin, but his lips pressed against her harder, more desperate. She wrapped her arms around his neck, inviting him for more, and heard the *click* of the door unlocking, feeling the cool against her back as the door opened.

They manoeuvred inside, a few uncoordinated steps—she would have stumbled if Nate hadn't kept her on her feet. Their lips still locked, Nate kicked the door closed and placed the scotch on the hall table, pressing her against the wall and sliding his hands up her back to tangle in her hair, exposing her neck for his kisses. It felt good—his touches, his kisses, his body pressing against hers. With each kiss, her legs grew a little weaker, and the moan that had been building in her chest escaped through her lips.

She wanted him.

And she wanted him *now*.

'Nate,' she urged.

'Hold on.'

He grasped the back of her thighs and lifted her effortlessly. She wrapped her legs around his waist and pressed her lips to his again as he carried her to his room. She felt, rather than heard, the rumble at the base of his throat and, before she knew it, she was laying on his bed, each item of clothing hitting the wall as it came off, his body against hers. The warmth of their bodies moving together, the fervour in their kisses, the tenderness he showed. It all felt … right.

It was the best damn whisky she'd ever had.

And it scared the hell out of her.

Chapter 2

She was gone.

Nate leaned against the doorframe, staring at the tussled sheets on his bed, and took a sip of his coffee. He chuckled at the thought that he'd just had a one-night stand with a sexy woman. Russ would be proud. But then, he sobered. He hadn't *wanted* to just sleep with this woman and send her on her way, never to see her again. What they'd done was something different to what he'd had with other women. With her, it was entirely unique, closer to what he would actually call making love. He wanted to get to know her, take her on a date, start fresh. Maybe see if they had something.

It sure as hell felt like they could last night.

But it clearly wasn't what she was thinking.

He must have read the signs all wrong. He must have thought there was something there that wasn't. God, when had he ever been bad at reading signals? Maybe she'd just distracted him from thinking rationally or logically. Or maybe, she was cunning enough to play him without him realising it. He chuckled to himself. That would be the first time he's been played. And she was most definitely a worthy opponent. If Russ found *that* out …

'Judging from this bottle, things either went really well or terribly wrong.'

Nate blinked, turning his head to see his friend standing next to him, holding up the bottle of whisky that had been sitting on the hall table all night. 'How do you keep getting in here?'

He moved back towards the kitchen to top up his coffee—and so Russ didn't pick up on what he'd been thinking.

'You gave me a key, remember?' Russ said, following him and putting the whisky on the bench.

'To use in *emergencies*,' Nate said, pouring the dark liquid into a fresh cup, and topping up his. He handed the fresh cup to Russ. 'I'd take it back off you if I didn't need a backup key somewhere.'

Russ took the cup, shaking a finger at him. 'This *is* an emergency,' he said. He spread his arms out, indicating towards the whisky. 'My best friend left the bar with a bottle of whisky and a pretty girl. I had to make sure you got laid. And since you did, it's no longer an emergency.'

Nate shook his head. 'What makes you think I got

laid?'

'I can smell it.'

'You can't smell it,' Nate said, pinching the bridge of his nose with his thumb and forefinger.

The coffee was slowly starting to ease the throbbing ache in his head. He wondered if Wren felt the same. *Wren.* Her name intrigued him. He'd never met someone with that name before. It was unique, yet, strangely, suited her perfectly. Too bad he didn't even have a last name to go with it or any chance of finding her—women rarely frequent the same bar after a one-night stand, according to Russ.

'I can smell sex a mile away,' Russ said, sipping his coffee. Considering Russ was a bit of a player, Nate had no doubt about that. 'And you, sir, had sex. So, did you get her number, or kick her out?'

'Neither,' Nate mumbled.

Russ looked at him blankly. 'Well, it has to be one or the other. She's not here, so did you kick her out?'

He shook his head. 'She left on her own,' he said. '*Before* I could get her number.'

'Ahh, so the legends are true.'

'What legends?'

'That there *are* players in the female world.'

'I'm not sure she's a player,' Nate said.

'What were you doing when she left?'

Nate shrugged. 'Having a shower.'

'Did she have a shower?'

Nate's brow furrowed. 'No, she was asleep when I hopped in.'

'Did she tell you she was leaving?'

Nate shook his head. She hadn't said anything to him. She hadn't waited for him to finish in the shower—even though he was only in for a few minutes. Heck, she didn't even wait for the sun to come up.

Russ nodded. 'Player.' He picked up the bottle of whisky. 'I guess you won't be needing this anymore.'

'I'm keeping that bottle,' Nate said, sipping his coffee, staring at the bench. Either Wren regretted sleeping with him so much that she didn't want him contacting her ever again, or Russ was right.

She's a player.

***

'All right, I'm here. What's the emergency?'

Kassandra placed her sunglasses on top of her head and seated herself opposite Wren in *HotSpot*—the café she frequented that had the best coffee within walking distance and an all-day breakfast menu. Wren was already on her second coffee by the time her best friend—and work colleague—got there. To be honest, she'd rather have something a bit stronger than coffee, but it was a bit early for that.

'I had sex.'

Kassandra stared at her blankly, blinking slowly. 'You dragged me out of bed early on a Saturday morning to tell me *that*?'

Wren looked at her watch. 'It's not early, it's … nine.'

'On a Saturday!'

'Well, I was hungry.'

'Clearly! You obviously worked up an appetite. So … was it good?' She waggled her eyebrows.

Was it good? Of course it was good. It was *too* good. Way too good for a one-night stand. But that's all it was. At least, that's what she gathered when he snuck off for a shower without saying anything.

Wren didn't speak but felt the heat spreading to her cheeks. She smiled and lifted her eyes—an attempt at making her answer obvious. Kassandra's brow creased.

'What was that?' she said, waving her hand towards Wren.

'What?'

'That weird look you just pulled.'

Wren pointed to her face and tried to replicate the look. 'That?' Kassandra nodded. 'I was just—'

'No.'

'No?'

Kassandra shook her head. 'We really need to work on your expressions, Wren. How on earth did you manage to find someone to sleep with?' Her eyes widened. 'Wait, weren't you supposed to be getting married today? You move fast, girl.'

'It's not my fault that Griffin couldn't work out which way he swung until a week before the wedding.'

'And you decided to celebrate your new-found freedom by *having sex* the night before you were supposed to get married?'

Wren shrugged. 'I was … drunk. It's not like I planned to hook up with anyone. I just felt like a few drinks.'

'Alone?'

Wren nodded.

Kassandra rested her head in her palms, her elbows on the table, and shook her head. 'You *are* bad at this, aren't you?' She dropped her hands, refocussing on Wren. 'All good, though. You were with Griffin for a long time and there wasn't much happening there. It's natural to overlook these things when you've been out of practice.'

Wren scoffed. 'You would know.'

'I know how to work the bars, Wren, *and* the men.'

'I don't need to know details.'

'You do if you're going to jump back into this.'

'I'd rather *ease* back in,' Wren mumbled.

'Bit late for that, honey,' Kassandra said, flashing a mischievous grin. 'I'll teach you everything you need to know. Starting with this new guy. Name?'

'Nate.'

'Nate, who?'

'Nate from Marketing.'

'Nate from … *what*? You didn't get his last name?'

'No.'

'Phone number?'

Wren shook her head. How could she? He didn't give her a chance to.

Kassandra rubbed her forehead. 'So, let me get this straight. You met a guy. You had some drinks with him. You had *sex* with him—*good* sex. And you have no way of contacting him or knowing who he is?'

Wren shrugged slowly. 'Well, I might be able to find his house again,' she mumbled. 'Or the bartender! The bartender is his best friend, I could—'

'No.'

Her brow furrowed. They were the only two ways of getting in touch with the guy. How else was she to contact him? If she wanted to, that is. But she'd got the signal that he didn't want anything more, so what would be the point of it?

Kassandra sighed. 'You can't just go around trying to find him. That's stalkerish.'

'Maybe he doesn't want to be found.'

'How did it end?'

'Kass!'

'The night, Wren, when you left! What did you think I meant?'

Wren shook her head. She'd learned to jump to the dirty conclusion around Kassandra—it was what she was getting at most times. 'He didn't say anything,' Wren said. 'He just went and had a shower. So, I left.'

'Did you say anything?'

Wren shook her head. Should she have? Should she have asked him if he wanted her to leave? She thought it was just the done thing—that the girl was supposed to leave while he had a shower. That's what always happened in the movies, at least. Besides, even though it was *really* good for her, maybe it hadn't been for him. Maybe it was best that she had no way of contacting him, and he had no way of contacting her.

That way, she couldn't be disappointed.

She couldn't make a fool of herself.

And she could move on with her life.

'Well, congratulations, Wren,' Kassandra said, her eyes teasing. 'You just had your first real one-night stand.'

Wren forced a smile, but her chest felt heavy and she'd lost her appetite. She sipped her coffee while Kassandra ordered one for herself. How was she supposed to do the whole finding-a-guy thing? It had never been much of a priority for her. She didn't even have the faintest clue of where to start. But, at least, she was starting the next chapter on a high. A very … *big* … high. She sipped her coffee again, hoping Kassandra didn't see her cheeks redden. How could she keep moving forward when her mind was on a guy she didn't know?

'So,' Kassandra said, refocussing on Wren after the waitress left. 'How *did* it end?'

***

Monday couldn't have come quicker. Wren had made sure she kept herself busy over the weekend and far away from bars—any bars. *Especially* Nate's bar. Somewhere over the weekend, she'd started thinking of it as his bar. Obviously, it would be one he'd frequent. He'd worked there before, his best friend was still there, and he probably just liked the bar. Heck, it was a nice bar. *She* liked it. But she couldn't go there. Not if he didn't want to see her again. And if she did go there and happen to accidentally bump into him, how would she be able to look at him without remembering their night together?

Memories of his touch and their … intimacy … had reappeared in her dreams, and she'd even found her mind drifting in that direction when she was well and truly awake. Just the thought of him sent a blush to her cheeks. She had no hope of concealing it if she ever saw him again. What would be the courtesy, anyway? Do they ignore each other? Do they say hello, ask how things have been and move on? Kassandra was right—she *was* bad at this. But she didn't exactly fancy the idea of getting advice from Kassandra—she was the true female version of a player, though she preferred to say she was just having a bit of fun.

Wren scoffed. She would bet any day that Kassandra had a bit of fun with it. In fact, she *knew* that she had a *lot* of fun if her stories were anything to go by.

'Wren, what are you still doing in here?'

'Hmm?'

'The meeting,' Kassandra said as if reminding her. Wren looked at her questioningly. 'Did no one tell you about the meeting? Shoot. Durgan's announcing the position in a few. Hurry up.'

Wren's eyes widened. 'The position? *The*

position?'

'Yes, Wren. The one you've been working for. Looks like he's just going to announce it in front of everyone. Come on.'

Wren sprung to her feet and followed Kassandra out of her office. She didn't know Durgan was going to be announcing it today—and with no warning! She thought he would have at least talked to her before announcing it in front of everyone, but if this was how he wanted to do it …

'God, everyone's here,' Kassandra mumbled.

She was right. Durgan was making the announcement in the big room with all the open offices where all the new people start when they first get employed at *Stanza Marketing Agency*—it was the only room that could fit all of their employees. Wren felt the nervousness in the pit of her stomach. This was the promotion she'd been waiting for—the one she'd been working so hard for, jumping through hoops, and working ten times harder than anyone else in this building. She heard Durgan talking, and Kassandra grabbed her wrist, pulling her against the wall to get closer to the front of the room. Her eyes were on her boss, and as she neared the front of the room, his eyes flicked towards her, lingering for a moment, stalling his speech, before he focussed on the rest of the room.

What was that look about? She'd expected a smile, the kind of look a boss gives someone he's about to promote. But that look hadn't come. Durgan cleared his throat.

'You've all been waiting for this announcement long enough, so I won't take any more of your time,' he started. 'I know that many of you have been working hard for the marketing manager position, but unfortunately, there was only one spot available.'

Many? She scanned the room. She wasn't sure who else showed interest in it, but she was the only one who was remotely qualified to do the position.

'So, without further ado, meet your new Marketing Manager—' She took a step forward. 'Mr Hoffman.'

Mr *who*? She stopped in her tracks, watching as he moved from the front of the crowd to stand by Durgan. And that's when she saw the face she thought she'd never see again. The same square jaw sporting the same three-day growth that he clearly maintained, the same smile that made her heart flip. She grabbed hold of Kassandra's arm, pulling her back towards the wall.

'Wren?' Kassandra's face showed nothing but concern. She knew what that promotion meant to Wren, and since she didn't get it … but Kassandra didn't know the half of it.

'N—Nate,' she whispered, not taking her eyes off the man who stole her promotion.

'Your Nate?'

She nodded, unable to form any words. Her Nate? Hardly. The Nate who she'd slept with, thought she'd never see again, and who *stole her promotion*? Abso-freaking-lutely. She heard

Kassandra swear under her breath and try to pull her back, but she wouldn't budge. Not until she'd had a chance to tell Hans Durgan *exactly* how she felt about having her promotion swiped out from under her.

***

Nate had been looking forward to starting his new job—to actually be utilising his degree in a well-renowned company. He'd spent a lot of time swapping between making sure he was ready for this job and thinking about that night with Wren. He'd succumbed to the fact that he'd probably never see her again, even if that night was the best night of his life. At least the memory of her would never be tainted. But he also wasn't sure he could feel the same connection with anyone else.

He focussed on the crowd standing in front of him and waited for the claps to end. He'd expected that there would be a few disgruntled employees who weren't happy with Hans Durgan hiring from outside of the company for this position, but he also knew they'd get over it. Eventually. But as he scanned the room, he didn't see any disgruntled employees.

'Would you like to say a few words?' Durgan prompted.

Nate cleared his throat. He was never good at speeches, but he could not let himself fail at giving one within the first hour of his new job. Especially one where he'd be required to give speeches from time to time. God, he hadn't thought *that* part through when he decided to study marketing.

'Good morning, all,' he started, scanning the room slowly. Eye contact—he'd read it was important in speech making. 'Hans tells me that I've come at a busy time, but I trust that you'll all be patient with me as I learn the swing of things. But I—' he stalled when he saw her and could practically feel the shards boring through him.

Wren.

The Wren. The sexy woman he'd slept with and had left without a trace before he could get her number. What the hell was she doing here? And why was she giving him that look? She. Looked. Pissed. She clearly recognised him. Why else would she be glaring at him like that? Unless …

His mind drifted back to that night and he felt his heart drop. *The promotion.* She'd talked about hoping to get a promotion soon. Was that …? *Shoot.*

'Aww hell,' he breathed, hoping no one else heard. She was hoping to get this job. *His* job. The one that she'd been working hard for and he took out from underneath her. It was only a matter of time before the bombshell that was her would go off, he was sure of it. He took a deep breath, suddenly feeling not as confident in his speech. 'I … umm … I'm looking forward to working with each of you and getting to know you *all* on a … professional … basis. Thank you.'

'Mr Durgan, I need to talk to you.'

Nate felt his body stiffen as he heard her voice. She didn't just look pissed. She *was* pissed. And she had every right to be. But not at him. How was he to know that he was taking the job that she'd worked hard for? The crowd was dissipating from around them, and he kept his focus on Wren, but she refused to look at him. She was tunnel visioned on Durgan.

Durgan's wide eyes flicked towards Nate before focussing on Wren as she came to a halt in front of them. 'Wren! I was wondering when you'd—'

'What the *hell*, Durgan?' she yelled, throwing her arms in the air. '*Everyone* knows I've been working my ass off for that job, and you'd rather give it to some *random* than someone who knows the company inside out?'

Durgan put his hands out, facing his palms towards her. 'I assure you that Nate is not just a random, Wren. He's qualified for the position.'

'So am I!'

Durgan sighed. 'Look, Wren, the truth is I need you where you are.'

Wren's eyes widened, and she blinked once. 'Are you freaking *kidding* me?'

Her voice reached a pitch that was higher than what sounded normal. Nate felt like he should say something, but what could he say? It's not like he was going to quit the job he just started. And he was fairly sure that anything he had to say would fall on deaf ears.

'You're the best social media manager I've ever

had, Wren,' Durgan said. 'I can't afford to not have you in that position.'

Ouch. Nate's eyes widened, and Wren looked like she'd had the wind knocked out of her as she processed what Durgan just said. If only there was something that Nate could say or do to make her feel better about this arrangement. But there was nothing. Nothing would make her happy about not getting the promotion she'd been working towards.

'Now, I've made a decision,' Durgan continued. 'And I have things to do. So, if you need anything else, take it up with your new marketing manager.'

Durgan left without another word. Wren still looked … shocked. He ached to make her feel better, but he knew he was at a total loss to do so. He didn't know this woman. Sure, he'd slept with her. But he didn't *know* her. He only knew the drunk version that was disappointed about being jilted. He only knew the shape of her body and the way she moved against him—like she hadn't been loved in a long time. This woman standing in front of him was something else. This was a woman who most definitely regretted sleeping with him. But he'd never regret that night.

'Wren,' he said, reaching out to touch her arm without thinking.

She shook him off. '*Don't* touch me.'

He placed his palms out in surrender. 'I didn't know you worked here.'

'And I don't care,' she said flatly.

Her eyes bore through him with a look that didn't

suit her. He preferred the look she'd given him that night much more than this. He'd take desire over despise any day. She spun on her heel, her hair swishing, and stormed away from him, a woman with a dark high ponytail falling into step beside her.

He exhaled, realising he must have been holding onto his breath. He was certainly in for a rough ride.

Chapter 3

Wren tapped her fingers on her desk, staring at her computer screen. She was never up for the promotion. Durgan had never even *considered* her for that position. He'd always wanted her to stay exactly where she was.

So, why the hell had she been working her ass off for so long to get it?

Had Durgan simply thought that she was good at her job? That she was happy where she was? Sure, she didn't *hate* her position, but she also wasn't a big fan of it, even if she *was* the best this company had ever had at it. She'd worked her way up from the bottom, and now she was stuck. With no future promotion in sight. No chance for progression.

And Nate in the position she always wanted.

He'd be a fool to leave a job that good. Which is why he'd probably never leave. And she'd be an idiot to leave her job, especially with how scarce job opportunities were on the Gold Coast. And there was no guarantee that the next job would be as well-paying and good as this one had been. There was no working around it. She would have to see Nate every day that she was here. And she wouldn't have to simply *see* him, she'd have to work closely with him. *Very* closely. Especially since he was the head of the managers. He was technically her new boss.

Wren groaned.

Trust her luck that the only guy she's ever slept with without at least going on a few dates first was now her boss. She was starting to regret her decision to sleep with that nice, funny guy from the bar, even if it had been good at the time. Truth is, she still felt it. When she felt his eyes resting on her—she felt the wave it sent through her body. The way he said her name. The way she couldn't even *look* at him without her cheeks reddening and her stomach flipping at the sheer sexiness of his face. The way his touch sent a pulse through her body that should definitely, most certainly, absolutely *not* be there.

She rubbed her eyes, taking a deep breath. She had to work this out. She had to put on a brave face. She had no choice but to work with him, and she *had* to keep things professional. Workplace relationships can end very badly, and even worse the closer the professional relationship is. And Wren and Nate would be working together much more often than she was comfortable with.

'Bad timing?'

His voice startled her, and she banged her knee against the desk. She clenched her jaw to keep from crying out in pain. Even though it hurt like hell. She rubbed the throbbing on her knee and glared at him.

'What do you think?'

He moved closer to the desk and she bit her tongue, reconsidering her initial thought of telling him to leave. 'I think we got off on the wrong foot.'

She scoffed, then cleared her throat. God, why did she have little control over her reactions with him? It had never been a problem before. She shifted some papers around her desk to make herself look busy, even though she knew it was just making more of a mess. 'Well, you *did* steal my promotion.'

His brow furrowed. 'I didn't—' he sighed. 'I only applied to a job that was being advertised. I didn't even expect to get it and I'd applied well before I met you.'

She felt her heart drop. 'He … he advertised?'

He nodded. Wren took a deep breath, focussing back on the papers in front of her. Durgan had always intended to hire someone outside of the company. Why else would he have advertised? Her vision started blurring, but she blinked back the tears. She had to keep her brave face on. She couldn't let Nate see how that news affected her.

He rested his hands on the back of the chair opposite her desk, leaning forward a little. 'I know this isn't … ideal,' he said. 'But we have to work together, and I need you to show me the ins and outs of this job, especially since—'

'Since I've been doing your job for the last few months?' He nodded. 'What makes you think I want to help you?'

'I don't,' he said. 'But I need someone to show me the ropes and, according to Durgan, you're the best there is.'

'But apparently not good enough,' she mumbled.

He sighed. 'What can I do to make this easier?'

'You can quit and make sure I get your job.'

She never intended to *actually* say it, but she did, and she wasn't sure how she felt about it. There was a little bit of wishing she hadn't said it, but there was also the satisfaction that she had. He stared blankly at her for a moment.

'That's not happening.'

She spread her hands out across the desk. 'Then, there's nothing you can do.'

She busied herself with clicking on her computer—mainly making the mouse cursor make squares across the desktop which was surprisingly satisfying—but she could still feel his eyes on her. It was … unnerving.

'What if I got you a pay rise?'

Her eyes flicked up towards him. 'Not even three hours on the job and you already want to pay me out? Sorry, Nate. You can't buy me.'

His jaw clenched, and she was certain that she saw a muscle twitch. Sure, it may have been a bit of a jab at their night together, but she couldn't help it.

He brought out the worst in her.

'Oh, I wouldn't want to.'

His response surprised her. What the hell was that supposed to mean?

'But it's not a payout,' he continued. 'You wanted this job, you didn't get it. I did. The least I can do is negotiate for a pay rise for you because you *deserve* it. Not because I'm trying to be nice or make up to you or whatever. Because that's not what I'm trying to do. Just remember that *you* are the one who left without a trace, not me.' He pushed off the chair and headed towards the door.

'You're nothing but a player.'

Nate scoffed, his stare cold. 'Funny, I was going to say the same thing about you. Be in my office in an hour, no later.'

She pressed her lips together, trying her best to keep herself together. 'I want to forget it ever happened.'

He paused by the door, glancing back at her. His expression was still cold, but there was something else there—something she couldn't quite place.

'I don't.'

***

She knew how to get on his nerves.

She knew how to find that one spot to keep picking at that would drive him mad. And it all came back to that blasted night. She thought *he* was the player?

Nate rubbed his chin, feeling the stubble against his palm. How the hell was he going to get out of this one? He just had to make it through the day. And the next. And the next. And every damn day until either she moved on or he found somewhere else to work. But the thing is, he'd been looking for months for a job like this, and they just do not exist. The chance of another coming up anytime soon was incredibly slim.

She puzzled him, confused the hell out of him. He was sure there'd been something else there that night, something special. And he'd hoped it'd still be there if he ever saw her again. But here they were, working with each other, and she clearly hated his guts. He didn't blame her. He *did* take the bottle of whisky that she'd been drinking from home with him. He may have *hoped* that she would have joined him inside. But what happened after that was out of his control. That was two people wanting the same thing, and there was no denying that.

But now? It was like that person didn't exist. The whole idea of being someone totally different when drunk definitely applied to Wren. He would never regret something so incredible as that night. But she did. And that only meant it wasn't as good for her as it had been for him. He pushed down the hallway and banged his fist against the door before opening it and walking into Durgan's office like he owned the place. *He* was the one that really had some making up to do, and Nate was going to make sure it happened.

'Nate, everything all right?' Durgan's eyes were

wide. 'Usually my employees wait for a response before barging into the room.'

'We need to talk,' he said, coming to a halt at the desk. 'About Wren.'

Durgan nodded slowly and indicated to the seat next to Nate. He sat. 'Honestly, I didn't think she'd take it so hard. She usually gets over things quickly.'

'You gave her job to someone else. How did you think she'd react?'

'Are you saying you don't want it because it hurt someone's feelings? You'll have to toughen up, Nate, if that's what you're worried about because that's what this type of job involves.'

Nate shook his head. 'I'm saying that she deserves more. She's been working hard for a promotion that you had no intention of giving her.'

Durgan's eyes narrowed. 'How do you know that?'

Because she said it right before he slept with her. 'People talk when you look like you don't know what's going on.'

'I was going to give it to her,' Durgan said, leaning back in his chair. '*If* I couldn't find someone else. Which I did.' He indicated towards Nate. 'And I hope you're not going to make me regret that decision.'

Nate's chest tightened, but he kept his poker face on. 'She should be rewarded for her hard work.'

'As the new marketing manager, what do you propose?'

'A pay rise.'

'That's not happening.'

'You want your employees to respect you, don't you? Rewarding hard work is what will get you that.'

'Is this speaking from experience?'

'In a manner of speaking,' Nate said, shrugging. 'Recognising and rewarding hard work ensures longevity and keeping morale high. Right now, Wren needs recognition, even if she didn't get this job.' He rose to his feet, straightening his suit jacket. 'She'll be in my office in less than an hour and you know what I want to hear.'

Durgan studied him for a moment. 'You better not make a habit of this, Hoffman.'

Nate nodded his head, heading towards the door. 'I'm only doing what should have already been done.'

He didn't know if it would work. He didn't know how generous Durgan would be in showing appreciation for Wren's hard work. And he had no idea how well it would go down with her. His aim was to at least call a truce with Wren. But lack of recognition to people who worked hard was a pet peeve of his. He'd always promised himself to make changes if he ever had the power to do so. Now he did. But he also hadn't expected the person he'd be advocating for to be someone who regretted sleeping with him.

***

'I don't need your charity!' Wren stormed into his office—two minutes past the hour he gave her—

looking almost as pissed as she had when she realised she didn't get the promotion.

'You're late,' he mumbled.

She pointed his finger at him. 'Yes, and that's *your* fault. I would have been on time if Durgan hadn't pulled me into his office.'

He lifted his eyes up towards her. 'What did he say?'

She flopped into the seat across from his desk. 'Oh, not much,' she said sarcastically. 'Except that he's giving me a *pay rise*.'

'Good.'

'*Good*?' she repeated. 'Didn't you hear what I said before? You. Can't. Buy. Me.'

'I'm not trying to,' he said, putting his pen down and focussing on her.

'Then why the *hell* did you negotiate for a pay rise when I told you not to?'

'Because you deserve it, Wren, which is what *I* told you before.'

'Oh, I know I deserve it,' she said curtly.

'Then why would you be so upset about getting a little extra money?' He could feel his heart quickening, frustration nudging him closer to the edge. Why did it have to be a big deal? Why couldn't she just be thankful and move on?

'Because …' She diverted her gaze, her brow furrowed. 'I … I didn't want it to come from you.'

'It came from Durgan, not me.'

'But it was *because* of you.'

He studied her for a moment. She'd relaxed into

her chair a little, though she still looked stressed. Exhausted, even. God, no wonder she was a totally different person in the bar. She was actually able to let her guard down for a little.

'I didn't do it because of …' He tilted his head, hoping that she understood what he was saying. The blush creeping to her cheeks confirmed it. He cleared his throat. 'I'd do it for anyone who didn't get recognised for their hard work. It's … kind of my thing. And hopefully, I've shown Durgan how important recognition is and I won't have to keep reminding him. It just happened that my first advocacy case turned out to be you.'

She stared at him for a moment, as if considering everything he was saying. She hesitated, but she held his gaze with those intense blue eyes that he hadn't been able to resist that night at the bar. He felt something stir within him and squashed the feeling. It wasn't the time or the place, but God, it would be hard to resist her.

'So …' she started, hesitantly. 'It had … *nothing* … to do with that … umm … *thing* … we did?'

He shook his head. He couldn't promise that everything he did would have nothing to do with that night, but he could guarantee that that particular issue didn't. At least, not entirely.

She sighed, leaning back in her chair. 'Good.'

'Good.'

***

Good.

Because the last thing she wanted was any kind of pity or apology payout, especially when it came to her work. She didn't want handouts. She worked hard to get to where she is. And she still couldn't shake the thought that his advocacy for her might have had *something* to do with their night together, even if he denied it. It couldn't purely be a coincidence.

But then, maybe he was telling the truth. She didn't know him. She didn't know his ethics, his passions, his virtues. She knew nothing except for how terrifyingly right they felt together that night. How *good* it felt to have their bodies moving in unison and to have him filling her so … perfectly.

But she had to forget that. She had to forget about their night together because he wasn't just a one-night stand. He wasn't just some guy she slept with to get over the fact that she was going home to an empty house because her ex-fiancé led her on for so long. And maybe, if she hadn't been avoiding all of it when Griffin was picking his things up from her house that night, she wouldn't have let her guard down. And she never would have had any kind of involvement with the incredibly sexy man who was now working with her. Everything would be professional. Except for the inevitable appearances he'd make in her dreams because she was sure he had a habit of doing that in any sane woman's dreams.

And she had no doubt that his smell would stay

with her, forever making her brain fuzzy. Especially when he was standing so damn close to her, trying to see the computer screen as she walked him through the database and programs they used. He'd given her his chair so she could show him, and he was basically leaning over her, resting his hands on the arms of the chair. She could practically feel his body heat penetrating through her clothes, and she tried to ignore the pull she was feeling—the urge to lean back, just a little, to rest her head against his chest. She could feel his breath in her hair—all entirely accidental, she was sure. And she didn't know what the hell she was thinking when she purposefully crossed one leg over the other, knowing it often pulled her knee-length skirt up a little.

It wasn't her. This behaviour was against her entire work ethic. No involvement with any work colleague. No dates, no kissing, no innuendos, and *especially* no sex. Not even so much as a flirtatious smile. She shook the fuzz from her brain, shifting to the edge of her seat to move further away from him, adjusting her skirt to cover as much of her thighs as possible. She had to get control of the situation. She couldn't have what happened between them compromising her work ethic. Strictly professional.

But maybe her work ethic had already been compromised the second he walked into this building.

Chapter 4

Nate was a man on a mission. He'd already told Russ that he'd meet him at the bar and talk to him while he worked. He figured he needed the true player's advice about how to deal with working with Wren. He'd been the last to leave, being distracted with learning the system and learning names and positions. The last thing he wanted was to call one of the other managers by the wrong name.

But Wren—she was one he couldn't forget.

He hadn't missed the way she'd shifted in her seat, her skirt riding up a little when she was showing him the programs they used. Or how she leaned her head back just enough for him to catch the sweet berry scent of her shampoo. He also didn't miss how she adjusted herself to sit further away from him. He knew that this first day involved more close proximity with her then the rest would. She was showing him the ins and outs of the company and, as far as he could see, no one knew it better than she did. The thought that tomorrow would be less time with her had him both relieved and disappointed. He stepped outside of the building and slapped his hand against all of his pockets, making sure he had everything.

Keys.

Wallet.

Phone.

He exhaled, turning back inside the building. Trust his luck to forget his phone. He took the elevator back up to his floor, still amazed that he worked on a floor that he needed to take an elevator to get to. Even as a kid, he'd never even dreamed that he'd be dressing in a suit and have an office of his own. His parents hadn't been supportive of his move to the city. They'd wanted him to work the farm. Being the oldest of two boys, his future had been set out for him. His brother would have had more freedom. That is, until Nate left for the city to forge his own life.

He hadn't heard from his dad or his brother since. His mum spent the first month trying to convince him to come back home. Then, she gave up. And he hadn't heard from her since. Did he miss them? Sure. More than anything. They are his family. But he wanted more for his life than to work the farm. They didn't have to cut him away. They didn't have to ignore his phone calls in that first year of being away from them. They could have answered his letters giving them an update on what was happening, his change of address or phone numbers—he'd sent letters because he wasn't sure if they'd changed their numbers.

Would they be proud of him now?

Maybe. Probably not.

Did it bother him?

Not anymore. It had, to start with. And he'd wondered if he should go back to the farm and make amends, spending every damn day doing something that didn't make him happy. But it wasn't an option. His dad had never been the forgiving kind. His brother followed in his footsteps. Even if they did accept him back, he'd never be able to make it up to them. Then again, if he'd been recognised for working his hands to the bone instead of being hounded to work harder, maybe he would have stayed. Or at least, he might have had more respect for his dad.

It didn't take him long to find his phone, and once he had it, he headed back towards the elevator, surprised to see one of the other office lights on from the corner of his eye. *Wren's office*. He should have ignored it. He should have stepped into the elevator and forget he ever saw the light on. But he didn't. Instead, his feet moved him closer to her office, curiosity getting the better of him. And when he saw she was in there, her jacket draped over the chair opposite her desk, the top few buttons of her shirt undone—ones that had been done up earlier that day—and her hair brushing against her chin as she studied the paperwork in front of her, he should have walked. She hadn't seen him, he could have left without her knowing he was ever even there.

But he didn't.

***

His knock startled her, and she slammed the textbook closed, pulling a pile of office paperwork on top of it. She glanced at the window. The sun had set some time back and her eyes felt heavy.

'Hope I'm not interrupting,' Nate said, leaning against the doorframe. 'I saw your light was on, thought I'd check in.'

She blinked up at him and her breath caught. His hair was tousled, and he'd taken his tie off, the top few buttons undone to display a small tuft of chest hair. She swallowed. She knew what lay under that shirt, and it was surprisingly sexy. She shook the thoughts from her mind, remembering that *her* top few buttons were undone, and crossed her arms over her chest.

'Wh—what are you still doing here? Work finished hours ago.'

A mischievous smile flickered across his face as he pushed off the doorframe and eased his way into her office. 'I was about to ask you the same thing,' he said. He held up his phone. 'I forgot my phone, so had to come back in. But yes, I was here late.' He spread his arms out, his smile widening. 'You caught me. I was trying to get used to the programs.'

She smiled. 'It's easy once you get used to it. To be honest, I ... I did the same when I first started here.'

'No kidding,' he said. 'So, since you're already adept at the programs, what are you doing here this late?'

'Oh, nothing, really. Just ... work.'

She bit her lip, hoping that she was a better liar than she felt she was. He eased towards the desk, leaning back against it, and shifted the paperwork she'd put on top of her book. His eyebrow lifted. 'Business accounting?'

She shrugged. 'Just a little ... light reading.'

'It's a textbook.'

She sighed, letting her arms drop, and rubbed her forehead. 'I'm ... studying. It's easier to do it here than at home. Fewer distractions. I started on the Bachelor when I thought I had a chance at getting ... your ... job.'

His brow furrowed. 'How did you manage to get a job here without being qualified?'

'I have a diploma. And my wits.'

He chuckled—a sound that made her heart flip. 'That would do it.'

'I guess there's no reason for me to even bother with it now,' she said. 'I've clearly reached the top of my career.'

'Mmm, you never know,' he said, tilting his head from side to side, glancing over his shoulder at her.

'Durgan might leave and you might get his job.'

She scoffed. 'Hardly. They can't afford to have me leave this position.'

He smiled an easy, relaxed smile. 'You should really take that as a compliment. Your job is basically secured for life.'

She laughed, rolling her eyes. 'Great.' He held her gaze for a moment before she dropped her eyes to the textbook in front of her. 'You know, I try my best to understand this stuff, but I just can't wrap my head around it. I don't even see how this is related to marketing. I really should save myself the trouble ...'

'I can help if you want.'

Help? It was tempting. He had said that he'd done his Masters. But the thought of him being so close to her, spending more time with her, trying to help her understand her studies? It terrified her. How would she be able to concentrate with him showing her when she couldn't even keep her mind straight when he was in the room?

'Oh, I ... can't ... don't ... I don't want to bother you,' she mumbled. 'Besides, you look like you're going out.'

He raised an eyebrow. 'It can wait.'

'No, really, I—'

He moved around to her side of the desk and flipped the book open to where her bookmark was.

'It's no trouble, Wren.'

She took in a sharp breath, feeling her heart quicken. She didn't have much room to move, and she could feel the warmth radiating from his body and his scent that still lingered in her memory. God, she could not have him helping her. Any attempt would be futile. It would just batter at the wall that she'd built between her and workplace relationships until it fell down, one brick at a time.

'Here,' he said, scribbling something on a post-it note and sliding it towards her. 'Remember that formula, and you'll be fine.'

She glanced down at the formula. 'It can't be that simple.'

'It's not, technically,' he said. 'The terms can be used interchangeably. But that is what everything comes back to.' He tapped on the formula to emphasise his point.

She glanced up at him, squinting, holding his gaze. 'Are you messing with me?'

He laughed, his eyes widening. 'I am actually being very serious about this,' he said. 'I can explain it to you more if you ever let me help you again.'

He'd turned so that he was leaning back against the desk again, facing her. It's like he was …
searching … her. Looking for something, but she couldn't tell if he'd found what he was looking for. He'd stopped laughing, but he kept his easy smile on his face. God, it only made him sexier.

'I … umm…' She cleared her throat. 'I don't think that's a … good … idea.'

His brow furrowed, the smile dropping from his face. 'Why not? You're helping me here, it's only fair that I help you.'

She rose to her feet, but he didn't move. 'You've

already helped enough.' She hadn't meant for it to sound rude, but it had. And she was sure she saw a flicker of something—hurt—flash across his face. 'It's late. I should ... leave,' she whispered.

He scoffed, shifting his legs for her to move past, but she could still feel his gaze on her, even as she walked away from him. 'You're pretty good at that.'

She spun on her heel, closing the distance between them until they were only a foot apart. 'What's that supposed to mean?'

'You know what it means.'

He stood up straighter, his stare intense, almost throwing her off balance. What was he on about? Of course, she knew *what* he was talking about, and it annoyed her more than anything. Throughout the day he'd been hinting at it whenever it came up. Well, more like jabbing. Accusing. Was there even really a name for it?

'Was I not supposed to leave?'

'You're a grown woman, you can do what you want.'

'You had a shower without saying anything. Didn't that mean you wanted me to leave?'

'It meant I wanted *a shower*.'

Her jaw dropped. The distance between them had reduced to only a few inches. She could smell the addictive sweetness of his breath and returned his intense stare with one of her own.

'You mean—'

'I thought you were asleep,' he said. 'I didn't want to wake you.'

'Y—you didn't want me to … leave?' She barely recognised her own voice.

He shook his head slowly. 'But I figured you must have wanted to, since you left pretty quickly.'

She squeezed her eyes shut, rubbing her forehead with her thumb and forefinger. 'Oh, God,' she whispered. 'I *am* terrible at this.'

'What do you mean?'

She laughed—awkwardly—and spread her arms out, looking up at him. His brow was creased, and he almost looked … concerned. 'You know, Kass said I had no idea and she was right. Clearly, she was right.'

'You've lost me,' he said shaking his head.

'It's been a while, Nate,' she said. That freaking awkward smile was still on her face. 'No, not just a while.' She shook her head. 'A *long* time. And never … like that. So, congratulations, Nate. *You* were my first official hook up.'

He grabbed hold of her arms, urging her to focus on him. 'Wren, I didn't … I don't just hook up with people either. It's not really my scene. But with you … I don't know … there was something different about you.'

She scoffed. 'I was drunk and lonely. That doesn't make me any different to anyone else.'

'It's not th—'

'I can't—' she dropped her gaze, pressing her palm to his chest to keep the distance that was becoming incredibly more difficult to keep between them. She squeezed her eyes shut, trying not to make a fool of herself. She didn't know why it hurt to say it, but it did. 'That night was a mistake, Nate,' she whispered. 'I want ... I *need* to forget about it, and I can't unless you forget about it, too.'

***

She blinked up at him and her blue eyes shimmered like the waves in the ocean they looked like. How had things got so out of hand? He hadn't meant for the conversation to even get back to this, but he'd been the one to bring it there. Because he couldn't keep his damn mouth shut. Truth is, his mind had been concocting a plan to take her out more rather than trying to forget about her. As long as she was around him, he'd never forget their night together. And even if he never saw her again, he'd still never forget it.

'No,' he said flatly.

'It was a mistake.'

'Like hell it was.'

Her lips parted, and she took in a shaky breath. 'Nate—'

'You can do what you want, but I'm not going to forget it ever happened.'

'Why not?' She sounded frustrated. Much like he was feeling.

'Because it was too damn good!' There. He said it. 'If I really have to spell it out for you, Wren, I'm not going to forget it because it was *too damn good,* and I still have half a bottle of whisky sitting on my bench to remind me.'

'Y—you kept it?' she whispered.

'What else was I going to do with it?'

'I don't … I—' she snapped her mouth shut, studying his eyes. Was she really at a loss as to what to say?

He could see the rise and fall of her chest as she took deep, shaky breaths, her open buttons allowing him a clear view of her cleavage. Her hand was still pressed to his chest, shooting a warmth from her fingertips to below his belt as she pressed them against his muscles. Her fringe fell over her left eye just so, a few strands stuck to the corner of her mouth. He lifted his hand, sweeping the strands to behind her ear and sliding his hand to the back of her neck.

Before he could even think about it, he'd pulled her close, taking her mouth with his, his tongue dancing with hers like they had that night. Except, now, there was a lot less drunkenness and a whole lot more of something else. He'd almost expected her to slap him. But she didn't. He'd been sure that she would have pushed him away and yelled at him for literally sweeping into her life and messing it up from every angle. But she didn't.

Instead, she wrapped her arms around his neck, meeting his kisses with an intensity of her own and pressing her body against his. She was addictive. Alluring. Sexy as hell. And he would never be able to resist her. Never. Not that he'd ever want to. She lowered her hands and started unbuttoning his shirt. He didn't need to be asked twice. He lowered his hands to her thighs and picked her up, her legs wrapping around him, and sat her on the edge of the desk, pushing everything but the computer onto the floor.

'You know, it's not like in the movies,' she mumbled against his lips. 'I'm going to have to clean that up myself.'

'I'll help you.' *In more ways than one.*

He fiddled with the remaining buttons on her shirt—thank God there were only a few—and slid it off her shoulders, exposing her dark blue silky bra and magnificent body that he couldn't wait to feel against his again. She slid his hands under his open shirt and traced the lines of his body, catching his lip between her teeth and fuelling the fire even more. He felt the rumble of something awakening inside of him, pushing him so far away from control that it would be a miracle if he ever got it back. He slid his hands up her thighs, under her skirt, and hooked his fingers on her panties, shimmying them down her legs, and moved his hand back up her legs until he reached the sweet spot.

She was ready for him.

And he sure as hell was ready for her.

Before long he was where he wanted to be, his hands on her hips as he moved, her legs clenching around his hips in welcome and her back arching as she moaned.

He should have walked.

He shouldn't have gone into her office.

But he did.

And, God, he was glad he did.

Chapter 5

'I slept with Nate.'

'I'm sorry, but I'm getting this weird feeling of déjà vu.' Kassandra settled herself in the seat on the other side of Wren's desk. 'Honey, I *know* you slept with Nate. We've been through this.'

Wren groaned. 'No. I slept with Nate—*again*.'

'When?'

'Last night.' *On this desk.* She tilted her head, squeezing her eyes shut. 'And this morning.' *In the file room.*

Truth is, the morning one involved no talking. Just a look. A simple smile when he caught her eye. A nod of his head towards the empty file room. Then it was on. Everything was a flurry of arms and legs and clothes, and they were finished and dressed just in time for the first file-room users to arrive. It was too close for comfort. Way too close to actually being caught in action, and then what? Everyone would think she's fraternising with the new manager because she didn't get the job. Durgan would probably retract her pay rise—if he didn't fire her first—and she'd take the title of Office Skank from Legs—she wasn't sure what her name was, since she never actually had any regular contact with her, but she had legs as far as the eye could see.

Kassandra blinked at her, her eyes wide and her lips pursed as if analysing the situation. 'Huh.'

Huh? That's all Kassandra had to say? 'Kass, I need help!' she moaned.

'I'd say,' Kassandra said. 'You're a freaking sex addict.'

'He works with us.'

Kassandra shrugged. 'He's practically our boss.'

Wren dropped her head into her hands, her elbows resting on the desk. 'Don't remind me.'

'No, seriously, Wren,' Kassandra said, leaning onto the desk. 'Durgan doesn't care for office romances. That's why no one here is together and anyone that's been involved has been—' she pointed her thumb over her shoulder.

She furrowed her brow. 'What about Legs?'

'She hasn't *actually* slept with anyone here, Wren. She just has new stories about sleeping with people who don't work here every week. Like the delivery guy.'

'Isn't that … technically … the same?'

She shook her head. 'He doesn't *work* here. He just hangs around hoping to get back in her pants.' Kassandra leaned back in her chair. 'Big difference. But you? You are in dangerous territory, girl.'

'But it's different with us.'

'Only because you screwed him before you knew he worked here. But you've screwed him twice since, and this is his second day.'

Wren sighed, leaning back in her chair, staring up at the ceiling. She knew what she *had* to do. Even if she didn't want to. God, she didn't want to. It had been a long time since she'd been *that* intimate with someone. Griffin had always wanted to wait until they were married—despite living with her—and she knew why now. And she'd never been with anyone that made it feel *that* good. And Nate felt the same way, clearly, judging from their discussion last night.

If she didn't end it now, they would get caught.

They might still be caught as it is.

And there was no telling whose job would go—if not both.

'I have to end it, don't I?' she whispered.

Kassandra sighed. 'I hate to be the bearer of bad news—very, *very* bad news—but yes, you do.'

She closed her eyes, the disappointment affecting her more than it should. She couldn't sleep with the guy anymore. So what? She'd already spent years without it. But it was like an addiction. Now that she'd had a taste of him, she wanted more. But she also didn't want to lose everything she'd worked hard for.

'We'll find you someone else, honey,' Kassandra said sympathetically, rising to her feet. 'And we'll make sure he's not starting work here anytime soon.'

Wren laughed, but she wasn't really feeling it. How could anyone else compare to Nate? No one had ever made her feel alive like he did. No one had ever been so attentive, so … exciting. And now she had to give up the only good thing she'd had in a while.

'Weren't you … here … last night?'

She nodded her head. Kassandra's eyes dropped to the desk and her finger followed suit. She nodded again. Kassandra screwed up her face to feign disgust, but Wren saw the smile tugging at her lips.

'Eww.'

***

'I slept with Wren.'

'That's old news.'

Nate took a sip of the beer that Russ slid across the bar to him. 'Again.'

'What the *hell* is your problem, man?' Russ teased, leaning on the bar. 'I thought you didn't get her number.'

'I didn't.' He took another sip. 'That new job I got?' Russ nodded, his brow furrowed. 'She works there. Turns out I got the job she wanted.'

'And she still slept with you?'

Nate nodded. 'Again.'

Russ shook his head. 'I wish I had your luck with

women.'

Nate scoffed. 'What are you talking about? You have a new woman in your bed all the time.'

'True, but it does get hard trying to find someone you haven't already slept with.'

'I bet it does.'

'*So* hard.'

Russ winked at him and moved down the bar to serve the group at the end. Nate took another sip of his beer and turned to scan the room. He may not have had Wren's number the first night, but he made sure he got it the second time. And he couldn't have been happier to get a message from her to meet her at the bar. But why go to the bar? They hadn't needed drinks the last two times. Honestly, he couldn't be happier how it all turned out. There was still something about her that he couldn't quite work out, but he'd be lying if he said their ... rendezvous ... hadn't been fun. Maybe one day she might let him actually take her out beforehand.

He wouldn't complain if she didn't and their rendezvous continued. But he'd actually have to get to know her properly one day, right? Especially if he wanted any kind of longevity in ... whatever they had. She walked through the door and scanned the room, and his heart almost stopped beating. She was wearing tight jeans and a silky purple shirt. He felt that primal urge deep within him awaken again, but he subdued it. *Not in public*. Though those jeans would look *much* better at the end of his bed ...

He waved at her when she looked in his direction

and she started beelining towards him. He met her halfway, sliding his hand around her waist and pulling her close for a kiss on her …

Cheek?

She freaking cheeked him!

Sure, maybe she wasn't ready for the whole public displays of affection, he could get over that. But the way her voice shook when she spoke? That had him worried. Whatever this was, certainly wasn't a date. And he had a feeling it wasn't going to end well.

'I … umm … we need to talk.'

That never ends well. *Never*. He wasn't ready to give up their … thing. But maybe she wanted to talk it out—work out what, exactly, it was they had. Did they have a title? Were they more than just friends with benefits? Heck, he barely even knew her well enough to refer to her as a friend. He nodded, taking her hand, and leading her towards an empty table at the back of the bar.

'Do you want a drink?' He slid onto the seat next to her.

'N—no, I … no, thank you.'

He furrowed his brow. Something was definitely off, and he could see what was coming. He stretched his arm around her shoulders, hoping to change her mind, but not holding his breath.

'All right, what's on your mind?'

'I … ahh—' she covered her face with her hands, clearly trying to compose herself. She took a breath. 'Oh, God …'

'Wren?' he prompted.

'I … umm—' she dropped her hands, looking up at him, her eyes glistening. 'I can't do this, Nate. We can't … this whole … thing … between us—I can't do it.'

He retracted his arm—it clearly didn't work anyway. 'Ahh.'

She shifted in her seat to get a better view of him. 'I'm sorry, Nate, but you have to understand,' she continued. 'It's not you, it's—'

'*Seriously*?'

She shook her head, confused. 'What?'

'You really are bad at this, aren't you?'

'Excuse me?'

'"It's not you, it's me'? You don't need to give me that bullshit, Wren,' he said flatly. 'Just tell me what's going on. Are you freaking out?'

'No, I—'

'Can't identify a good thing when it's right in front of you?'

'Nate—'

'Did your ex decide he was straight again and wants you back?'

'That's not fair.'

Okay, maybe it was a bit too far. He didn't know why he reacted like this to her wanting to end things. Maybe it was because it was too good to give up and he seemed to be the only one to see that. Or maybe it's because he was still convinced there could be something else there—an attraction like that *had* to have more to it. It couldn't just be … this.

'Well, it can't be worse than any of those. So, talk to me, Wren.'

She sighed, focussing on her hands in her lap. 'It's … Durgan.'

Durgan? What the actual hell? He hadn't seen that coming—the thought hadn't even crossed his mind. But now it did. And it made him sick to his stomach. Was it his fault? Was it from his advocating for higher pay? If Durgan *dared* to do anything to Wren, he wouldn't hesitate to—

'Nate?'

He caught Wren's stare, her brow furrowed. 'You're going to have to … give me … a bit more than that, Wren, because that sounds a *whole* lot worse than it probably is.'

'What do you—' Her face paled, like she'd seen a ghost, then was replaced with a look of pure disgust. '*Oh*. Oh! Eww! Why would you even—'

Thank God. He sighed, relieved. 'What about him then?'

'Well, not *that*,' she said, shuddering. 'He doesn't … approve … of workplace relationships.'

He furrowed his brow. 'Did he say something to you?'

'No. Well, not yet. It'd be a matter of time if this—' she moved her finger between them. 'Continued. But people have lost their jobs because of it. Well, no one really knows if it was because of *it*, but it's a bit too … coincidental.'

'It's none of his damn business, in my opinion.'

She sighed. 'Look, Nate, you might not be worried

about your job, but I've worked hard to get to where I am. I'm not going to throw that away.'

He put his hands up between them, his palms facing her. 'All right, so we keep it on the down low.'

'No, Nate, it can't happen.'

'Sometimes?'

'No.'

'But we work together.'

'So, we'll be … colleagues … friends.'

He raised an eyebrow. '*Friends*?'

She nodded, her lips pursed. If he could just close the distance between them … 'With rules.'

He felt his eyebrows shoot up. 'You want … rules.'

She shrugged. 'It's that or nothing.'

'Rules it is, then,' he said, hating himself as he said it. He'd never really liked rules—especially when it came to relationships or … friendships. But he was just about willing to do anything to make sure Wren stayed in his life. And if that meant he had to follow some rules, then so be it. 'What are we talking?'

She pointed to her fingers. 'The obvious, I think. No kissing. No romance stuff. No sex.'

'*No sex*?' God, this woman was going to be the death of him.

'That's what got us here in the first place, Nate.'

'Fine,' he grumbled. 'Is that it?'

'No hand-holding. No dates. No drunken late-night calls.'

He scoffed. 'Would I do th—' Her eyebrow raised. 'Okay, I'll make a note. Go on.'

'No flirting. No innuendos.'

He laughed. 'In your en—' he started, breaking off when she scowled. 'No innuendos, right. I wasn't sure I heard that properly.'

'And no ... close proximity ... unless it's otherwise unavoidable.'

He pointed across the table. 'So ... I should move then.' She nodded. He eased out of the chair and sat across from her. 'No flirting, really? Flirting is completely harmless.'

'Not for us.' Her cheeks reddened.

Yeah ...

This wasn't going to work at all. But he'd play her game. And when she was ready to break all of her rules, he'd be there to break them with her. No questions asked.

She sighed. 'Well, since that's sorted ... I should be going. Pleasure doing business with you, Nate.'

She held her hand out across the table. He raised an eyebrow and took her hand shaking it. 'Pleasure was mine.' He leaned a little closer. 'And, ahh, you just broke one of your rules.'

Her cheeks reddened, and she retracted her hand quickly, crossing her arms. 'Starting now.'

'How about one for the road and we start after that?' He didn't think it would work, but it was worth trying.

She laughed, shaking her head. 'See you tomorrow, Nate.'

'See you tomorrow, Wren.'

God, Russ would get a laugh out of this.

***

I did it. You're no fun.

She hit send and waited for Kassandra's reply. She knew that she had to end the ... intimate ... side of her relationship with Nate. She just hated that it had to be so soon. And where had the whole friends-with-rules thing come in? She couldn't be friends with the guy without wanting something more. She could barely be around him without keeping herself from him. Why would she ever think they could be friends?

Because she wasn't ready to have him out of her life completely.

They worked together—as long as that continued, he'd always be a part of her life. But with this whole friend arrangement, she basically guaranteed the extra involvement. The permission he needed to push into her social circles—not that there was much to let himself into. To organise things that friends do and have her there with him. Heck, she might just organise some things herself. Her phone dinged, and she opened the message.

I'm just looking out for you.

She sighed, putting the phone down and resting her head against the back of her couch. This wasn't going to work. She could feel it in her bones. But she was sure as hell going to try to make it work. It had to. The idea of not having Nate in her life was a much less pleasurable alternative.

Even breaking it off with him was bad enough.

And the rules they—she—made? Ridiculous! Every single one of them. She was almost ready to forget about it all and risk her career, the life she'd built for herself, just to enjoy a little longer with him. He hadn't seemed in any rush to get rid of her. And she would have enjoyed their rendezvous as often as they came.

But she couldn't.

Not anymore.

She closed her eyes, seeing Nate's gorgeous smile, feeling his touch as his fingers traced her cheekbone. The tingling that his lips left as they kissed her neck and the pulsing through her body when he slid his hands under her shirt and around to her back, pulling her closer. The way he whispered her name. The way his name sounded on her lips. She shifted in her seat, opening her eyes, and staring up at the ceiling, a groan escaping from her throat.

He was going to be the death of her.

And only being friends with him was going to kill her. Slowly. And agonisingly.

Chapter 6

'Camping.'

'*What*?'

The week had passed without much interaction between Nate and Wren. Sure, she'd been avoiding him, for the most part. But there were times—like meetings—where she couldn't just avoid him. At least there were other people in the room every time she couldn't avoid talking to him. Truth is, she was worried that if they were alone in a room together again, their rules would go straight down the drain. Like they had in her dreams.

It hadn't been easy—avoiding Nate all week. And it hadn't been easy to hide her blush when she saw him, especially when the images she'd dreamed about kept popping into her head at inopportune times. If only they didn't work together, they might have had a chance. But, on the other hand, they hadn't really … talked. There was definitely a physical connection. A very … intimate … and unavoidable … physical connection. But she didn't even know where to start talking with the guy. And it certainly wouldn't be easy to develop a friendship based on their fling.

She'd managed to avoid him for the most part of four days, but here he was, in her office, standing across from her, blurting out this ridiculous idea.

'We should go camping,' he said, his eyes wide.

She raised an eyebrow. Camping was a *terrible* idea. The two of them together, alone, in the middle of the bush, spending the night? The idea was doomed from the start.

'I came across an article about another big company doing a camping trip to improve morale and it was a total success. It not only improved morale, but there was also an increase in production and teamwork was improved.'

Oh, for the *company*. She shook her head. 'I don't think that's a good idea. Half the people here would kill each other.'

'That's the whole point,' he said. 'Well, not the killing each other, but the improving … *professional* … relationships.'

Wren sighed. 'I'm not sure, Nate.'

'I'm going to pitch it to Durgan, I just thought there'd be a better chance of it happening if you're on board with it.'

She laughed. 'Do you really think anyone's going

to go for it?'

He shrugged. 'We can make it compulsory.'

'That wouldn't be a good idea. Could you imagine over a hundred disgruntled employees stuck in the middle of nowhere with each other?'

He stretched his arms out. 'Maybe it can just be the management team, then. More of a proper … team-building … activity.'

'We all work fine together.'

'Come on, Wren,' he said. 'It could be fun. And it'll give us a chance to do the whole friend thing with other people around.'

'Ahh.'

So, there *was* an ulterior motive to his suggestion. She sighed, rising to her feet, and walked around to the other side of her desk. They were close enough for her to feel the nerves tingle in her stomach—heck, he only had to be in the same room as her for that to happen—but still far enough apart to have some distance between them.

'Nate, we don't need to … push … this … friendship.'

'I was simply listing it as an extra benefit of a team-bonding activity.'

'I think the less time we spend together, the better.'

'I disagree.'

He'd stepped closer until they were only a few inches apart. She lifted her chin to catch his eyes with hers and felt her breath catch in her throat.

'I—close proximity,' she whispered. 'It's … umm

... against the rules.'

He raised an eyebrow, taking a step back. 'Right. The rules.'

'We don't need to ... plan ... things, Nate,' she said. 'It's just a period of adjustment. It'll come naturally, I'm sure.' She felt like she was trying to convince herself more than convincing him.

'No, what comes naturally is—'

There was a knock on her office door, making them both jump back.

'Coffee time!' Kade said, walking towards Wren, his eyes shifting between her and Nate.

Kade worked at *HotSpot* and often brought coffees up for some of the workers—Wren included. She didn't know how he did it, but he always seemed to know when she needed a coffee—mostly Friday afternoons when she didn't get a chance to go to the café herself. He was a tall, lanky guy, with a head of shoulder-length blond dreadlocks that he usually had tied back into a ponytail. His bandana and jovial countenance were always bound to make her day. And he made the best damn coffee she'd ever had from a café.

'Is it that time already?' she said, taking another subtle step away from Nate.

'I should ... go,' Nate said, rubbing his hand over his chin. 'I'll talk to Durgan, Wren, see what he thinks about the idea.'

He glanced briefly at Kade and left the room. If Wren saw correctly, it was almost like he was sizing him up. Kade brought the coffee over to her and she took it from his outstretched hand.

'He new?' Kade said, moving his head towards the door.

She nodded. 'He's the new marketing manager.' She waved her hand. 'He wants to take the management team on a camping trip for a team-building activity. It's just … ridiculous.' She didn't know why she felt the need to justify why she was in the same room as Nate—especially to Kade.

'It doesn't sound like such a bad idea,' Kade said, shrugging. 'Work camping trips *have* been shown to improve morale.'

She pointed her finger at Kade, smiling. 'Oh, that's not fair!' she said. 'You've known me longer, you should be on my side.'

He flashed a coy smile. 'Always on your side, Wren,' he said. 'Speaking of, aren't you … umm … supposed to be on your honeymoon or something?'

She sighed. It had been such a big week she'd almost forgotten she was supposed to be honeymooning. 'Yeah, it didn't work out.' She moved back behind her desk, shifting some papers.

'You left him?'

'He left *me*.'

'Damn,' he said softly. 'Well, for what it's worth, you don't look like you're heartbroken.'

'I'm not.' It was the truth. Still, didn't mean she wasn't disappointed that her plan was falling behind. 'Really, I'm fine. It was never meant to work out.'

He rested his hands on the back of the chair on the other side of the desk. 'You know, you should have some fun. Celebrate your freedom.'

She raised an eyebrow. 'It's not that exciting.'

His coy smile widened, his lips curving higher on his left side than his right. 'You've been working hard, you deserve it,' he said. 'I'm going surfing tomorrow morning. You should come.'

She shook her head. 'I can't surf.'

'Ever tried?'

'Once,' she said, squinting. 'I failed miserably.'

He laughed. 'All right. Well, come along anyway and enjoy the beach. Maybe we can … hang out … when I'm done.'

'Mmm, I don't know …'

'Come on, Wren,' he teased. 'Live a little.'

She sighed, bowing her head. 'All right, fine.'

'Yes?'

'Yes,' she laughed. 'I'll come enjoy the beach.'

'Great,' he said, his smile widening even further. He plucked a business card off her desk and tapped it to his forehead. 'I'll let you know when I'll be there.'

She nodded, watching as he left, exhaling once she was alone in her office. What a day. She rubbed her forehead, taking a sip of her coffee. It was made to perfection, as usual. But there was something about his suggestion that had her chest tighten. Had she inadvertently agreed to a … date … with Kade? *Shoot*. Surely, not. She would just be enjoying the sun on the beach while he surfed. There'd be barely any contact between them. Just two people in the same place at the same time. That's all.

She sighed, putting her cup on the desk. Maybe

she shouldn't go alone. Not that she didn't trust him—he did make her coffees, after all. That kind of responsibility is almost like trusting him with her life. But she didn't want to give him the wrong idea. And she certainly didn't want to risk the quality of the coffee.

***

Durgan actually agreed, to Nate's surprise. He'd been thinking about it all week and had come up with a total loss of things that would be considered friend things for him and Wren. From what he could see, Wren was a pretty private person. There were no social circles for them both to coincidentally be a part of. And people at their work didn't seem to do things outside of work—apart from the newest people and the interns. But Wren was not in those circles.

In fact, she was near on impossible to find outside of work. His guess was that she spent most of her time at home—that is, if she wasn't staying late at work studying. He'd resisted the urge to stay back and find out. But after how it went last time, he wouldn't be surprised if she never stayed back again. Especially since it could mean that their rules would be violated.

The only way they could get to know each other without violating their rules is if they were in a group. Which meant that he had to organise it all and make sure she'd be there. First of all, his idea was to get people from their work together in a situation where everyone would be forced to get along. Maybe some friendships would be made. At the least, he'd be able to see who she was willing to spend time with.

But he hadn't once expected that Durgan would actually go for a camping trip for all the management team. He'd imagined lots of convincing, negotiating, coming up with a new idea altogether. But there was none. Durgan couldn't have been happier for Nate to plan it. He'd even suggested it would be a paid trip to guarantee the numbers.

Now he just had to tell Wren it had Durgan's approval and reassure her *again* that it had nothing to do with them being friends. Even though it had everything to do with it. He'd been heading towards her office at the end of the day when he saw her and Kassandra out of the corner of his eye in the tea room. He backtracked, standing by the door—close enough to hear whether he would be interrupting something important without being seen.

'Tomorrow? It's a date,' Kassandra said.

'So, you'll meet me there?' Wren said.

'Of course I will. I don't want to miss all the hunks emerging from the water with their boards.'

'Mmm, I should have known that was the appealing factor for you.'

'Burleigh Heads, right?'

'Nine o'clock. And Kass, *please* don't be late.'

He heard footsteps heading towards the door and moved away as quickly as he could—well, as quickly and *subtly* as he could manage. He hadn't meant to hear that much of their conversation, but he couldn't have been more thankful that he did. He ducked back into his office, hoping that Kassandra and Wren hadn't seen him and grabbed his things from the office. He knew where they were going to be and what time. Now, he just had to make it look like bumping into them is a total coincidence.

***

'You *are* joking, right?'

Nate furrowed his brow. 'I don't think I've ever been more serious.'

'Dude, you have these … rules … and honestly, it doesn't really sound like she wants to hang out.'

Nate waved his finger at his friend. 'See, that's where you're wrong, Russ,' he said. 'She only *thinks* she doesn't want to hang out. But I'm going to show her that we can actually be … friends … and do things together without the awkwardness.'

Russ leaned on the bar. 'You've slept together. It's going to be awkward. You can't change that.'

'I can try.' Why wasn't Russ as excited about this as Nate was?

Russ rubbed his forehead. 'Planning a work camping trip? Showing up somewhere where you *know* she'll be and acting like it's a coincidence? How can that *not* be awkward?'

'It'll work.'

At least, he hoped it would. Truth is, he wasn't

sure how he'd be able to pull off seeing her at the beach as unintentional. Especially since he was sure he was terrible at lying. And the camping trip? Well, he did intend to spend as much time with her as he could. But he'd respect her decision—her rules. Sure, he hoped she'd come around and forget the rules. But he wasn't going to push her. And he also wasn't going to remove himself from her life because she was scared to see what they could have. Russ raised an eyebrow.

'But I need your help.'

'I'm not going to help you ruin something that should come naturally.'

'You will,' Nate said. 'Because it can't come naturally if she keeps avoiding me and pushing me away.'

'You're desperate.'

Nate shrugged, his lips curving to one side. 'Will you help me?'

Russ shook his head slowly, but he was smiling. Nate knew it wouldn't take long to persuade him. 'Why do you need my help?'

'She has a friend.'

'Ahh.' Russ poured a beer and slid it across to Nate. 'Nope.'

'Come on, Russ,' Nate urged. 'She's your type.' Russ's eyebrow almost reached his hairline. 'I mean, if you *had* a type, she'd be it. But I just need you to be a distraction. Just to … be there … and not make me look so desperate.'

Russ sighed. 'There's no way you're not going to

let me go with you, is there?'

'I will drag you there if I have to.'

'Fine,' Russ said, shaking his head. 'I'll go willingly. But just this once. You know my rules.'

'Rules shmooles.'

'What are you, twelve?'

Nate grinned. Could Russ really blame him for getting a little bit excited about his plan falling into place? Besides, it wasn't *entirely* desperate, right? He just had to get them over this bump and maybe the rest will come naturally. And if not, he'd keep trying until it did.

Chapter 7

'I can't believe you talked me into this.'

'It's not like you needed much convincing.'

Nate drove slowly, trying to identify any car that looked like one he'd seen at work. Truth is, he didn't know what Wren's car looked like, or what kind of car she would have. For all he knew, he and Russ could be prowling the beach looking for them for hours without finding them. Heck, they might have even cancelled their beach trip. How was he to know? He was starting to become less convinced it was a good idea and starting to believe Russ.

What had driven him to the point of thinking that this would be okay?

In what world would she believe it was purely a coincidence?

'Any woman in her right mind won't buy it.'

'You're probably right,' Nate said.

'Do you even know if they're here or what they're doing?'

Nate shook his head.

He pulled the car into the next free car park. He'd just about given up on his idea, and the stirring in his stomach made him want to run for it. But it was a nice day, and they were already here. Why not enjoy the day in the sun and the water?

'But you're still going ahead with it?' Russ said, climbing out of the car at the same time as Nate.

Nate sighed, grabbing his footy from the back of the car. 'Okay, I admit, I'm an idiot for thinking it was a good idea.'

'So, *now* you admit it.'

'*But* we're already here, and it's a nice day. Why waste it?'

They heard a thump from a few cars over and a woman's voice. 'Son of a bee-atch!'

Why did that voice sound familiar?

Nate glanced around the back of the cars to see a woman bent forward, her bikini bottoms on full display, rubbing her shin with her hand— presumably, she'd hit it against the towbar of her car. He headed towards her, Russ on his heel.

'That looks painful.'

'I've had this car for almost three years and still can't get used to the bl—' She turned to face them, shooting herself upright in surprise. 'Oh … ahh … it's Nate, right?'

Nate nodded. He hadn't *officially* met Kassandra, but he recognised that ponytail from the office. If she was here … that meant that Wren probably was, too. Maybe bumping into Kassandra first would make it more convincing. Her eyes shifted slowly to Russ, looking him up and down.

'Have we met?' she said, dropping one of her shoulders so her sleeve slipped down her arm and puffing her chest out a little.

'Pretty sure I'd remember if we had,' Russ said, sidling closer towards her.

She seemed to consider him for a moment before her lips curved into a smile and she stretched her hand out towards him. 'Kass.'

Russ took her hand, holding it long enough to make Nate feel slightly uncomfortable. 'Russ.'

Nate watched the two eyeing each other for a second and cleared his throat. 'So, Kass, we weren't expecting to see you here. Are you by yourself?'

'Oh, no, I'm meeting—' she hesitated for a moment. 'Wren.'

He widened his eyes, and he struggled to keep his poker face on. 'Wren's here?'

Kass's eyes flickered between him and Russ. 'Umm … yes. Somewhere,' she mumbled. 'I should go. I've just got to … find her.'

She reached into the back of her car and loaded her arms up, struggling to close the boot of the car. Russ reached up, pressing down on the boot until it closed.

'Thank you,' she said, sighing. 'Ahh … the keys.

They're in my … my … bra.'

Russ's eyebrow shot up, his lips curving into a smile. Nate cleared his throat, taking some of the stuff from Kassandra's arms.

'We'll come with you,' he said, nodding to Russ to get the rest of her things.

'Oh … I mean, you don't have to. Were you meeting anyone else?'

She reached into her shirt and pulled out her keys, locking the car. She chucked the keys into the tote bag Russ was holding for her.

'Just us.'

'Umm … well, I don't know. Wren's only expecting me.'

'I'm sure it'll be fine,' Nate said. Kassandra opened her mouth as if to say something, but Nate kept talking. 'Besides, I … umm … forgot to mention something to her at work yesterday. I mean, I was going to text it to her later, but she might prefer to hear it face to face.'

'And you clearly need help carrying all this,' Russ offered.

'Right,' she said slowly. 'All right, I guess we'll all go find her then.'

Nate smiled, falling into step beside Russ, Kassandra on the other side of Russ. Maybe his plan was going to work after all. And at least now, he didn't look—or feel—so desperate.

***

Wren looked up from her book, taking in the beauty of the waves and the sun shimmering on the water. Kassandra had messaged that she was here—and that was almost fifteen minutes ago. Surely it wasn't that hard to find where she was. She scanned the surfers riding the waves, looking for the neon green shorts and yellow bandana holding back Kade's dreadlocks. Once she located him in the distance right before a big wave hid him from sight, she closed her book and glanced down at her phone— still nothing else from Kassandra.

Wren chuckled. Kassandra had probably already found her *hunk* and was off flirting with him. She wouldn't be surprised if she had. She had a knack for those kinds of things. Wren would have felt awkward about her being late if Kade had stuck around. But almost as soon as they met up at the beach, he started his surfing, leaving her in charge of his things. She took her hat off, stroking back the stray hairs that had stuck themselves to her face, scanning the beach again.

She exhaled in relief to see the familiar ponytail and loose off-the-shoulder shirt heading towards her. She was next to a giant of a man who seemed to be carrying her things, bumping into her shoulder every few steps. She sighed, shaking her head. Of course, she'd found her *hunk* already. And as usual, she'd overpacked for the beach. But there was another man walking next to Kassandra's hunk. He walked with a gait that looked a little too familiar and was holding a footy. By the time she could tell who it was, they were already within earshot.

'Oh, God,' she whispered, dropping her hat on Kade's things.

What was *he* doing here? And why was he with Kassandra? Kassandra waved, and Wren waved back, glancing back to the water to find Kade's whereabouts, but he couldn't be seen. She stood, making sure her beach shirt covered as much as it could—thankfully, she'd opted for modesty.

'Look what the cat dragged in,' Kassandra said, pulling her shirt off and tossing it next to Wren's things. She wasn't so much one for modesty.

The giant's eyes were glued to Kassandra's body, and Wren recognised him from the bar—Russ, Nate's best friend. Admittedly, Kassandra did seem to be flaunting her body a little for him. She shifted her gaze to Nate.

'This is a surprise,' she said, squinting.

'A good one, I hope,' he said.

She bit her lip. Did he know that she'd be at the beach with Kassandra? Surely not. The only way he could have known is if he'd overheard her conversation with Kade or with Kassandra. Kassandra was the one who told her she had to break it off with him, she wouldn't have *invited* him, would she? She supposed it wouldn't be so awkward if it was just her and Kassandra. But she was here with another man. She diverted her gaze to her friend.

'Kass, a word?'

She didn't wait for a response before yanking Kassandra far enough away from the guys to be out of earshot.

'What are *they* doing here, Kass?' she hissed.

'How the hell should I know?' Kassandra yanked her arm from Wren's grip. 'They were in the carpark when I got there.'

Wren sighed. 'Okay, but why did you bring them *here*?'

Kassandra shrugged. 'They wanted to say hello,' she said, crossing her arms. 'I didn't think it would be a big deal. Besides, I needed help carrying everything down here.'

'Well, if you didn't *overpack* for everything, you wouldn't have had that trouble.'

'Why are you mad at me, Wren?'

'I'm supposed to be here with Kade.'

'Didn't stop you from begging me to come with you,' Kassandra said, glancing back at the guys. They were both talking, but Wren could tell they were watching them, even if they were trying to be subtle.

Wren bit her lip. 'They have to leave.'

'Come on, Wren,' Kassandra said, dropping her hands on Wren's shoulders. 'Have you even told Kade that I was coming?' Wren shook her head. 'Okay, so what's wrong with two more people?'

'My best friend is *very* different to the guy I've slept with, Kass.'

Kassandra leaned closer. '*He* doesn't know that.'

Wren rubbed her forehead. Kassandra had a point. Kade didn't know that she'd slept with Nate, and it wasn't exactly something she planned on advertising. On the other hand, she hadn't wanted this outing to be date-like with Kade. And having other people around would definitely make it more casual. Or at least, make it seem that way. It still didn't hide the fact that she felt awkward having Nate here—that she didn't *want* him to see her out with another man—and she didn't know why.

She was the one who brought the rules into things.

She was the one who distanced herself from Nate.

Why should she feel awkward hanging out with him, especially with other people around?

'Look,' Kassandra said, softening her tone. 'Give me some time to figure out if I want to give hunky my phone number, and when Kade gets back, I'll try to get them to leave.'

Wren shook her head slowly. 'He can't see me with Kade.'

'Why the hell not? You're not *with* Nate, Wren. Just trust me.'

'I'm not like you, Kass.'

Kassandra shrugged, raising her eyebrow, and flashing a mischievous grin, before spinning on her heel and walking back towards Nate and Russ with an obvious bounce in her step. God, sometimes she wished she was more like Kassandra. She wished she could hide her feelings better or compartmentalise her life. She wished that she'd never let herself go that night at the bar—that she'd never let her guard down. She'd always had standards, but where were they that night? She supposed she'd lost faith in her standards when she picked the wrong kind of guy to spend her life with.

She sighed, following Kassandra back, quickening her pace to catch up. She glanced at Nate while she walked. His brow was furrowed, and he was focussed on her. She took a shaky breath, dropping her gaze as she reached them. Kassandra was already talking to Russ, and it looked like she had every intention of giving him her number and no intention of getting rid of him.

'Everything all right?' Nate said, his voice quiet, making her heart flip.

She pressed her lips together and hummed. 'All good. Everything is—I'm fine, really. I just didn't expect Kass to … have company.'

Nate's lips curved to one side and his nose crinkled. 'To be fair, she didn't have much of a choice.'

'What do you mean?'

He shrugged. 'Well, when she said that you were here, I said we'd come with her.'

Of course he did. 'Nate—'

He put his hands up between them, his palms facing her. 'I legitimately wanted to tell you something. I didn't get a chance to yesterday and figured you should hear it from me. And also—' he leaned in a little closer, nodding with his head towards Russ and Kassandra, who had both moved far enough away from them to not be within earshot. 'He wanted to find out what her deal was.'

Her eyebrows pulled together as she studied

their friends. 'I'm pretty sure she's doing the same.'

'Does it bother you?'

She flicked her gaze back to Nate. 'Kass will do what she wants. I'm used to it now.'

'I wasn't talking about her,' he said, clasping his hands around his footy. 'Does it bother you that *I'm* here?'

She swallowed the lump in her throat and dropped her gaze. 'I ... umm ... what did you forget to tell me?'

She glanced back up at him in time to see something flicker across his face. It was clear she was avoiding his question. She was never good at hiding what she thought. Despite her best efforts, she was an open book, and he was reading every damn word. He hooked the footy with one arm and ran his free hand through his hair.

'Oh, it was just ... camping.'

'Didn't we talk about that?'

'Well, not ... entirely,' he said. 'Durgan approved it, for the management team. He even wants to pay everyone to be there.'

'Oh.'

Oh? That's all she could say? Maybe him being here bothered her so much more than she realised.

'Wren—'

'Well, I hope I'm not missing the party.'

Kade laid his surfboard on the ground near them and draped his arm across Wren's shoulders. She felt her cheeks flush, despite the cool of Wade's body, and noticed Nate's body stiffen. He stood tall, and any emotion that had just been on his face was gone. Kade waved his finger towards Nate.

'Hang on, you're that new guy at Wren's work, aren't you?'

Nate nodded slowly, squinting as he studied Kade. 'Coffee guy, right?'

Kade laughed—a sound that, for some reason, made the hairs on Wren's skin stand on end. He dropped his arm from around Wren and stretched his hand out. Nate took it. 'Kade.'

'Nate. Nice dreads.' It sounded more like a jab than an actual compliment, but she was sure that Kade either didn't notice or brushed it off. 'I was just … telling Wren something. Work talk.'

There was so much wrong about this whole scene—Kade putting his arm around her when it wasn't clear if it was a date or not, Nate's sudden change in demeanour to seem almost … possessive … dominant. It was like a silent war was going on between the two and there was likely nothing that Wren could do to change it. But she'd give it a damn good try.

She cleared her throat. 'Durgan … umm … agreed to do the camping trip.'

Nate's eyes shot towards her. 'You told him about it?'

'He was there,' she said, shooting a warning with her own eyes. 'Kade actually agreed with you.'

He shifted his eyes back towards Kade, who shrugged. 'Sure, camping's been shown to improve morale in the workplace.'

'Hmm.'

That was it? Nate had nothing else to say? God, she wished she could get inside his head and find out what the hell he was thinking right now. Her imagination was going wild, and she hoped that he wasn't thinking half the things she was.

'What else has she told you?' Nate continued.

'Nate—' she warned.

'Wren! Oh, God, sorry, I didn't—hi, Kade.' Kassandra drew out her greeting to Kade. 'Nate.'

Nate raised an eyebrow. 'Kass.'

Russ mouthed something to Nate, and he shrugged slightly—probably in hopes that no one saw, but Wren did. She glanced over at Kassandra, her eyes widening. Kass nodded.

'Umm … we should probably … get going,' Kassandra said, grabbing hold of Russ's arm. 'Leave you two to the rest of your … come on, boys.'

'Oh, you don't have to run off on account of me,' Kade said. 'Friends of Wren's are friends of mine, right?' He indicated towards Nate's footy. 'We can play for a bit.'

Nate scoffed. 'Sure.' He tossed his footy to Russ. 'You in, Wren?'

She bit her lip. How much harm could tossing the footy to each other be? 'All right.' Kade started moving further away to put some distance between everyone. 'But don't go easy on me and Kass because we're girls. We know how to handle our balls.'

She regretted it as soon as she said it, knowing it came out entirely different to how she meant it to sound. Nate's eyes widened, his lips curving into a grin. 'Oh, I know you do,' he said, loud enough for only her to hear. She scowled at him as he started running backwards. 'Handy with balls—I like that.'

She glanced over at Kade. It was obvious he heard the last bit—Nate had said it loud enough for all of them to hear. Russ tossed the ball to Kade, who kicked it to Wren. She kicked it towards Kassandra but ended up with it going somewhere between her and Kade.

'I thought you said you were good with balls!' Nate called out.

She flipped him the bird and heard him laugh. Her cheeks felt hot. She could feel Kade's eyes on her, his gaze shifting between her and Nate. Nate certainly wasn't making hiding their history easy. In fact, she was sure that the only person in this group who didn't know was the only person she was supposed to be here with. The ball started flying quicker and their harmless game was getting more competitive. She could feel her stomach tightening as the ball was being passed harder and faster between the three guys and, before she knew it, Kassandra had launched herself onto Russ's back.

'You're supposed to pass it to *me*, ass-hat!' she yelled, clutching to Russ as he laughed, throwing the ball in one last attempt to get it back to the guys.

It fell short, Nate and Kade both running towards it to catch it. It looked like Kade was going to get there first, but as the ball was lined up to land in his hands, Nate launched himself towards the ball. It was almost in slow motion, and she could have sworn that she heard the crack of Nate's elbow colliding with Kade's face. Kade fell to the ground, his hand clasping his face and for the split second that Nate glanced over at Wren, she saw a flicker of something that shouldn't be there.

Something that told her it wasn't entirely an accident.

Chapter 8

'I'm *sorry*, Wren. It was an accident.'

It wasn't an accident.

There wasn't even an ounce of anything that could be called accidental in it. Sure, maybe he *shouldn't* have led with his elbow. Maybe he *shouldn't* have purposefully placed himself closest to Kade in case the opportunity presented itself. And maybe he *shouldn't* have enjoyed it as much as he did. But he couldn't stand the thought that Wren might have seriously been seeing this guy. Seeing Kade put his arm around Wren like he was sending Nate a message—it got to him more than it should have. Thing is, *he* wanted Wren.

He wanted to feel her body against his again. He wanted to take her to the beach, or to the movies, or out for dinner. He wanted to be the one she defended like she defended Kade now. And maybe he didn't realise how much he wanted it until it was too late. Now they had these stupid rules and the stupid idea that Durgan had any influence on anyone's relationships.

But he and Wren weren't together. They weren't anything. They were supposed to be working on being friends, but he might have blown that opportunity up, too. He let the thought of Wren being with anyone else get the better of him, but he had no say in it. Wren was free to do what she wanted and be with anyone she wanted. But it didn't mean it didn't bring out the worst in him.

'You should be apologising to Kade—he's the one you hit, not me.'

She was refusing to look at him, even though she stood next to him in line at the kiosk. He glanced back at Kade sitting at the bench with Russ and Kassandra. He'd said he was all right, but Wren insisted that she get some ice for him and Nate figured he had some making up to do.

'I *have* apologised to him, and he said it was all good. Nothing's broken, just bruised.'

'It's *not* all good, Nate.' She glared up at him. 'I know it wasn't an accident.'

'Wren—'

'No, you didn't like him from the start,' she said, turning to face him properly. Her stare bore through him like icicles, penetrating straight to his heart and making everything cold. 'I saw how you looked at him when he brought me coffee yesterday. I saw how your demeanour changed when you realised I was here with him. You got all … possessive … and aggressive … and *jealous* … and you had *no* right.'

'*Jealous*?' he scoffed. 'Did you want me to be? Were you *trying* to make me jealous, Wren?'

Her eyes widened. 'Why would I *try* to make you jealous, Nate? You weren't even supposed to be here!'

'How was I to know you were going to be here with another guy? He clearly thinks this was a date. I thought you were only meeting up with Kass.'

Her mouth dropped open and she quickly snapped it shut. 'What did you just say?' She spoke through clenched teeth and he knew he'd said too much.

'I said he probably thinks that you two are dating.'

She shook her head. 'Did you *know* I was going to be here?'

He bit his lip. 'We bumped into Kass in the carpark and she told us th—'

'*Before* that, Nate.'

He raised his hands in surrender between them. 'Okay, sort of,' he admitted. 'I *may* have overheard you and Kass organising it in the tea room yesterday, but I swear I didn't know—' She rubbed her forehead with her hand, dropping her gaze to the ground. He held her shoulders, urging her to understand. 'Wren, I didn't know you were here with … with him. I wouldn't have come if I did.'

'Bullshit.'

'What?'

'I don't believe you, Nate,' she said, lifting her chin to stare him straight in the eyes. 'If you knew, you would have simply found a way to make sure it wouldn't happen.'

'Wren, I—'

'*Wouldn't you*?' she repeated.

He didn't respond. Because he would have. Heck, he would have searched the work database to find out where she lived, and he would have taken that bottle of whisky over and spent the night. He would have made damn sure that she didn't end up anywhere alone with another man. He would have given her a reason not to.

He searched her glistening eyes, looking for any kind of hope that he hadn't screwed up his only chance of having her close. But it couldn't be found. She was slipping through his fingers and there was nothing he could do about it. And it was his own damn fault. She swiped at a tear.

'M—maybe this friend thing isn't going to work,' she said softly.

'Wren—'

'No, seriously, Nate. If I'm here with another man, it's none of your business. It doesn't matter if it's a date, or whatever. It's *none* of your damn business.'

'You can't be serious about him, Wren. He's a hippy.'

'He's a nice guy,' she said, her jaw set. 'Which you

would know if you got to know him. And it's ... *so* ... much more than I can say about you.'

'Wren,' he pleaded. 'I'm sorry. I am. I was just trying to—'

'God, Nate. We've been through it all already. You *can't* force this.'

'I'm not trying to.'

'Then what was with *that*?' She indicated towards Kade.

He pinched the bridge of his nose with his thumb and forefinger. She was dead set on what she wanted. And nothing he said or did would change that. 'I don't know,' he mumbled. 'I got carried away. It won't happen again.'

'You're right. It won't.' There was something in her voice that made him look at her again. And it was exactly what he didn't want to hear. Ever. 'Because this isn't going to work, Nate. We can't keep doing this.' She tried blinking back a tear, but it fell through her lashes, and he fought the urge to wipe it away. 'What we ... had—' She diverted her gaze towards the ocean. 'It's written in the sand, Nate. All of it. It's just going to wash away with the next tide. We need to forget about it.'

'Wren,' he started.

'*Please*, Nate,' she said, shaking her head. 'Don't say that you can't. I'm not giving you a choice.' She turned towards the kiosk and asked the worker at the register for some ice, but he couldn't find the urge to move.

It hit him like a brick. Sure, he might have acted

like an idiot, and he might have done things he shouldn't have. But how could he not? He needed Wren in more ways than she knew and knowing that he might not have her drove him crazy. But he should have played it smarter. He should have listened to his head and let it happen naturally. But he couldn't. He was scared of losing her.

But now he had.

And it was his own damn fault.

***

Maybe it had been too harsh. But she was furious. She didn't have time or patience for jealousy and games. And she wasn't ready to risk her job for something that clearly wouldn't work out. The fact they couldn't even be friends without something going wrong proved that. She was relieved it was their turn in the line to be served when it was. She wasn't sure she could keep looking at Nate without crying.

God, he made her feel like a fool. He drove her crazy in more ways than one. She hadn't wanted this beach trip to be a date with Kade. And it certainly didn't feel like it when it became a group thing. But the way Nate acted? How could she explain that? Wren grabbed the bag of ice from the kiosk worker and turned back to where Nate was standing.

He was gone.

She scanned the crowd around her but couldn't see him anywhere. She sighed, walking slowly back towards the bench. She'd thought that he might have gone back to sit with the others, but by the time she got there, Kade was alone. Had he really left without saying anything more? But what would he have said to that? She'd basically told him that she didn't want him in her life—which is the total opposite of what she really wanted.

It made her heart ache, telling him that. Much more than it should have. And now that he'd left, she wished she hadn't. But the reality of the situation is they couldn't be together. Their work didn't allow it. And even if it did, could they really base their relationship on a drunken night? Sex isn't the only important thing in a relationship, no matter how good it is. Was. Because it was never going to happen with Nate again. Maybe they might work out how to be friends. That is, if he ever gave her the chance. But she was convinced that chance had been burned. She handed the bag of ice to Kade.

'You know, they say a raw steak is best for a black eye,' Kade said, bumping his shoulder against hers as she sat next to him.

'Sorry,' she mumbled. 'That's all they had. How are you feeling?'

He shrugged. 'It's nothing, really. It'll be fine.'

'Show me.'

He moved the bag of ice from his face and she gasped.

'That good, huh?' he teased.

'Well, it's not *fine*. It's already bruising.'

He pressed the ice back against his face. 'I've had

a black eye before, believe it or not. It's not that bad.'

A smile pulled at her lips. 'Did you get into a fight or something?'

His nose crinkled. 'No, I rode my bike into a streetlight. Hit my head right here—' he pointed to his forehead, just above his left eyebrow. 'Gave me a black eye for about a week.'

'How old were you?'

He shrugged. 'It's been a long time. I was about … twenty-five years old.' Her eyebrow shot up. 'Okay, so it was a few months back. Remember when I didn't bring your Friday coffee that time and you came for it?'

She nodded. 'They told me you weren't there that day.'

He leaned closer. 'I was out the back. I just didn't want you to see me with a black eye.'

She laughed, slapping her hand against his shoulder. Why would he have been worried about what he looked like even back then? She thought they were friends—as much as two people whose relationship was based on coffee could be friends. But had he wanted to be more all this time?

'Careful!' he teased, clutching a hand to his chest. 'I'm a wounded man.'

She laughed again. 'So, that's the only time you've ever had a black eye?'

He nodded. 'But you're the only one who knows how I *really* got it. It did make for good stories though. I might have to come up with some more stories for this one.'

'You've never been in a fight before?'

He shook his head. 'Love, not war, right?'

'Hmm,' she hummed, diverting her gaze towards the ocean.

'Wren, I wanted to ask you something,' he said, his tone serious. She glanced back at him. He'd removed the ice from his face. 'The café is catering for a bush dance tomorrow night at the community hall. It's to raise money for drought relief for our farmers.'

'It's for a good cause,' she said.

He nodded. 'You should come with me.'

'Oh, I don't kn—'

'Your friend—Kass—and the guy she was with are coming.'

'And … Nate?'

'I didn't get the chance to ask him. So, will you come?'

She bit her lip. What were the chances of Nate being there if Russ was going? And what were the chances of him wanting to be anywhere she was after what she said to him? Slim to none, most likely.

'Come on, Wren. You can help me concoct a story to explain my black eye.'

'Okay,' she said quietly. 'Every little bit for our farmers helps, right?'

'Exactly.'

Her brow furrowed as she studied the bruise coming up on Kade's face. 'I'm sorry about your eye.'

His lips curved into a smile and he pressed his

palm to her cheek. She felt her cheeks flush, her body heating up—and not in the way it did with Nate. He held her gaze, and then, started to lean in. She felt her chest tighten and turned her head in time for his lips to press softly against her cheek. He paused then pulled away. She took a shaky breath.

'Sorry, I just … I—' she stammered, twisting her hands together.

'No, don't be. *I'm* sorry. I misread,' he said flatly, directing his gaze towards the kiosk.

They sat in silence, but her mind was a warzone. This was very dangerous territory for her. She'd never had anyone—*anyone*—show an interest in her except for Griffin. Well, not that she'd noticed, at least. And in just over a week, she'd slept with Nate and almost kissed Kade. What the *hell* was wrong with her? She was turning into Kassandra. She loved her best friend—she did—but she didn't want to be like her. Kassandra was so much more confident and … free … with using her body and picking up men. She was basically an expert.

But Wren didn't want to be like that. Wren wanted to find the right guy and let things take its course. She didn't want to move from one guy to another. She didn't want to hook up with handsome strangers and never see them again. She wanted so much more.

'How old did you say you were?' she said, her brow furrowing.

'Twenty-five. You?'

'Twenty-nine.'

He chuckled. 'Always had a thing for the older ladies.'

'Hmm.'

She bit into her lip. She really couldn't say the same for younger men. She'd always wanted a man older than her. She never wanted to feel like a cougar or to be the more mature one by far. She'd figured a man older than her should at least have the same maturity level as her.

And age differences were one of those things that you just can't change.

Chapter 9

'I slept with Russ.'

Kassandra barged through the door and walked straight to the kitchen, grabbing a mug from the cupboard, and pouring coffee into it. Wren blinked, closing the door, and took a sip of the coffee in her hand.

'Please, come inside,' she muttered.

'Oh, I did, Wren. Trust me.' Kassandra took a sip of her coffee.

Wren pulled a face. 'Ugh. Too early. Too much information.'

Kassandra moved around the bench and flopped onto the couch. Wren leaned against the edge of the wall, rubbing her forehead. It had been a long night. A night where sleep was impossible, and she would have preferred to smack a book against her head until she passed out. Maybe it would knock some sense into her.

How could she talk to Nate like that? How could she cut off all ties with him, even though she desperately wanted to tangle all the ties together and make something out of it? She *worked* with the guy. It's not like she'd never see him again. It was awkward already, this was only going to make things worse.

Then, there was Kade.

And their sort-of date turned into a group thing. And what she was *sure* would be a date tonight. And the fact he was younger than her and was, indeed, more of a hippy than she'd realised. After the silence that followed their awkward age discussion, he delved into further details of his love-not-war motto. And all about his free spirit. And green peace. And reduce waste. And every other damn cause that he spent his time researching and fighting for.

Sure, she cared for the environment, and she felt like she did the right thing by recycling everything that could be recycled and not buying things with excess packaging. She just wasn't into making a big deal about things. But that was her. Head down, keep working, be left alone. She had nothing against those who were courageous enough to fight for their causes. And Kade was nice enough. She could just see it wasn't going to work with him. They were too … different. He wanted to travel; she was focussed on her career. He never wanted to be tied down with kids; kids were definitely in her life-plan. Always had been. Their very lifestyles were different.

It came down to their only common interests basically being coffee. And it turned out that he didn't even *like* coffee. He only liked *making* it. He'd responded by saying that opposites attract, but she wasn't so convinced.

Kassandra flipped herself upright, facing Wren. 'It's almost noon. What do you mean it's too early?'

Wren took another sip of her coffee, blinking her eyes until they didn't hurt as much to have them open. Kassandra waved her finger at her.

'You're not dressed.'

'No sleep,' she muttered.

'Nate?'

She nodded. 'And Kade.'

Kassandra bit her lip. 'I saw you talking with Nate when you were getting ice. It … didn't … look good.'

'It wasn't,' she admitted. 'I was mad, and I let it out on him.'

'Oh, honey, you were more than mad.'

'I might have been too hard on him.' She sighed, moving over to the couch to sit next to Kassandra. 'It ended badly. I—I think I messed up, Kass. With all of it. The rules, being friends, all of it. I cut him away and now I'm not convinced it was the right thing to do.'

'Durgan would have had your job if you didn't end things with Nate.'

'Screw Durgan!' she yelled, swiping at her eyes. 'It's his fault I'm even in this position. If he'd just given me the promotion like he was supposed to—'

'Durgan didn't make you sleep with Nate.'

'I wasn't *supposed* to see him again, Kass. How was I to know that he'd got my job? We didn't go into detail with our backgrounds, it just … happened.'

Kassandra bit her lip, pulling Wren into her arms. 'It's messed up,' she said, shushing Wren. 'Just apologise to Nate tomorrow and maybe you can at least get along at work. It's for the best.'

'If he'll let me,' she muttered.

Kassandra laughed. 'In the meantime, I'm cutting you off one-night stands. They are clearly not for you.'

'It wouldn't be the same if I did, anyway.'

Kassandra pulled her to arm's length and looked her straight in the eye. 'Wren?'

'It was different with Nate, Kass,' she said, her voice cracking. 'I mean, it's been a while, but I know that none of my other times felt like it did with him. And now I—I ruined that.'

'Oh, honey.' Kassandra stroked her hair. 'You're in way over your head.' It looked like she wanted to say more, but she hesitated.

She chuckled. 'You can be honest with me, Kass. I think I need it.'

'I'm not sure you want to hear what I have to say.'

'Kass—'

'*But*, since you insist,' she continued. 'You just broke up with Griffin—you were supposed to be getting *married*. It's only natural that you're going to have a … lost … stage. One-night stands don't mean anything. That's the beauty of them.'

'But I'm not a one-night stand kind of girl.'

'I know,' she said. 'But you were desperate, and you'd hit a point of insecurity. And Nate was there. That's it. That's all it can ever be, trust me.'

She sighed. 'You're the expert.'

Kassandra's eyes flickered. 'That's right. I *am* an expert. Remember that. You might end up as friends with Nate, but if it happens, it'll happen with time. The plus side is you have a nice guy who *wants* to be with you, and he doesn't work with us.'

She studied her hands. 'It's not going to work with Kade.'

'Why not?'

'He's a hippy. And he's younger than me.'

'So?' Kassandra smiled. 'I've been with hippies, and I've been with guys younger than me, and *trust me*, they can be a lot of fun.'

'I don't want fun. I have a plan. I … *had* … a plan.'

'Give him a go, Wren. You need time to adjust to being single again. You *need* fun. Did he ask you to go to the dance with him tonight?' Wren nodded. 'And you're going?' She nodded again. 'So, let yourself have a bit of fun. Without Nate.'

Maybe Kassandra was right.

And maybe Wren was moping more about this whole Nate thing than she should. Still, it didn't stop her wishing things could be so very different. And the ache in her chest certainly didn't help.

***

'I slept with Kass.'

Russ pushed past Nate, grabbing the coffee out of his hand as he passed.

'Help yourself,' Nate mumbled. He headed to the kitchen to make another. 'Why are you telling me this?'

Russ looked at him quizzically, leaning against the bench. 'Isn't that what we're doing now? You told me, so I tell you?'

Nate shook his head. 'What's your point, Russ? You sleep with women all the time.'

Russ took a gulp of coffee, holding his finger up to Nate. 'But it's different with Kass.'

'How?' Nate pinched the bridge of his nose with his thumb and forefinger and stared into the dark liquid gold in his cup.

'I'm seeing her again.'

Nate flicked his gaze up towards his friend, his eyebrow raised. 'You never do that.'

'I know.'

'So, why this time?'

Russ shrugged. 'We're going to that dance tonight. We sort of agreed to go before we … you know.'

Nate's brow furrowed. 'What dance?'

'The fundraiser dance? At the community hall?'

'What are you on about?'

'Kade didn't tell you?'

'I left before you, remember? You said you were

going to leave with Kass, and I left while Wren was getting ice.'

'Ahh,' Russ said. 'So, you missed that conversation.' He finished the rest of his coffee. 'The café where Kade works is having a bush dance tonight to raise funds for the farmers. He invited me and Kass, and I assume he was going to invite Wren. I'm sure he would have asked you if you came back to the group.'

'Doubt it,' he muttered. 'I'm sure he doesn't want me there. Wren doesn't.'

Russ stood straight. 'Why's that? Did she tell you?'

'In a way,' he admitted. 'Not about the dance specifically. But everything in general.'

'I'm sure she didn't mean it.'

Nate scoffed. 'She was pretty clear. I pissed her off. I pushed it, and I blew it. It's over.'

He stared at his coffee a moment longer then took a gulp. The words hurt as he said them. He'd tried to avoid thinking about it all night—to no avail. Wren didn't want him. She didn't want to be with him. She didn't want to be friends with him. And no doubt, she didn't even want to be seen with him. And he probably deserved it. He wasn't usually the kind of guy to fight people. But Wren clouded his mind to a point that he couldn't think straight. He knew she shouldn't affect him as much as she had. He knew his chest shouldn't feel tight every time he thought of her.

She'd made her feelings clear.

And if she wanted to be with Kade, who was he to stop her? He couldn't call her his. And nothing he said would hold any value with her. He just had to let her go. Even if it hurt like hell. But how could he forget about someone he has to see every day?

'That's not like you, Nate.'

'What?' He glanced up at Russ. His brow was furrowed.

'The whole defeatist attitude,' Russ explained. 'You're usually the one with a plan. All optimistic and stuff.'

'People change,' he muttered.

'Not like this. Do you really think she was serious?'

'She seemed pretty serious.'

'So, what are you going to do?'

Nate considered his coffee for a moment and shrugged. 'I'll give her what she wants. I'll stay out of her life as much as possible. Interactions will be minimal. Strictly business.'

Russ shook his head slowly. 'Is that some kind of reverse psychology attempt?'

Nate frowned. 'No. I'm serious, Russ.'

'Like hell you are,' Russ said. 'You're going to go to that dance tonight, do your thing, and win her back.'

'I'm not going to chase her if she doesn't want to be chased.'

Russ's eyes gleamed. '*All* girls want to be chased, Nate. They just don't realise it.'

'That sounds a little on the creepy side, Russ.'

Russ laughed, grabbing a piece of paper, and scribbling something on it. 'Well, if you're not going to do it for Wren, do it for me. I acted as a buffer for you yesterday, I need you to do the same for me.'

Nate scoffed. 'You don't need my help.'

'I do. Because if I end up sleeping with Kass again, it breaks all of *my* rules.'

'So, why go at all?'

'Because I said I'd be there. And I'm no liar.'

Nate shook his head. 'You're one complicated man, Russ.'

Russ pushed off the bench and headed towards the front door. 'Life is a whole lot simpler than you think, Nate. You just have to let it happen.'

'I have no intention of going to that dance!' he yelled after him.

He heard no response other than the front door closing behind his friend and studied what Russ had scribbled on the paper. It was the details for the dance. He sipped his coffee and turned his head to where the bottle of whisky still sat on his kitchen bench. If only life could be as simple as Russ made it out to be—if all he had to do was hold the bottle of whisky out to Wren, and all would be forgiven. That they could move on to what they could have been.

But it wasn't.

Life wasn't simple. It was a first-class bitch that threw things at him left, right, and centre. And there was nothing to do about it except for taking it as it comes. He was used to that. He was used to not drawing the best lot. He was used to working hard for anything he wanted and accepting what he got. He was used to taking things into his own hands. And maybe it was time he realised that things with Wren were doomed from the start. And that's just the lot he drew.

***

'Where are you?'

'Hmm?'

Wren flicked her eyes up to meet Kade's—one eye bruised from the accident. They'd been standing in the waltz position while the band described the steps for what she gathered was a quick-stepped dance and Wren hadn't heard any of it. They'd danced the circle and line dances, but when it came time to dance specifically with Kade, she just didn't feel right. Sure, it was fun, she supposed. As much fun as it could be when her mind was entirely elsewhere. On someone entirely different to the man she'd come to the dance with.

She couldn't help but think of how it didn't quite feel right having her hand in Kade's. Of course, he was a good dancer, and they seemed to get the moves right—for the most part. It's just that she still hadn't felt right after what she said to Nate.

She knew that she shouldn't feel a tightening in her stomach when she thought of what she said to him. She knew that she shouldn't miss him as much as she did. But she also knew that Kade couldn't possibly be right for her if she couldn't think about him when he was standing right there, holding her.

'You're miles away, Wren. Did you catch any of the steps?'

She glanced across the room, seeing Kassandra and Russ standing close together, their eyes on each other rather than the band. Kassandra was smiling. It looked more natural than what Wren usually saw on her face when she was with a guy. The rest of the hall was filled with people wearing jeans and flannelettes, some sporting broad-brimmed hats. Wren closed her eyes, shaking her head slightly.

'Sorry, I just … I need some air.' She pushed back in an attempt to move outside, but he held onto her arm.

'I'll come with you.'

She tried to tug her arm from his grip, but her attempt was weak. She could feel her body heating up, her skin prickling, and beads of sweat forming on her forehead. She just needed to get outside, get some air. Allow the cool breeze to snap some sense into her.

'I'm fine, I just need to … I need some oxygen, that's all.'

She pushed through the doors, breathing in the cool air, and leaned against the outside of the building, her eyes closed. Where had her life started to go wrong? Everything had been going well. Her life plan was on track. Then Griffin ran off, and Nate entered the picture. And now she couldn't even dance with a friend and truly enjoy it.

She remembered all the times she'd spent with

Griffin—and all the times they hadn't. How had she not seen the signs sooner? They'd been friends, but had there really been anything more? Sure, maybe she'd been fooled for a long time. Or maybe she just refused to believe it wasn't going to happen. Admittedly, there had been times when she wondered if Griffin really was right for her. But she was too damn focussed on her plan to convince herself that there might be someone better suited for her. And now? Now she wondered if there was really anyone out there for her. How could she focus on anyone else when all she could think about was Nate?

'Is it something I said?'

Wren opened her eyes, focussing on Kade. His brow was furrowed, and his arms were crossed. She shook her head. 'No,' she said. 'I just … I'm not feeling very well. I don't think I had enough water yesterday and I'm paying the price for it now.'

It was possible. She found it very easy to become dehydrated when she'd been to the beach. Something with the heat and the sea breeze. But she also knew that she'd made a conscious effort to stay hydrated yesterday, and her turn was more likely to be related to her conversation with Nate and the fact that she had no damn sleep the night before. And apparently, Kade suspected it, too.

'You don't look like you're dehydrated,' he said. She avoided eye contact with him. She was a terrible liar, and it was clear that he knew it. He sighed, shifting his gaze to focus on something behind her, in the direction of the carpark. 'You're not into this, are you?'

She lifted her gaze to focus on him and, when he returned his eyes to her, there was a coldness in them. A seriousness that wasn't usually there. Her chest heaved. 'You're a nice guy,' she whispered.

'I'm not a fool, Wren,' he said. He lifted his hand, rubbing his forehead. 'I figured it was too good to be true. Why would a girl like you agree to go out with a guy like me?'

She reached out to him, but he stepped back. 'Kade, you deserve better than me. I'm not in the right place right now. I have a lot to sort ou—'

'It's Nate, isn't it?'

His words pierced through her like shards of ice. How had she got herself into this mess? She dropped her gaze to focus on the sidewalk beneath her feet. 'I'm sorry,' she whispered.

He was silent for a moment, and when she looked up, he was looking towards the carpark behind her again, his jaw tense. 'I suspected it, you know,' he said, his tone cold, distant. Almost like he wasn't talking to her. 'At the beach. I hoped it wasn't true. But don't worry—I won't get in your way.'

'Kade—'

He shook his head. 'Maybe you should find someone else to make your coffee for you.' He stared straight at her, his expression cold. It sent a shiver down her spine.

The door swung open behind them and one of the waitresses popped out. 'God, there you are.

Kade, we need your help. We're understaffed, and Kasey is going out of her mind.' She paused, looking between Kade and Wren. 'I hope I'm not interrupting anything,' she finished hesitantly.

Kade raised an eyebrow. 'Nope. We're done.' He turned and started to follow the waitress back into the hall. He paused at the door, flicking his eyes back towards her—and behind her. 'You'd be good together. Perfect, even.' His tone was flat, and it made Wren's breath catch and her brow furrow.

He went back inside without another glance and she got the feeling she wasn't welcome to go back in either. Just as well she'd only brought the things inside that she could fit in the pocket of her jeans. She closed her eyes for a second before widening them again. Why had he kept looking behind her? Slowly, she turned on her heel until she saw him— standing a few meters away—with the bottle of whisky in his hand.

Chapter 10

He hadn't thought it would have happened that way.
He'd had no intention of going to the dance. Then,
he couldn't get that damned bottle of whisky out of
his mind. How could he possibly forget about what
he and Wren had when he had the constant
reminder sitting on his kitchen bench? But he
couldn't bear to simply toss it. He'd considered it. He
could save them both the trouble and avoid the
temptation by simply pouring it down the sink and
throwing the bottle in the bin.

But he couldn't. He'd had the lid off, about to
pour it down the sink, and couldn't bring himself to
do it. He'd put the lid back on and put the bottle
back on the bench, considering it for a while.
Throwing it out felt more like he was throwing away

everything he had with Wren—the nights they'd spent together, the connection they could have had, the relationship they could have pursued.

So, he decided to give it to Wren, and she could decide what to do with it. She could throw it in the closest bin and he'd never have to know. And if he ever found out, he at least knew exactly where she stood—if she really meant every word she said to him. He figured the dance would be a better place to do it than at work. Work was too risky. And he had no idea when or if he'd ever see her outside of work again.

And if Kade just happened to see him giving the bottle back to Wren, maybe he would know that Nate was backing down. Maybe Wren would have to explain to Kade what went on between them, or maybe she wouldn't and act like it never happened. Truth is, it hurt to see her with someone else. But she wanted to move on, and he wasn't going to stop her. She could ask for anything and he would give it to her. This was no exception.

He hadn't expected to overhear their conversation or be walking towards the hall from the parking lot when they came outside. He'd slowed his pace once he saw the look on Wren's face—how she'd leaned against the building, her eyes closed. He could hear the band leader describing steps and starting the music slowly. Had something happened? God, if Kade had done anything to hurt her … He stopped walking once he was within earshot.

She gave some excuse about being dehydrated.

He agreed with Kade—he'd seen her drinking plenty of water while they were at the beach. Though, he couldn't speak for after he'd left. She didn't look overly dehydrated, from what he could see, anyway. He didn't have the best angle of her. But he could tell in her stature that something was definitely on her mind.

He felt something catch in his throat once he realised that Kade had noticed him. He stood up straighter, lifting his chin to stare at him straight-on, half-expecting him to say something. But he didn't. Kade's focus drifted back to Wren. He watched the exchange—was Kade ending it with her? He heard Wren apologise, saying that Kade deserved better, and his chest tightened when he heard what Kade said next.

'It's Nate, isn't it?'

He'd taken a step forward, but he couldn't find the push to move any more than that. Wren's response was too quiet for him to hear but, judging by the way Kade looked at him when she answered and with the rest of their conversation, he could only imagine her answer. And he was feeling his decision to let her go start to slide.

What was he supposed to do? Was he supposed to turn around and leave before she realised he was there? Before she realised that he'd overheard everything? And leave her outside, alone, in the dark? He imagined that she'd have no intention of going back in there. Then again, he also didn't know who she came with or if she drove herself. It was the fact that she would probably be feeling vulnerable that made him lean towards leaving, and it was the fact that he still cared about her that made him want to stay. But before he could decide on an action, she'd turned around and was facing him. His decision was made for him.

'H—how long have you been standing there?' Her voice was shaky and her eyes weary. She folded her arms across her chest and kicked at a stone near her feet.

He slowly began to close the distance between them. 'Not long,' he said.

'Did … did you … overhear … any of that?' Her eyes flicked up to look at him through her long eyelashes.

He shook his head slowly. Why couldn't he tell her that he heard all of it? Why was his instinct to lie to her? Maybe to save her the embarrassment. Maybe to save himself. She released the breath that she'd been holding on to.

'It didn't look like it went too well, though,' he said, coming to a halt a couple of feet from her.

'It didn't,' she muttered. 'It wasn't going to work out with … Kade.'

He bit into his lip to stop the inappropriate smile that was trying to force its way onto his face. He furrowed his brow. 'Do you want to talk about it?'

She shook her head. 'What's there to talk about? It didn't work out.'

'Because he's a hippy?' He'd spoken before thinking it through that time, and he held his breath for her response. She hadn't been happy with him saying that at the beach, but she actually smiled this time. It was slight, but it was there.

'Because he's a hippy,' she said quietly, a ring in her voice. 'Among other things. We had too many ... differences.'

Do we?

Her shoulders dropped and she moved her arms so that she was twisting her fingers together in front of her. 'I'm sorry, Nate,' she whispered. 'About yesterday. I was just ... I don't know what came over me.'

He pressed his lips together, studying her eyes. She looked sincere, and only a moment ago he was questioning what they had, convinced that he didn't have another chance with her. Now, there could be. Especially with how her conversation with Kade went. But now that she was apologising to him, there was something that made him hesitate, that made his chest tighten. He really didn't know what kind of woman she was, and he didn't want to be the guy she tossed away and kept coming back to. He didn't want to be the rebound. But then again, he was only ever the rebound with Wren. Everything they had was based on her being a jilted bride. How had he never seen that sooner?

'I didn't mean it,' she continued. 'I was too harsh on you, Nate. I was caught up in all of it and I ... I still want to be friends with you, if you'll let me.'

His head dropped back enough to look over her head. How could he move from being a rebound to a friend? Before he realised that that was all he was, he would have agreed in a heartbeat. But now? Now, he didn't know what to say. He didn't know what to *think*. Looks like she'd played him after all.

'I don't know, Wren,' he whispered, closing his eyes, and pinching the bridge of his nose with his thumb and forefinger.

She took a shaky breath. 'Nate,' she whispered.

He shook his head, looking down at the hand he had draped by his side—at the whisky. He stepped forward, holding the bottle out to her. 'I thought I'd give this to you,' he said flatly. 'Just in case you wanted it.'

She took it from his hand, studied the label and glanced up at him. 'This is—'

'*The* bottle, yes,' he said, shifting his gaze. He caught a glimpse of her eyes glistening before he looked away. 'I couldn't … forget … with it there in view. So, you should have it.'

She laughed—a light, quick chuckle. But it didn't have as much heart in it as she probably meant for it to have. 'Couldn't you put it in a cupboard or something?' Her voice was shaky, and he risked a glance at her. She was blinking quickly as if trying to stop tears from flowing.

He shook his head. 'It's not that easy.'

He knew she understood what he was saying. She swiped at her eyes with the back of her hand and nodded. 'Are we still friends?'

He considered her question for a moment and nodded. He might need some time to wrap his head around it, to let the whole rebound thing slide. And he'd follow the rules to a tee. But he was sure that, somehow, they could start over. As friends.

***

There really were no words to describe the relief she felt when he nodded. She hadn't broken it beyond repair. They could still be friends. He wasn't going to leave her life for good. She gripped the bottle of whisky tighter between her hands. Why had he given it to her? Had he planned on forgetting her as he implied? Had he planned on moving on, taking himself out of the picture?

God, she hoped not.

She knew it was foolish and silly of her to want it so much. She knew it was selfish to not want him to forget about her. About what they had. Especially since she was the one that said that she wanted to forget about it. But she hadn't regretted a conversation—or anything for that matter—as much as she regretted what she said to Nate. And for what? She gained nothing but misery from it. She'd unknowingly been self-sabotaging any chance she had of being happy. She wondered if Griffin knew that about her. Maybe that's why he stuck around with her as long as he did.

The door to the hall opened behind her, and a couple walked out towards the parking lot. They were laughing, enjoying themselves, and didn't even glance at Wren and Nate. Everyone was oblivious of them. No one even knew they were there or that there was this unspoken battle between them. As the door swung closed, she could hear the song switch to the hokey-pokey.

Nate cleared his throat, and she shifted her gaze from the couple who had just got in their car, back to Nate. He'd taken a couple steps back. He was distancing himself, putting space between them, and she knew it shouldn't hurt as much as it did. He'd agreed to be friends, so why was it still so difficult?

'I should ... umm ... I should go,' he muttered, running his hand through his hair, his muscles flexing under his shirt. 'Enjoy the rest of the dance, Wren.'

'I wasn't really planning to go back in,' she said. 'I don't think Kade wants me to. But I'd consider it if I had someone to dance with.' She indicated to his outfit—jeans and a dark blue flannelette shirt, the sleeves rolled up to his elbows—that suited him much more than she'd imagined it would. 'You're dressed for it.'

'Ahh ...' He hesitated, diverting his gaze. 'I'm not sure that's a good idea.'

'Why not?' she said, shrugging one of her shoulders. 'Friends can dance. And Russ is in there with Kass, so we won't be alone.'

He shook his head. 'I don't want to go inside.'

Her brow furrowed, and she felt her breath catch as she spoke. 'Why did you come here, Nate?'

He nodded towards the bottle of whisky in her hands. 'To give you that.'

'You could have done that tomorrow,' she

whispered. 'You're dressed for the dance.'

His lips pressed together, and his jaw was tense. 'In case I had to go inside to find you. But you were outside, I've given you the bottle, and now I will leave.'

She felt her chest tighten, and her vision started to blur. He turned and started to leave. 'Nate.'

Her voice cracked, and she wasn't entirely sure what she was going to say. It was as though her mouth had a mind of its own. He stopped, looking over his shoulder at her. He said nothing, but his eyes urged her to continue.

'Please stay,' she whispered.

He turned his body so that all of him was facing her, but he didn't move closer.

'We don't have to go inside,' she continued, feeling her hairs stand on end. 'We can stay out here, enjoy the music.' He took a step towards her, then another. 'Start afresh, as friends. Just for a moment.'

He came to a stop with barely a foot between them. The music transitioned to a slow song—another waltz. She felt her breath catch in her throat and felt that tingling through her body that being near him gave her. God, how could they ever just be friends when he made her feel like that? When he made her want to push herself onto her toes, lift her chin, and meet his lips with hers. Holding her gaze, he pried the bottle from her hands and put it by the wall. He ran his hand down her right arm and lifted her hand, wrapping his fingers around it, and tugged her close with his other, resting it on the small of her back. As if by instinct, she relaxed her left hand on his shoulder.

'Friends can dance?' he said, still holding her gaze.

His eyes were so intense that she couldn't bring herself to look away. She nodded, slowly, unsure. She wasn't as convinced about it now as she had been a moment ago. Friends could dance. It's been common knowledge for years. Probably for as long as dancing has been around. He started swaying her, leading with his left foot, and carrying out the steps like someone who knew what he was doing. She felt him press his hand against her back, pulling her just that little bit closer. It was possibly the most sensual and intimate dance that she'd ever had—Griffin certainly never danced this close with her. He never danced at all. Nate still held her gaze, searching her eyes. There was something in his eyes she didn't recognise. Uncertainty? Hesitation? She couldn't quite place it.

'Are you sure?' he asked, his eyebrow raised. She nodded again. 'It doesn't break any of your rules? Like the no-close-proximity one?'

'I'm sure I can make an exception.'

She slowly released the breath she'd been holding onto without realising. He flashed her a smile that she knew meant he noticed her shaky breath. *Damn*. She shifted her gaze, resting her head against her hand on his shoulder to avoid catching his eyes again. He continued leading them around in slow circles, his fingertips pressing gently against her back and the thumb of his other hand rubbing softly against her hand. She closed her eyes, just for a moment, and felt a smile creep onto her face.

If only it could be as simple as this.

If only they didn't work together, maybe they could have had something. They *did* have something. She could still feel it, despite the rollercoaster they'd already been on. They just had to settle for a friendship, with rules attached. She felt a weight in her chest and opened her eyes, realising that she'd shifted her hand further back and her head was resting directly on his shoulder. Had he realised? Or was he lost in the moment as she had been? As slowly as she could, she moved her head away from him, putting some distance between them. He tugged her closer again and she felt her breath quicken. He had noticed.

Friends could dance.

But not like this. Friends could not dance like lovers. *That* was in complete violation of the rules. The song changed again, to something faster-paced, and she heard the crowd inside grow noisier again. But Nate didn't let her go. He still held her in that waltzing position. She looked up at him and he held her gaze, his lips curving into a knowing smile that made her heart flip.

She opened her mouth to say something, but nothing came out. And all she could think about was her heart racing, the heat spreading to her cheeks, and the compelling urge to close the distance between them.

Chapter 11

It used up every fibre of his being to not give in to the urge. The urge to tell the rules to go get screwed. The urge to take her mouth with his and kiss her hard, thoroughly. To have her. To explore all of her body in more detail than he'd had a chance to.

She wanted it too, he could tell. The way her breathing was already choppy, the way her body stiffened just enough to show him that she had urges of her own. The way she looked at him with those blue eyes, darkening, even in the dim light. It took him a moment to realise they'd stopped moving, dancing. They were simply standing there, her hand in his, their bodies pressed together, studying each other, knowing what lay beneath. Fighting their inner battles. Fighting the urge.

He should pull away. This wasn't what friends did. Friends didn't hold each other like they wanted more. Friends didn't look at each other like they wanted to rip their clothes off and make sweet passionate love, gentle and rough, slow, and fast. He felt his jaw clench, an involuntary reaction to fighting the losing battle, and her lips parted even more. He could smell the sweetness of her breath that he was already addicted to. They were so close that their breaths were mingling together.

He should pull away. But he couldn't. He could close the distance, allow them to have what they both wanted. But he shouldn't. It would only mess things up more, keep them running in the same circle, fighting the same battle, stuck in the same cycle that was already pushing them to the edge. He had to do *something*. But he couldn't. He was frozen, torn between his addiction and doing things right. Torn between her and, well, *her*. He didn't want just one part of her. He wanted all of her. He saw the slow movement of her throat as she swallowed, the hesitation, the wanting.

'Nate,' she whispered.

God, even his name on her lips was pure ecstasy, feeding his addiction, fuelling his desire, draining him of every little bit of resolve, just to have her once more.

If the door hadn't opened behind them at that very moment, he would have lost the battle. But because it did, it gave him the strength to release her, take a step back. If it hadn't been Russ and

Kassandra, he might have found himself back where he was the second they were gone. But because it was, he and Wren were no longer alone. No longer in that moment where things could have gone either way.

And at *that* very moment, he both hated his best friend and was grateful for his timing. And he was willing to wager that Wren felt the same way.

'Ahh, so you *did* come,' Russ said, dropping his arm from Kassandra's shoulders.

Russ gave him a look that showed him he was grateful for Nate being there. After all, they were *both* in situations they hadn't planned to be in. Nate ran a hand through his hair, the reality of how close he'd been to blowing it catching up to him. He registered Wren taking a shaky breath, folding her arms across her chest, staring at the ground.

'Umm ... yeah,' he muttered. 'Figured I'd come and make sure you lot weren't having too much fun without me.'

Kassandra was squinting, shifting her gaze between him and Wren. She opened her mouth as if to say something, but Wren was the one to speak, surprising him. 'What are you guys up to?' she said, focussing only on Russ and Kassandra.

'Oh, we were just ...' Kassandra started, glancing up at Russ.

'Headed back to the bar,' Russ offered. Nate knew he was referring to the one he worked at.

'Right,' Kassandra said unconvincingly. 'The bar.'

'Hey, you two should come,' Russ said,

attempting to make it sound casual.

Nate's eyebrow lifted. He glanced over at Wren, who was looking a little … unsure. But what harm could there be in going to the bar? Sure, they hooked up in a bar. But they were alone that time. This time, they wouldn't be alone. And what better way to truly get to know someone than over a few drinks with other people around?

'I'm up for it,' Nate said, catching Wren's eyes. 'If you are. I don't want to be third-wheeling these two.'

'Oh, it wouldn't be third-wheeling,' Russ said, almost desperately. He glanced over at his friend to see Russ's eyes wide. Kassandra was glaring up at him.

'I'm not sure,' Wren said hesitantly.

'Has to be better than this, right?' Nate continued. 'You didn't look like you were going back in. And it would have to be better than just going home.' Even though *he* should just go back home.

Wren squinted, undecided, then turned to her friend. 'Kass?'

Kassandra sighed. 'Mmm, you should come,' she said, dropping her scrutinising gaze from Russ. 'Plenty of time to be boring the rest of the week.'

Wren's lips curved up, and he wondered if that's what she actually preferred. What *was* her usual boring night like? Was she a reader? Did she watch movies? Stay up late, or go to bed early? Order take-out, or cook her own meals? He didn't know *any* of that about her. But he also couldn't help but imagine himself doing whatever she did with her.

'All right, then, I'm in,' she said, a glint in her eyes as she glanced at him.

He felt his heart leap, even though he knew it shouldn't. But was that the first real step towards them being proper friends?

'What's the plan, then?' Wren said. 'The parking's not great on that street.'

'Nate's place is the best spot to park,' Russ said. 'If I recall correctly.'

Nate scoffed. If *he* recalled correctly, Russ's car was perpetually parked at his place. Wren looked at him questioningly, her brow creased. 'Is that okay?' she said.

'Well, it's not far from the bar,' he said. *As you already know*. Her eyes widened, and he was certain that he'd seen her cheeks tinge darker. Had she thought the same thing he had?

'It's settled then,' Kassandra said. 'We'll follow you home, then head over to the bar.'

Russ and Kassandra started heading towards their cars as if on a mission—no doubt they were—but he noticed Wren's slight hesitation before tagging along behind them. And he wasn't sure why it tore at his chest. Didn't she want to hang out as a group? For some reason, he figured she'd probably be okay with it if he wouldn't be there. And he had a good idea why.

***

Wren pulled up behind Kassandra's car in front of Nate's place—of all places! She glanced at the bottle of whisky on the floor of the passenger side, then up at his front door, memories of that night flooding back and making her cheeks heat up. What was she doing? Why was she here? She'd barely had time to adjust her thoughts from *trying* to give Kade a go, to accepting that she just couldn't.

And why?

Because Nate.

Because she couldn't stop thinking about him, feeling sick in her stomach at the thought of having lost him, the thought of being with someone else. The thought of letting someone else into her life after Griffin. And now, she'd agreed to go to the bar—*the* bar—with Nate. Sure, Kassandra and Russ were both there as well. They weren't *technically* alone. But they may as well be with the way those two had been looking at each other all night. Nate had been fortunate enough to not have to witness that look yet, but she was fairly certain that Kassandra had other plans for the night.

And if that left her alone with Nate, she wasn't sure whether she'd be grateful or terrified.

She'd been ready to kiss him before they were interrupted. And she was almost certain that he had been, too. Who were they kidding? Could they really be friends? Could she *deal* with them being friends? It was a long shot, but it's the only way it could go. With Durgan's rules and her wanting to keep the job that she worked hard for, even if she didn't get the promotion, they couldn't be more than that.

She squeezed her eyes shut, trying to compose herself even a little, and startled when there was a tap on her window. Nate, of course, since Kassandra and Russ had already started walking. *Damn it*. There goes her buffer. She took a breath, feeling a whole lot less confident than she hoped she looked, and opened her door, stepping out. The sooner they caught up to the others, the better. She couldn't trust herself to be alone with this guy. Especially when the flannelette shirt he was wearing only served to make him look *that* much sexier. *Damn him*. Did he know what he was doing to her? Probably not.

'You all right?' he said, leaning against her car as she climbed out.

'Mhmm, yep,' she said, her voice much higher than it should be. 'Just making sure I had everything I needed.'

'You sure?' His brow was furrowed, and he looked genuinely concerned. 'We could do something else if the bar's not your scene.'

And be by themselves, without Kassandra and Russ? Even if they were giving each other sexy eyes all night and driving Wren insane and even if the bar *wasn't* her scene—which it really wasn't—she couldn't be alone with Nate. Not if they even remotely had a chance of being friends, which was becoming much less believable by the second.

'Have you forgotten where we met?' she said, plastering a fake smile on her face. His grey eyes darkened, and it made her heart skip a beat. Stupid heart.

'Maybe that's why I suggested it,' he said, shrugging slightly, holding her gaze. 'Remove the temptation.'

This time, her lips curved on their own. Only slightly, but she was smiling. She knew it wouldn't remove the temptation. Heck, being alone with Nate would only make it worse. Removing the temptation would be removing him from the equation. And she wasn't sure she was ready for that, even if they couldn't act on it. She sighed, dropping her gaze, redirecting it towards their friends that were almost half a street ahead of them.

'You know, after tonight, I feel like I need a drink,' she muttered.

He said nothing. And when she glanced up at him to see if he'd heard her, he was studying her. His eyebrows pulled together, his eyes still dark. It sent a shiver down her spine, even though she wasn't cold. Then, he nodded—once, ever so slightly—then tore his gaze away from her. She felt her shoulders drop as she released a breath she didn't know she'd been holding onto. He pushed off her car, giving it a pat, and moved past her.

'Funny,' he said. 'I didn't picture you in a Barina.'

She frowned, looking over her car as she locked it. 'What's wrong with my Barina?' she said, walking quickly to catch up with him, then, falling into step beside him.

'Nothing,' he said, smirking that mischievous grin

that looked *so* good on him. 'It's just … small.'

'I'm not a big person, Nate,' she said, feeling her insides squirm when his shoulder brushed against hers.

'Didn't say you were,' he teased. 'Just figured you'd be in a more … *sophisticated* … car. You know, considering you drink whisky and all.'

Her eyebrow lifted. 'Hey, she goes all right,' she said. 'Besides, how do you think I can afford whisky?'

He pressed his lips together and nodded, as though considering her statement. 'Fair enough,' he said. 'Strangely, it makes sense. But red?'

She felt her lips curve higher. 'Red goes fast.'

'Not in the case of a 1.4 litre engine,' he said, his body pressing closer to hers as he dodged an overgrown bush. 'How do you go with long drives?'

She shrugged, staring down at the ground. 'I don't really … go … on long drives.'

She felt his eyes shoot towards her. 'Please tell me you're kidding.'

She shrugged. 'I'm usually too busy, or tired from working so hard and studying.'

'You don't ever take time off work?' He seemed surprised.

She shook her head. 'Why would I? I've got nowhere else to go. Not really. My dad lives nearby. I don't need to take leave to see him.'

'How much leave do you have accumulated?'

She shrugged again, for what seemed like the hundredth time in the last few minutes. Why did he seem so interested in how much leave she had?

Sure, it wasn't a touchy issue for her, but it also wasn't one she advertised. She was a workaholic. She didn't have plans to travel, no list of places to see. She did have plans, until Griffin left. She had travel plans—only for the honeymoon, but future travels didn't seem absurd—she had a life plan. Now? What did she have?

'A couple months. Maybe three,' she mumbled, feeling a heaviness in her stomach.

Had she really lost her life plan? Of course, it would be difficult to do the whole married with kids and a dog without a guy. But the rest of it? Her dreams she once had of seeing the world, her bucket list of things she'd once wanted to do. It all now seemed … silly. Had she lost herself somewhere along the line, or had she simply created a new identity? One that obsesses over work and things not going to schedule. One who was terrified of taking risks and doing what she really truly wanted. Which was what, exactly? Almost instinctively, she glanced up at Nate, feeling her breath catch in her throat. His eyes were wide in feigned shock. Or maybe it wasn't feigned.

'You have *three* months of leave?' he said. 'I've never made it past three weeks! Have you ever taken leave?'

She grimaced. 'Not exactly,' she said. 'A few days here and there if I can't avoid it. Mostly for exams or big assignments.'

'So, no holidays.' It was more a statement than a question. She shook her head. 'Sick days?'

'Rarely,' she said. His mouth fell open. 'I have a good immune system,' she added quickly.

He shook his head slowly, shifting his gaze to somewhere in front of them. Kassandra and Russ were out of sight, and she could see the bar a few doors up.

'Huh,' he hummed. 'Are you sure you're human?'

She laughed. And not a graceful, sweet kind of laugh. It was somewhere between a bark and a scoff. It only made him look more amused and her more embarrassed. 'I promise, you have nothing to worry about.'

'Sounds like something a non-human would say,' he said, nudging the door open and letting her in first.

'Okay, if I'm not a human, what am I?' she said, turning to face him once through.

He shrugged. 'I haven't decided yet. Do you have superpowers?'

'I do not.'

'And I suppose you can't morph yourself into different creatures or shapes, either.'

She laughed—a nicer laugh this time, since she was prepared. 'No.'

'Not a robot?' he said, squinting. She shook her head. 'Hmm, well perhaps you are human after all. Tell me, what do you do of an evening?'

'I go to bed, mostly, when I'm not studying,' she said. She didn't miss his subtle smirk. She frowned. 'I'm not boring, you know.'

'Didn't say you were,' he said, placing his hand on

the small of her back to lead her towards their friends. 'Besides, I *know* how boring you're not.'

His breath was deeper, low, loud enough for only her to hear. She felt his breath against the sensitive part of her neck, just below her ear, sending a shiver down her spine and leaving her wanting more. She felt the disappointment when his hand left the small of her back and he slid into the seat next to Russ, leaving only a spot next to Kassandra for her.

Oh, she knew what he was talking about. And she'd be lying if she said she didn't enjoy not being boring. But take that night and the few times after out of the equation and, well, her life was looking pretty boring. By the time she got home from work or finished with study, she was usually too exhausted to do anything else. She'd tried reading a book. She'd even gone to the trouble of buying a book that seemed entertaining and light enough to read when she was feeling too exhausted to do anything else. It was still sitting on her bedside table, bookmarked halfway through chapter one and collecting dust. She figured she'd have more time when she'd finished study or after her promotion. The promotion she didn't get.

Even if she and Nate were making headway on their friendship, it still didn't lessen the hurt and frustration that she didn't get her promotion. And she hated that that was what she was defining herself on. Then again, what did she expect? She'd put all her eggs in one basket—the one that seemed certain. And it failed her. She'd spent all of her energy chasing the one thing that was never even in the cards for her. And now? She couldn't even have the guy that she could have *fun* with. When was the last time she'd done something fun?

She blinked back the haze when she heard her name mentioned, only to be greeted with a concerned look on Nate's face. No, on all *three* of their faces. Kassandra nudged her, and Russ was holding a shot glass and a bottle of tequila, readying himself to pour it.

'Sorry?' she muttered.

Nate frowned. 'I said they've got tequila,' he said. 'Are you happy with that, or do you want whisky?'

Whisky? So they could have a repeat of the night they met? 'Tequila is fine,' she said. After all, maybe it was time to add a little *fun* into the mix.

Russ filled the shot glass and handed it towards her. She downed it, surprising herself with the burn, and started coughing. It took her a moment to realise she was the only one that drunk hers and the others looked shocked.

'What the *hell*?' she forced out. She frowned at the wedge of lime that Nate held out to her.

'Take it, Wren,' he said. 'It'll help.'

She took the lime from his hand and sucked on it, surprised it was an actual improvement.

'Haven't you ever had tequila before?' Russ said, licking the back of his hand near his thumb.

Kassandra licked her hand as Russ picked up the jar of salt. What kind of weird ritual was this? 'She doesn't sway much from the whisky,' she said, holding her hand out towards Russ. Russ tipped some salt on her hand, then tipped it on his.

She flicked her gaze back towards Nate, his lips curved up in amusement. 'Ever heard of lick, sip, suck?'

She looked at him questioningly and he took the salt from Russ. He did the same weird ritual that Kassandra and Russ both did—licked his hand, tipped some salt on it. Then, he lifted his shot glass and put it in the same hand as the one that he'd licked. In his other hand, he held a wedge of lime. She bit into her lip, the burn only just starting to subside. This is why she liked whisky. No big preparation to have a drink, no harsh burn—at least not for her—just enough to warm her insides.

He lifted his hands in front of him and nudged his head towards them. 'Watch,' he said. 'Lick.' He licked the salt off his hand in a way that looked a lot more seductive than it probably should. He made another noise as he downed the shot, which she assumed was him saying *sip*. Then, he bit into the lime, sucking the juice from it. 'Suck.' As if on cue, Kassandra and Russ followed suit, minus the commentary. 'Makes tequila a lot more tolerable,' Nate added, pouring another round of shots. 'Want to try again?'

She grimaced. Here she was thinking that she was all sophisticated and only did sophisticated things and drunk sophisticated drinks and now—*now*—she was licking her hand and taking shots.

'What the hell,' she muttered, licking her hand, and holding it out to Nate. She saw something flicker in his eyes as he tipped some salt on her hand and she couldn't describe what it was, but it made her heart leap and a smile creep onto her face.

Yep. She was screwed.

Chapter 12

'Wren, I'm cutting you off.'

'Wait, where are you taking my bottle?'

Nate pushed the tequila bottle to the end of the table, just out of reach of a very drunk, very slurry Wren. He wasn't entirely sure how the past few hours had progressed, but between dancing and getting up from the table for various reasons, he'd managed to end up on the same side of the table as her. He was still surprised that Wren didn't know how to drink tequila to start with. Then, he was surprised how *quickly* she took to it. He wasn't sure she had the whole party-girl thing in her.

He scanned the room around them, looking for Russ and Kassandra and coming up empty. They'd disappeared some time ago. To dance, he'd assumed. Now, he wasn't so sure. But he was hoping he'd see him so that he could get him to take the bottle back to the bar. He certainly didn't want to let drunk Wren out of his sight or leave her open to advances from other people. Maybe it was the ex-bartender part of him. Or maybe he just simply cared too much to have something happen to her. He'd lost count of the number of shots she'd done, but he knew when to stop. And she was well past that point.

'Y'know what, Natey,' Wren slurred, pressing her hand against his cheek. '*You're* the one who's no fun.'

He smiled, pouring her a glass of water from the jug that Russ made sure they had before he disappeared with Kassandra and handed it to her. 'Drink.'

She obeyed, taking a sip, then pushing the glass away. 'Ugh, what is *that*?' she said, pulling a face.

'It's water,' he laughed. 'And you need it. You've had too much to drink.'

'*I'll* be the judge of that,' she said, sitting up straighter and frowning, trying her best not to slur her words. He'd be lying if he said it wasn't cute. She made grabby hands for the bottle of tequila. 'Gimme.'

He held her hands back, realising that the bottle wasn't as far out of her reach as he'd thought. 'Trust me, Wren. I should know when someone's had enough. And you, my dear, have had enough.'

'*Why* should I trust you?' she said, shaking her hands free of his grip, and slapping his hand uncoordinatedly, pouting. '*You* stole my *job*.'

'I didn't—' he started, shaking his head. He pinched the bridge of his nose. 'Actually, no. We're not going to do this here.'

She waggled her finger between them, her eyes drooping. 'But it's true,' she said, drawing out the words. She pressed her finger to her chest. 'I'm *not* boring. See? I cannot be not boring.'

His eyebrow lifted, and his lips curved. 'You just said you're boring.'

She squinted, leaning forward until she was almost resting her forehead on his shoulder. 'I said I'm not *not* … not … boring.'

Her head dropped to his shoulder and he patted her hair. 'I know what you're trying to say, love,' he said, freezing at his accidental slip of the word. She didn't seem to notice.

'Shhh,' she said, pressing her finger to his face. 'I'm sleepy.'

He groaned, still unable to see Russ anywhere in the room. But it didn't matter. He didn't fancy lugging a deadweight back home, so if they were going to leave, they had to leave before Wren fell asleep. *Damn.* So much for being an innocent night. How had he let her get so drunk? Truth is, he wasn't solely to blame. He was sure she was taking swigs directly from the bottle for every shot she had. And then there were likely times when he wasn't looking …

'No, don't sleep,' he said, nudging his shoulder as her head felt heavier.

'Why *not*?' she whined, rubbing her eyes.

'Because we have to get you home,' he said, easing himself out of the seat and catching her from falling out onto the floor. God, *how much* did she have?

'I can live *here* now,' she mumbled, staggering to her feet.

He sighed, wrapping his arm around her waist to keep her upright, grateful she wasn't wearing heels. It was much harder to keep a drunk woman in heels upright. He grabbed the bottle of tequila and guided them both towards the bar. Once there, Wren flung herself on the bar and waved towards the new bartender, Jess. Russ was right, she *was* prettier than him. But only by default—him being a guy and all. Sure, she was attractive, but she had nothing on the drunk woman hanging off his arm.

'Hey, lady!' Wren called out. 'Can I get a hells yeah?' Jess walked towards them, raising an eyebrow. 'A *whisky*,' Wren corrected, squinting at the shelves behind the bar, then pointed to the top row. 'That one.'

'Ignore her,' Nate said, handing Jess the bottle of tequila. 'She's had enough. Is Russ still here?'

'I saw him leave with some girl. Pretty, dark hair. Dressed like you two,' she said, squinting at him. 'Have we met?'

'I don't think so.'

'Hey, you're *pretty*,' Wren said, pointing to Jess. 'How do you get your hair like that?'

'It's a … bun,' Jess said, shaking her head, smiling.

She focussed back on Nate, her eyes questioning. 'I've seen you somewhere.'

'I did work here,' he suggested.

She pursed her lips, then, as if it just came to her, clicked her fingers. 'Nate the Tank! I knew I've seen you before.'

He felt his body stiffen. Thank God Wren was too drunk to properly remember this conversation tomorrow. Wren scoffed, resting her weight against him. 'Nate the *Tank*? What kind of name is *that*?'

'A stripper name,' Jess said.

'A *stripper* name?' Wren repeated laughing.

Jess looked at him puzzled. 'You haven't … *oh*, you haven't told her.'

'I don't tell *anyone*,' he said through clenched teeth. Truth is, he'd only done it a few times, filling in on the rare occasion when none of the real strippers were available. Seems those few times were memorable for some people.

'Sorry,' Jess muttered. 'Didn't realise it wasn't common knowledge.'

'Wait, are *you* Nate the Tank?' Wren said, bumping against him again. He frowned, hiking her upright. 'You *are*! Hey, lady,' she said, turning back towards Jess. 'I banged Nate the Tank!'

'All right, that's enough,' he said, leading Wren towards the door and preparing himself for the dizziness she'll feel as soon as she takes a lung full of fresh air.

'Where are we going?' she whined. 'I want to *dance*!'

'We're going home, Wren. We can dance another night.'

'*Fine*,' she huffed, letting him drag her out the door. She clutched to him tighter once they were outside, as he'd expected. 'Woah.'

'You okay?'

She held up a finger. 'I'm going to be si—nope,' she said, snapping upright, laughing. 'I'm okay! I'm just going to go … that way,' she added, spinning towards the other end of the street.

'This way,' he said, correcting her course.

God, he wouldn't mind having non-drunk Wren now, like this, his arm around her, going for a walk in the cool of the night. But it wasn't how it was. Instead, he had a very drunk, very verbal Wren who was very reliant on him to keep her upright.

'*You* need to lighten up, Natey,' she said, resting her head on his shoulder after a few moments of random mumbling. 'You feel so … *tense*.'

He laughed. Him, tense? Might have something to do with being so close to someone he was so desperately attracted to and knowing that *any* advance would be beyond wrong. That was bound to make any guy tense.

'I once … licked … a cow,' she muttered, her head getting heavier on his shoulder.

He lifted his shoulder a little to make sure she didn't fall asleep. They were almost back to his place. He was sure he'd be able to carry her the rest of the way if he had to. But he also noticed that she already felt a whole lot heavier drunk than she had any other time he'd had the pleasure of being this close to her. He already felt his own head starting to throb after the few shots of tequila he'd had. Wren was in for a hell of a morning tomorrow.

'A cow?' he repeated, trying to keep her talking.

'Well, a steak,' she said, her words drawing out. 'But it comes from a cow, right? So, *technically*, I licked a cow.'

He tried not to laugh, but it didn't stop the smile. He walked her up towards the door of his house. 'I'm going to let you go, Wren,' he started.

She pouted, her eyes looking like she was about to burst into tears. Heck, a single tear already started rolling down her cheek. '*Why*?' she said. 'Don't you like me anymore, Natey?'

What? He tilted his head, wondering what the hell she'd be thinking when he realised what she'd got from that. Did she *like* him liking her? 'Not *that*, Wren,' he said. 'Physically. I have to unlock the door, so you're going to have to stand by yourself.' He wiped the tear from her cheek, his thumb lingering. God, if only she knew that he could never let her go *that* way. Not really. This woman was something different. Even if her mood swung uncontrollably when she was drunk. But if that was her worst ...

'Oh,' she said, straightening up and leaning against the post out front of his house. Then, she laughed. 'I've *got* this,' she said.

He smiled, plucked his keys from his pocket, and unlocked the door. But when he turned back to Wren, she was gone. 'Bloody hell,' he muttered.

He scanned around him only to find her trying to get into her car. Head first. As if trying to *lay* into her seat. He sighed, walking towards her until he was standing at the driver side door. She'd managed to pull her legs in by then and was kneeling on her seat, reaching over to the passenger side floor, her perfect ass on display.

'Wren, honey,' he said. 'You're not driving home.'

She wiggled her ass back a bit and peered over her shoulder towards him. 'I know,' she said sweetly, a mischievous look in her eyes.

She kept wiggling backwards until she almost slipped out of the car. Well, she would have, if he hadn't been standing *right there*. Instead, she'd managed to wiggle herself back against *him*. He grabbed onto her hips to steady her and let out a breath. God, this woman was going to be the death of him. The number of times he'd imagined having her like this … minus the being so-drunk she probably had no idea what she was doing.

'Wren, stop moving,' he forced out through clenched teeth. 'Let me *help* you.'

'Oh, I got it!' she shrieked, flinging herself backwards out of the car.

He only just managed to catch her. She'd moved so quickly that if his hands weren't already on her hips, he was sure she would have met the asphalt instead of his chest. He wrapped his arms around her waist to help her stand, but she didn't move. Instead, she batted her eyelids up at him. It was then that he realised she was clutching the bottle of whisky to her chest.

'Wren,' he started.

'It was lonely,' she said, pouting, patting the bottle gently. 'It didn't want to be by itself.'

He sighed, hoisting her up so she could support herself—relatively—and grabbed her keys off the car seat. He locked the car and hooked his arm around her waist to guide her back to the house, confiscating the bottle before she got it to her lips. She groaned a protest, but he couldn't let her get *drunker* than she already was. He couldn't believe it had ended up like this—looking after a very drunk Wren who had no filter. And him *not* being as drunk. And the bloody friends rules. Trust his luck.

Getting her inside proved to be a more difficult task then he'd thought, but he'd got her there in the end. Even if it was collapsed on the couch muttering something about the stars. Convinced that she was going to stay put, he went to the kitchen to get some water, his own throat feeling dry, put the bottle of whisky on the bench, and rummaged through his medicine box until he found the paracetamol. As he swallowed the pills, he felt a hand creep up his back and over his shoulder until it reached his chest.

'Natey,' she whispered seductively. '*Nate the Tank.*'

He closed his eyes, taking in a breath, harnessing every little bit of restraint he could find, knowing that if he didn't do the right thing now, he would regret it for a long time. But damn, she didn't make it easy. He stilled her hand and turned slowly as she pulled on him, only to have her placing his hands on her breasts. Her *bare* breasts.

Heck, *all* of her was bare. *Bloody hell*. He flicked his gaze up to the ceiling, lifting his hands to her shoulders. An act that *should* be innocent, but somehow still felt incredible. Hell, simply *touching* her was going to be the death of him.

'Wren,' he said, gritting his teeth. 'Where are your clothes?'

She shrugged, moving her body under his hands as if trying to move closer. He kept her at arm's length, even though it was killing him. Slowly, miserably. 'I don't *need* clothes,' she said quietly, tugging on his shirt, pulling him towards the bedroom.

Bedroom. The exact place he needed her to be, and the same place he had to *leave* her. Damn it. He'd imagined it was going to be hard enough with her clothes on, and now, it was going to be worse. He released her shoulders and focussed on her eyes, being *very* careful not to let his eyes drop to the rest of her body so he wouldn't lose himself. He closed his hands over hers and smiled.

'Let's get you to bed, Wren,' he said, leading her towards his room.

'Oh, I like the sounds of *that*,' she chirped, practically bouncing next to him. But it wasn't what she was thinking. And he'd never hated tequila more in his life than at this very moment.

He released her hands once he was inside the bedroom and rummaged through his drawers, finding a shirt that she might find comfortable enough to sleep in. Then, he turned towards her and almost had the wind knocked out of him as her body slammed against him, her lips on his, moving, pressing with a desire that blew every rational thought out of his mind. He tried not to reciprocate. He tried not to move his lips against hers or encourage her in any way. And it near on killed him.

He wanted her.

God, he wanted her.

But not like this.

He lifted his hand, cupping her cheek, pulling her away. It felt like he was ripping a part of him off himself. Her brow was furrowed, and she was pouting, her troubled eyes searching his.

'You don't want to do this,' he said, surprising himself that it was almost a growl.

Her shoulders dropped, and she took a step back, her eyes glistening. She sniffed. 'Don't … don't you … want … me … anymore?'

'It's not *that*. Trust me,' he started.

'You don't like me.'

'I *love* you, Wren!'

What the *hell*? He froze, letting the thought catch up to him. Letting the very reality and the dangerousness of it catch up to him. God, *he* must be drunker than he realised. Her eyes were wide, and he knew he had to say something—anything—to make her forget he'd let the L-word slip.

'Of course I *like* you,' he corrected, holding out his shirt for her to take. 'But I also don't want you hating me tomorrow.'

'I wouldn't *hate* you,' she muttered, taking the shirt, and turning away from him to put it on.

He wished he could believe that. He dropped his gaze to the ground, his hands folded across his chest, the fact he'd told drunk Wren he loved her when he didn't even know it himself still ringing clearly in his head. He knew that he was wishing she wasn't so drunk earlier, but God, now he couldn't help but *hope* she was so drunk she wouldn't remember.

She turned back towards him and he let himself look at her now that she was dressed. In his shirt. Looking sexy as hell. And found himself wishing he didn't have a conscience. And then he found himself wishing he could go back to *that* night and make a few changes. Like skipping the shower so he'd be there when she woke up. So she wouldn't run away. Or holding off—somehow—on hooking up with her until *after* he started his bloody job. Something— anything—that would mean it could be different now. That he didn't have to risk her *hating* him or regretting anything to do with him.

But he couldn't change things.

And he wouldn't take that night back, because it was the best damn night of his life.

'Tuck me in?' she whispered, her arms folded across her chest as if she'd suddenly got self-conscious.

He hesitated a moment, then nodded. 'Hop in,' he said, walking to the side of the bed.

She slid in and snuggled under his blanket, resting

her head on his pillow. 'I bet Nate the Tank would have been more fun,' she teased.

His lips curved up as he tucked the blanket in around her. 'You're probably right,' he muttered.

She lifted her chin as if trying to move closer to him without moving the rest of her body. 'A kiss goodnight?' she said, batting her eyelids.

He pushed a smile onto his face, even though he certainly didn't feel like smiling. 'I don't think so, Wren,' he said, brushing the hair from her eyes. Then, he left her in his bed, stopping at his door when she spoke.

'Why not?'

He looked back at her. She was sitting up, watching him. But she was settled in bed. She wouldn't be getting out. And he wouldn't be joining her. Even if he'd never felt like doing anything more.

'Because I won't stop.'

Chapter 13

He was on her.

No, he was all over her.

His hands moving up and down her body, as though he didn't want to leave any inch of her untouched, his lips rough against hers. Just the way she wanted it.

His tongue moved against hers in a dance that joined them together. His body moved with hers as one. This is what she wanted. This is what she needed. To feel him fill her with his entirety. To feel the friction between them turning into sweat—his, hers, she couldn't tell. She didn't care. Because it wasn't gross like this. No, not when it felt so amazing, so incredible. Not when he was where he belonged, and she was in his arms, where she belonged.

She kissed him back with a ferocity that matched his, her hands clutching for his shoulders, his hair. Anywhere she could grip onto as he pushed her closer to the edge, her body tightening from the core. Their breaths were hot and heavy. He broke the kiss, only to trail across her jaw and down to nibble on her neck. She threw her head back, granting him better access, feeling his stubble scrape across the tender part of her neck. It didn't hurt like she thought it would. No, it only served to push her closer to the edge.

The edge that she was aching to throw herself over and take him with her.

She heard a moan, though wasn't sure if it was him or her. Perhaps both. Then, the moan turned into a pulse, a throb. Her head. Her head was throbbing. And there was another sound. A piercing. A tune of some kind.

She forced her eyes open, and he was gone. She was alone, the blanket still heavy, the weight of clothes still against her body. She squeezed her eyes shut, and rubbed her forehead, realising that the throbbing was very much not a part of the dream. Neither was the tune. Whistling, to be precise.

She froze, her hand still on her forehead. *Why* was there whistling at her place? It was then she realised that this bed didn't smell like hers, that the blanket felt a little different to hers, that her clothes felt different. She clutched her hand to her chest and padded it around until she was convinced it was a shirt. Not hers.

The throbbing eased enough for her to hear the sound of running water with the whistling, a tune that somehow seemed familiar, though she couldn't work out how. She propped herself up on her elbows and scanned the room. A room that looked more familiar than it should.

Nate's room.

Hell.

She tried desperately to remember the night before—what happened, what they did, even though her being in his bed made her assume the worst. But she came up empty. She remembered the dance, remembered seeing Nate there, and Kade saying something about them. She remembered going to the bar with Nate, Kassandra, and Russ. She remembered tequila. Then, nothing. Well, not entirely nothing. Snippets. Snippets that she couldn't tell if it really happened, or if it was part of her very detailed, very realistic dream.

Dancing.

Something about a stripper.

Nate's arms.

Kissing him.

She sat up straight, flicking her legs over the side of the bed. She had to leave. She couldn't stay here. Not if she couldn't remember what happened last night. Not if what she *thought* happened did. *Shoot.* So much for staying friends. She felt her stomach churn, and steadied herself, letting her eyes drift to the bedside table, her gaze falling on a full glass of water and a couple of pills still in their foil packet. And a note. She lifted the note and read it.

For your head.

She sighed, holding the note gingerly in her hand before placing it back on the bedside table. She flipped the packet to check it was paracetamol and took them, even though she was convinced nothing would help this damn throbbing in her head. As she swallowed the pills and followed it up with a drink of water, her mind went back to the whistling in the shower, and her eyes drifted to the pile of folded clothes at the end of the bed—her clothes—her keys and purse sitting next to them.

He'd been thoughtful enough to leave her some painkillers for her head. And to fold her clothes and put her things somewhere she'd see them. It had to be him. Because she knew that she surely didn't make them that neat last night. Especially since she couldn't make them that neat when she was sober. Should she tell him that she had to go? Much to her demise, she had to go to work today—as did he. And she had no intention of rocking up in jeans and a flannelette shirt.

Her eyes drifted to the closed door to the ensuite, and she heard the sound of running water stop. She didn't have long to decide, but she didn't need it. Because her flight reaction jumped into effect. She couldn't let him see her like this. Sure, he'd seen her in less than this in this very bed, but the circumstances were different. She knew what she was doing then. She *knew* she'd slept with the guy. This time, she had no idea what happened. She jumped off the bed and gathered up her things, deciding she didn't have enough time to change before he'd be out.

She let her eyes linger on the glass of water by the bed, his thoughtfulness still tugging at her. Then, she left. Perhaps more reluctantly than she had last time, but possibly even more embarrassed.

***

Nate banged on his friend's door, a plan set in his mind. Had he been disappointed that Wren wasn't there when he got out of the shower? A little. Had he been surprised? Not one bit. In fact, he'd half expected it. So, he wasn't the least bit surprised when he heard the front door close as he came out of the bathroom. And certainly not when he heard her little car start up a few moments later. But he *had* noticed that she'd taken the painkillers he'd left for her. And she was most likely still wearing his shirt, since it was nowhere to be seen.

He knocked on the door again, and this time, it opened for him to see a seedy looking Russ, wearing nothing but bed shorts and his slightly-too-long hair looking ruffled.

'Nate,' he said, taking a sip of the coffee in his hand.

'I have a plan,' Nate started, stopping when Kassandra came into view, still buttoning her shirt.

She smiled at Nate. 'Oh, hi, Nate,' she said. She

glanced up at Russ with a look in her eyes that could only be put down to pure seduction. 'Bye, Russ,' she drawled.

He looked down at her, that same look in his eyes and bent slightly as though to give her a kiss. She simply smiled and turned away, squeezing past the men and out the door. 'Later, Kass!' Russ called after her, only to receive a backwards wave of her hand.

Nate raised an eyebrow, nudging inside. 'Thought you said you couldn't sleep with her again,' he muttered.

Russ shrugged, closing the door behind them. 'What can I say? The woman is feisty.'

Nate grimaced, turning back to his friend. 'You leaned in for a kiss.'

'Which she didn't reciprocate,' Russ said simply, taking another sip of his coffee. 'It's my test to make sure they're not too invested.'

'Bullshit,' Nate said, smirking. 'I've seen women leave your place before and they never received such a formality. You're smitten with Kass.'

Russ frowned. 'Says the guy who's whipped.'

'I'm not—'

'Don't pretend like Wren doesn't have you wrapped around her little finger,' Russ said, heading back to the coffee pot to refill his cup. He pulled another cup from the shelf and filled it for Nate, nudging it across the counter towards him. 'Kass knows what she wants, and she goes for it. I like that. We're … like-minded.'

Nate scoffed. 'That's a pretty different view from

yesterday when sleeping with her would break all your rules.'

'Well, I've made an exception,' Russ said. 'Every guy should have a girl he can sleep with, no strings attached. Kass is my girl. Wren is yours.'

'No,' Nate said. 'Not every guy should have that. You might be that kind of guy, but I'm not.'

Russ squinted. 'So, you're telling me that you didn't sleep with Wren last night?'

'No, I didn't,' he muttered. 'Was that why you left? You intended on making sure I slept with her?'

'No, I *intended* on sleeping with Kass,' Russ said, frowning. 'I didn't give a damn what happened with you and Wren. You understand.'

Nate rolled his eyes, sipping his coffee. 'Well, I didn't sleep with her.'

'But you wanted to.'

'Of course I *wanted* to,' Nate admitted. 'But I don't go back on my word.'

Russ studied him, squinting. 'You look tired.'

'I slept on the couch.'

His eyebrow lifted. 'She stayed the night?'

'She was too drunk to drive home,' he explained. 'Figured it was easier.'

'And *nothing* happened?'

Nate's mind flicked back to a naked Wren pressing her body against his, kissing him with so much want and need that he'd almost given in. 'No. Nothing happened,' he said, regretfully.

How drunk had she been? And how much would she remember? He wondered if he *had* done the right thing, or if he'd simply missed another opportunity to be close to her. He shook his head. He'd done the right thing. It had to be. But he couldn't help that little niggling that kept telling him that maybe she *really* wanted it. He'd fought that voice all night.

'But, I have a plan,' Nate said, bringing the conversation back to his original intention.

'Which is?' Russ said, feigning interest.

'I'm going to give her what she wants.'

'Sex?'

'Friendship,' he said, stretching his arms out, ignoring Russ's comments. 'I'm going to be the best *friend* she could have. I'll learn everything I can about her—' which he genuinely wanted to do. '—tell her everything about me—' well, as much as she wanted to know. '—and keep things friendly and professional. Sticking to the rules.' Her stupid rules. 'I'll make her laugh like a friend would. And make her comfortable around me. We'll spend more time together and she'll start to realise how much she *needs* me.'

Russ blinked, and took a sip of his coffee, rolling it around in his mouth thoughtfully before swallowing. 'Lame.'

'It's the perfect plan,' Nate said defensively.

'No, it's not,' Russ said. 'What about when the next guy comes along and woos her?'

'There won't be another guy.'

'You don't know that.'

'I do,' Nate said. 'Because that guy would see

how present *I* am in her life and he'll see exactly
what Kade did.'

'Which was?'

'That there's something more going on between
us,' he said proudly. 'Even if she doesn't see it.'

'Nate, I get that you're crushing on the girl,' Russ
said warily. 'But you're talking long-term here.'

'I am.'

'And you expect me to believe this is all just to
get her to *willingly* sleep with you again?'

'I don't expect you to believe anything,' Nate
said, polishing off his coffee. 'But I figured you should
know so you don't screw it up if you ever get the
chance.'

'Those rules don't apply to me, you know,' he
said.

'They do now.' Nate turned to leave. After all, he
had to get to work and set his plan in motion.

'I don't believe this!' Russ called after him.

'You better believe it,' he called back, smirking.

'You're *falling* for her.'

He paused, only briefly, then kept going. Falling
was an understatement. Throughout the course of
the night, he knew that him dropping the L-word
wasn't him being drunk. Somewhere inside, he knew
it was possible. Perhaps not *now*, but he could tell he
wasn't far off. Time be damned. He wasn't falling for
her. He'd already fallen. Hard and fast. And he didn't
need to be a genius to know that he couldn't live
without Wren in his life. Even if he had to wait for
her to realise it, too.

***

Wren popped another painkiller in her mouth and washed it down with a mouthful of water. Then, she picked up the dry biscuits she'd brought for her lunch and nibbled on it. She felt like hell. And going to work and staring at her computer screen for the first few hours of the day did nothing to ease her throbbing head.

Hell, what had she done? She'd managed to avoid Nate all morning so far—perhaps he'd been avoiding her, too. But she'd received an email from him earlier that morning saying he'd be in her office at twelve to discuss the camping trip. Which was five minutes away. She felt her stomach churn. Camping was the last thing she wanted to think about, especially since it was still a couple of weeks away. Surely they could discuss it on a day when her head didn't feel like it was going to explode.

She heard a tap on her office door that seemed a whole lot louder than it was and felt the heat flush to her face when she saw Nate's smile as he neared her desk. The bastard didn't even look like he'd been drinking last night. Then again, she was sure she'd had a lot more than him. It wasn't often that she let herself go like that, and last night was, unfortunately, one of those few times. The one before that was the first time she slept with Nate. She couldn't remember a time before that. She'd always been proper, sophisticated. Always had a plan.

'Coffee?' Nate offered, nudging the travel tray towards her.

'Thanks,' she said, feeling her stomach twist.

Though, she suspected this time wasn't because of her throbbing head. He lifted his other arm and plonked a paper bag on her desk that emitted a smell that was a little too satisfying. Especially since any smell that was slightly strong seemed to have her stomach churning.

'What's this?' she said, nodding towards the bag.

'Burritos,' he said, sitting in the seat opposite her desk and loosening his tie and top button. 'Helps with the hangover, trust me.'

He held her gaze, something flickering in his eyes that wasn't quite the same. His lips flicked up at the corner in a mischievous grin as he fiddled with his cuffs, rolling his sleeves up neatly to his elbows. But she was still stuck on the look in his eyes. It was almost … reserved … knowing.

She squinted, reaching for the bag. 'Have you had one already?' she said. 'You don't look hungover.'

She pulled out a burrito and placed it on the desk towards him and pulled out the other for herself. She saw that flicker in his eyes again. 'I didn't have as much as you,' he said, reaching for his burrito, and unwrapping the top. 'If you recall.'

Knowing. Because he knew something. Something about last night that she clearly didn't. And he knew she couldn't remember. *Damn it!* She sighed, fiddling with the end of the wrapper as she slowly tore it back. 'I don't,' she muttered. 'I mean, I don't remember *much* after the first few … shots.'

He took a bite of his burrito and rolled it around in his mouth, chewing slowly, methodically. She took a bite of her own, wondering about his new angle. Had she said something last night that put distance between them? Had he simply … had his fill of her?

'I see,' he said finally. 'Well, I also would have shown you my secret hangover cure when you woke up.' He spread his arms out to the side. 'But alas, no Wren to be seen.'

She felt her jaw set, finding it difficult to swallow her mouthful. He was sore about her leaving again? But he didn't look as bothered by it as he had the first time. Then again, she was starting to find that he held his frustration close, hiding it until he can't any longer. He reached for his coffee, his expression still calm. Teasing, even.

'It's not becoming a habit, is it?' he said, lifting his eyebrow as he looked at her.

She forced her mouthful down and rested the bottom of her burrito on her desk. *Depends how often I keep waking in your bed*, she thought. She froze, flicking her eyes up towards him when she realised she'd said it out loud. Damn the stupid throbbing in her head making it harder for her to know what she's thinking or saying. His eyes flickered again, his lips curving up as if instinctively. Then, his face grew neutral, as though he was trying not to have that stupid triumphant look on his face.

'I was embarrassed, okay?' she admitted. 'Having a bit of … déjà vu. I didn't want you to … to see me …

like that.' She bit into her burrito to make sure she wouldn't say anything else that she was supposed to keep to herself.

He considered her for a moment, and she waited for his response. Then, instead of talking, he took another bite of his burrito, seemingly uninterested in what she said. What the hell?

'That's it?' she said, surprised.

He looked up at her, his brow furrowed, rolling the bite of burrito around in his mouth. 'What?' he managed.

'You have *nothing* to say to that?' Hell, she'd managed to set herself up for a smart-alec comment and he said *nothing*?

He shrugged, swallowing. 'What did you think I'd say?'

'I don't know,' she said softly. 'Probably something about already having seen me naked … or something.'

His mischievous grin returned, but he still didn't comment on it. It only served to make her feel like he *had* had his fill of her. That he was content with what they'd done—whatever it was—and that he was almost … bored … with her. He took another slow sip of his coffee and sat up straighter, leaning forward slightly, his elbows resting on his knees. He looked up at her, making her breath catch in her throat at *those eyes*. The grey eyes that had warmth in them, but also held a hint of a secret. There was no coldness in them, not like she'd seen flickers of in previous conversations with him.

'What do *you* think happened last night, Wren?'

Her throat felt dry, her breathing ragged, her heart pounding. What did she think happened? There was kissing. There was her throwing herself at him. There was something about a stripper. There was touching. There was sex. Though, what *really* happened and what she dreamed happened were indiscernible. She couldn't tell which was which. And it was slowly killing her inside. This is why she stuck to whisky. Whisky had never let her down like that. With whisky, she at least knew what was real and what wasn't.

Chapter 14

'I don't … I don't … know.'

It was only a whisper, and her eyes were hazy. He fought the smile, relieved that she didn't know what happened. Heck, he was sure if she remembered *that*, then she would probably never talk to him again. Sure, they hadn't *done* anything, per se. Apart from her throwing herself at him and the fact he'd had a few goes at stripping coming out.

'I'm afraid I might have … stepped over our friends rule,' she said hesitantly. She was avoiding looking at him, and her cheeks had darkened.

Stepped over the rule? Hell, she launched herself over it and finished it with a tumble. But he wouldn't tell her that. Not if it would only do more harm than good. He sighed.

'Nothing happened, Wren,' he said simply. He couldn't help the niggling feeling in his chest that he'd just lied to her, but the relief that swept across her face made it worth it. He hoped.

'Y—you're sure?'

He nodded, sitting back in his chair again. 'It was all above board,' he continued. 'I mean, you were pretty drunk. So, you leaned on me for support while we walked home, but I'd say that still falls under a *friends* thing to do.'

'Nothing else … happened?'

He shook his head slowly, convincingly. After all, everything else was just minor details, right? 'You also left the whisky at my place and stole my shirt, but still. Friends do that all the time.'

She let out a breath—a slow, shaky breath. Relieved. He couldn't help the little ache that she didn't *want* anything else to happen. Especially since she was the one who threw herself at him. *Damn*. He reminded himself of his plan. She wanted him— drunk Wren was proof of that. Sober Wren, however, needed it to happen slowly. She needed a friendship first. The rest would come. With time. But God, he hoped it wouldn't be *too* long.

'Oh,' he added as though remembering something else. Her eyes flicked towards him warily. 'Russ and Kass hooked up again, too. Other than that, nothing really to report on.'

Her lips curved slowly at the corner. 'Again?' she said, lifting the burrito to her mouth. Her tongue slid along her upper lip as she eyed her food. God, he wished it was for him. 'Interesting,' she added slowly. 'Kass has a rule about sleeping with someone twice.'

'So does Russ,' he said.

She gave him a smile that made his chest tighten, a hint of mischief in her eyes as she took a bite of her burrito. Her moan almost made him want to forget his plan and launch himself across her desk until he'd had her again. Had her like he wanted to last night. How he wanted to since the moment he first laid eyes on her.

'Mmm, you were right,' she managed to say around her mouthful. 'This *is* good for the hangover.'

He smiled and polished off the rest of his burrito, thankful it had, at least, provided a buffer to get over the awkwardness between them. Now, to actually start with his plan. He rolled up the burrito wrapper and tossed it into the paper bag, nudging it to the side to clear some space in front of him. Then, he reached into his pocket and pulled out a sheet of paper and laid it between them.

'What's that?' Wren said, peering over her burrito at the paper.

'It's a list,' he explained, purposefully avoiding looking at her as she took another seductive bite of the burrito. 'To pass around to everyone. Things they need to bring to the camping trip. That kind of thing. On the back is a list of things that we'll need to provide for the group. Thought you might want to check over it, see if there's anything else to add.'

She shrugged lightly. 'I'm probably not much

help, then.'

He flicked his gaze up towards her as she sucked her fingers clean of the burrito juices and chucked the wrapper in the paper bag. God, it was going to be harder than he thought. The damn burrito was supposed to be innocent and she'd made every damn bite of it look seductive.

'I thought you'd be good with lists,' he said, dropping his gaze again.

'I am,' she said. 'But I wouldn't know what to bring on a camping trip.'

This time, he couldn't help but look up at her again, surprised. 'You've never been camping before.' It was more of an observation than a question.

She shook her head slowly. 'When would I have got the chance?'

'I don't know,' he said. 'When you were a kid, maybe?'

She lifted her shoulder lazily, her smile crooked. 'Never been.'

'Not with school?'

'I managed to be sick for that trip.'

His eyes widened. 'So, you *do* get sick!'

Her brow furrowed as if her mind was catching up. Then she smiled. 'You really don't forget what we talk about, do you?' Her tone was teasing.

'Why would I?'

He held her gaze for a long, tantalising moment. Too long. Much too long for friends. But there was something in her eyes that gave him just a flicker of hope. He cleared his throat, looking back down at the paper. 'It's mostly obvious stuff. Warm clothes, sleeping bag, basic toiletries—'

'Have you been?'

He looked up at her. 'Where?'

'Camping,' she said. 'Have you done it before?'

He eased back into his chair, away from the list. He knew it all anyway since he wrote it. 'I did,' he said. 'A lot. With my brother.'

She sat up straighter. 'You have a brother?' He nodded slowly. 'You just … you haven't talked about your family.'

He shrugged. 'Not much to say.'

'They're your family,' she said, her voice laced with disbelief, a hint of a laugh. Her brow furrowed, her face growing serious. 'Did something …'

He bit the inside of his cheek, reminding himself of the specifics of his plan. He'll learn all there is to know about her. He'll tell her all about himself. Even if it meant hitting the touchy issues.

'My parents own a cattle farm this side of Armidale,' he started. 'Like any farmer's dream, they had two sons. I'm the oldest. They're not exactly … supportive … of me wanting to live the suit life, working in an office, doing my own thing. They wanted me to take over the farm. So, you can imagine their disappointment when I didn't want to. I'm not in touch with them. Not my parents, not Leo. They made it clear I was practically disowned.'

'It's the twenty-first century,' she said quietly. 'They can't expect you to take over the farm, that's unrealistic.'

He looked up at her. Her eyes were wide in disbelief. 'That farm has been in my family for as long as it's been recorded,' he said. 'The men in my family don't have as much choice as you think, Wren.' In fact, if it weren't for Leo, it would have ended at Nate. Because he couldn't think of anything worse than spending his days somewhere he didn't want to be.

She opened her mouth to say something, then snapped it closed. He wondered what she'd wanted to say, but he suspected he already knew.

It's not fair.

You can do what you want.

You decide what you do.

He knew, because he'd thought the same things. He'd repeated them—and more—to himself to convince him he was doing the right thing for him. Even if his family didn't agree.

'I lost my family because I was chasing *my* dreams, Wren,' he said, picking at a bit of lint on his pants. 'I wanted to do something more. Be qualified to provide when the farm wasn't enough. The only people I cared about turned their back on me because I wanted to do something that would help *them*.'

'Still,' she said softly, drawn out. 'Family should be supportive. My dad doesn't care what I do as long as I'm happy.'

'Yeah, well, you're one of the lucky ones,' he mumbled. As he said it, he realised it wasn't the right thing to say. He sighed, looking up at Wren to see the troubled look on her face. No, annoyed. Frustrated. Angry? 'Wren—'

'No, you're right,' she said, her voice wavering. 'Only the *lucky* ones get to grow up without a mother and an empty shell for a dad.'

'I didn't mean it like that,' he said, holding her gaze, watching the fire burn in her eyes, watching it die down slowly. Hell, he'd be lying if he said that fierceness—that fiery look she'd given him—wasn't a turn on.

***

He'd pushed her to an edge she didn't know she possessed. Then, with the warm look in his eyes—the honest, caring, *genuine* warmth—he'd brought her back to safety. And in that look was the reminder that *he* was a genuine man. He hadn't taken advantage of her in her drunk state the night before, and he'd even been thoughtful enough to bring her hangover food.

Perhaps she'd snapped at him.

She blamed it on the headache that had formed instead of the throbbing, the still nauseated feeling in her belly. The burrito and coffee did help, a little. But she was still very aware that she was hungover, and she'd no doubt be feeling it for the next two days at least.

This is why she stuck with whisky. Whisky was safe. It didn't affect her the way that tequila obviously did. Sure, she got the mellow drunkenness from it if she had enough. But it was also the kind of drink that she *couldn't* have too much of. And it was never designed to be taken in shots like tequila. Rather, one drink would last a good while.

Whisky didn't make her feel like hell or snap at someone—who, keeping in mind, was *also* hungover, even if he didn't look the same as she felt like she looked.

But perhaps her hangover only made the reality of her situation more prominent. Even though she'd thought her and her dad had done fine over the years—she was alive, right?—when she looked back on it, he *was* an empty shell. A ghost of the man he used to be. Because losing his wife did that to him. He cared for Wren. He looked after Wren and helped her grow into the woman she now was, but he was not the same man he was before. She already suspected that when she saw how different—how happy—he looked in the photographs before Wren was born. Now, she knew it as fact. Her father had lived for her, but he hadn't *lived*. He had, however, never pushed Wren away when he had every reason to.

She couldn't comprehend why Nate's family pushed him away for wanting to do something different. But then, every family was different. And there were clearly some who were very much still deeply ground in tradition. Even at the expense of their son.

'I know,' she whispered, sighing, her shoulders

slumping. 'I'm sorry, I shouldn't have snapped. It's the tequila.'

He didn't say anything. His lips were pursed to one side, as if biting into the corner of his lips, his eyes studious. Then, slowly, he nodded and flipped his paper over to find a blank space at the bottom of the sheet. He reached across the desk and picked up the pen near her hand, his fingers brushing lightly against hers, sending a shock through her body. God, with all they'd been through in such a short time, she would have thought she'd be immune to his touch by now.

But she wasn't.

And she suspected she never would be.

'We need to talk about the team-building activities,' he said, continuing on from their earlier conversation as though they hadn't just talked about a touchy issue—clearly, for both of them. 'Otherwise, everyone will just be bored and the whole trip will be pointless.'

She sighed, plucking another pen from her penholder, ignoring the little niggle at the back of her mind wondering why he didn't just get a pen from there. She held the pen between two fingers and tapped the end of it against her desk. 'I thought you were all over this,' she said. 'Considering you'd managed to convince Durgan and all that.'

He chuckled, a light laugh that made her chest flutter. And his eyes held the same lightness, though, still holding onto that reservedness of before. 'Yeah, well, he agreed quicker than I thought he would,' he said. 'I was sort of relying on the pressure of trying to convince him to come up with actual ideas on the spot. I guess I blanked once I registered that I didn't have to go into detail.'

She lifted the pen to her lips, then waggled it towards him. 'I have a question about that,' she said.

His eyebrow lifted. 'Hmm?'

'Did *you* suggest that the trip be the weekend after next?'

His lips curved up to one side in a smile that made him look too damn cute. 'That was all him. Why?'

She pursed her lips thoughtfully. 'It's just not much notice,' she said. 'What if people had plans?'

His brow furrowed. 'Do you have plans?'

She opened her mouth then closed it again. Then, she rested her elbow on the desk, her chin in her hand. 'Well, not *me*, specifically,' she said slowly. 'But most people have plans on weekends. I mean, I get why it couldn't happen during the week since it's usually busy enough without taking the whole management team out of the equation. But why not a month or two away? Why two weeks?'

Nate sat up straighter, his eyes glazing over as though deep in thought. Hadn't he thought about it? It had practically been the only thing she'd been thinking about in regards to the camping trip. People had plans. And plans couldn't always be changed last minute.

'I guess Durgan just wanted it done as soon as possible,' he said.

She lifted an eyebrow as she studied him. 'Or maybe he's testing you.'

He lifted his chin, his eyes narrow, and his lips curved higher on one side, showing off his neat teeth—not quite white, but also nowhere near yellow. 'Perhaps he is.'

She nodded, her conspiracy theory running wild. 'It could be your big test to prove yourself,' she continued. 'You pull it off and get everyone to come, make it successful, increase productivity, yada yada, and you get to keep your job.'

Both of his eyebrows shot up. 'Is this the coffee or the tequila talking?'

She shrugged lightly, feeling her own smile creep onto her face. Heck, all of her felt light. And she wasn't sure where, in the course of this conversation, that had changed. He leaned forward again, propping his elbows on the desk, his hands clasped in front of him.

'All right, Wren,' he said, his side grin making her stomach flip. 'Will you help me pass this … test?'

She hummed. 'That depends.'

'On what?' he said, his expression amused.

'On how nicely you ask me,' she said simply, batting her eyelids.

His mouth dropped open in feigned shock. 'I brought you a *burrito*,' he said, emphasising his words.

'And that is a good start,' she said, lifting her chin decidedly.

Hell, she knew she was going to help him. And

she was sure he knew that, too. But there was something, somehow, that was different. It was like something ... *clicked*. She wasn't sure if it was because he knew when to change the subject or just something in the way he looked at her. But she'd gone from dreading seeing him in case she'd crossed a line last night, to being ... easy ... around him. Like a friendship with him would be ... easy. *They* would be easy.

'Speaking of plans,' he said casually, drawing her out of her thoughts. 'What *do* you do on weekends? Normally. Since you need notice.'

She thought he wasn't going to look at her when he said it. Then, his eyes flicked up to meet hers— only briefly—and she was sure there was a hint of mischief there, a bit of fun. Adventure. She bit into her lip.

'Oh, you know,' she said. 'The usual.'

'Which is?' he prompted, focussing on folding his paper up.

She shrugged, though she wasn't sure if he saw it. 'Just ... stuff.' She sighed. 'I don't know ... I don't really do much,' she admitted. His hands stopped moving. 'I usually sleep in on Saturdays, then go out for brunch. Sometimes with Kass. Mostly by myself, I suppose. Other than that, I don't really ... do ... much.'

Yet, somehow, she always managed to keep busy. She supposed she'd usually had Griffin around to do stuff with, even if he was just company while she did nothing. And the weekend just gone had been the beach trip with Kade and the dance and the tequila. The weekend before that had been, well … Nate. Truth is, this was going to be the first weekend she'd had with *nothing* happening since she found out about Griffin. And, frankly, she didn't know what she was going to do. But she also hoped it wouldn't be the moment where the whole Griffin thing hit her hard. She was over it, right? They'd been together for years and he was more like a housemate anyway … right? She bit into her lip, already feeling her mood dampening.

Should she have taken the time to grieve? Not so much for him, but for the loss of what she thought was an honest relationship, of her plans? She wasn't sure what was proper in this situation. She'd simply immersed herself back in her work instead of taking the time off she was supposed to have for her honeymoon. She'd had a few whiskies at the bar, hooked up with a guy she didn't know. Did that count? Part of her hoped it was enough. The other part of her wasn't so convinced.

'Well, how about this,' Nate said slowly, bringing her back to the present yet again. He waved the folded paper between them. 'I'll finish this list off on my own, so you don't have to worry about the boring stuff, and you let me join you for brunch on Saturday.'

She opened her mouth to say something—yes, no, she wasn't sure—but nothing came out. He tucked the paper back into his pocket and held his hands out, his palms facing her as though to ease her mind.

'It's all above board, Wren,' he said, his head bent slightly. Enough to look up at her through thick eyelashes that were, in her opinion, wasted on a man. Though she had to admit, it definitely added to his sexiness. She was sure she saw a glint of something in his eyes—part teasing, the rest that secretive look that intrigued her. 'No tequila, no whisky. Just two friends having brunch.'

She wasn't sure why that made her both smile and feel disappointed. Then, she realised it must be because he kept mentioning them as friends, except not quite in the same way as he had previously. It was as though he genuinely believed they were just friends—almost. Though, she wasn't entirely convinced that's all *she* wanted.

'You do know they have Bloody Mary's, right?' she said, smirking.

His eyes flashed with amusement, and his smile broadened. 'I'll have to make sure I'm on time, then.'

Chapter 15

'I'm in trouble.'

Wren closed the door behind her best friend. Had Kassandra ever been in *trouble*? She didn't think so. Her mind flicked back to earlier that week when Nate mentioned that Kassandra and Russ had hooked up again. She couldn't be pregnant … could she? If she knew now, it couldn't be Russ's. Kassandra sighed, turning on her heel to face Wren, her eyes widening as she read Wren's expressions.

'I'm not pregnant, Wren,' she said annoyedly. She pointed to the inner part of her upper arm. 'Arm bar, remember?'

Wren frowned. 'When was the last time you got that changed?'

Kassandra shrugged. 'A year ago, maybe?' She

shook her head. 'Doesn't matter. It's in date, and I'm not pregnant.'

'So, why are you in trouble, then?'

Wren got herself a glass of water from the kitchen, checking the time. She was going to be meeting Nate for brunch, and she didn't have much time to talk before she had to leave. As much as she'd drop anything to be there for Kassandra like she'd always done for Wren, she'd also been looking forward to this brunch with Nate. As friends, of course. Though, the way her stomach flipped when she thought of it and the way she smiled at even the memory of his cheeky grin, the intensity in his eyes, said otherwise. *Damn.*

The week had passed surprisingly comfortably, despite having to spend time with him working through some of the camping stuff, helping him *pass the test*, so to speak. She'd become convinced they could easily be friends. And that brunch was going to be their first *proper* friend thing to do. Alone. As friends.

Or perhaps her excitement for it and the nervousness in her stomach was because she wanted something more. And damn it if he wasn't a good person to do it with.

Kassandra's sigh brought her back to the situation at hand. She watched her friend's shoulders slump, her arms by her side, her brow creased. 'It's Russ.'

Wren halted the glass just before it touched her lips. 'What's wrong with Russ?'

Kassandra tilted her head to one side, then the

other. 'That's the problem,' she said. 'There's *nothing* wrong with him. He's a freaking master at what he does, and I can't for the life of me think of a convincing reason to break it off with him.'

Wren shook her head, showing that she hadn't properly understood. Kassandra started pacing, rubbing her forehead. 'When I sleep with a guy, I have to come up with a good enough reason for not seeing them again. You know, so they know it's not going to happen again, and they don't get attached.' She halted, staring at the wall. 'But Russ—'

'Is perfect?'

Kassandra turned towards her, her expression truly looking worried. Heck, Wren had *never* seen her best friend like this. She shook her head slowly. 'I should have known it was too risky,' she said. 'I'm careful to keep it simple, you know? Find a lonely heart, give them the night of their life, send them on their way. It's a process, and it's simple. But Russ—' she lifted an eyebrow nodding slowly. 'Oh, he's good. See, Wren, he's a player as much as I am. He knows what not to give away and, *damn it*, he gives *so* much.' Her eyes glazed over on the last few words.

Wren scrunched her nose up, trying not to think of what, in particular, he gave. 'Eww,' she said, coming up unsuccessful.

Kassandra smiled. 'Oh, yeah,' she said. 'He's good. Too good.'

Wren checked the time again, having a sip of water. 'I don't see what the problem is,' she said. 'So, you've slept with the guy more than you'd sleep with anyone else. Don't you think not sleeping with anyone more than once is a bit ... I don't know ... sluttish?'

'Thank you,' Kassandra said, her smile broadening, taking it as a compliment. Then, her face grew serious again. 'I'm in trouble because I don't want to *not* sleep with him again.'

Wren's eyes widened. 'My God,' she said. '*You* are attached.' Her friend nodded. 'Huh,' she added thoughtfully.

'What?' Kassandra said, frowning.

She shook her head. 'I just never thought I'd see the day.'

'This is serious, Wren!'

'No, it's not,' Wren said. 'Russ is a great guy.'

'Oh, yeah?' Kassandra said, folding her arms across her chest. 'And what do *you* know about him?'

'Well, he—' she tapped her finger to her chin, then, clicked her fingers. 'He stocks good whisky.' Kassandra's eyebrow lifted. 'And he's ... he's Nate's best friend, so he must be all right.' Her other eyebrow shot up. 'And he's *totally* your type, Kass! And your babies will look so *cute*!'

Her eyes widened. 'Oh, no. We are *not* talking babies here.'

'Too late,' Wren said, her smile lifting dreamily. God, how she loved teasing her best friend. 'Oh, I can see them now! Twelve cute little brown-haired minions. Your daughters will be leggy—naturally— like you. And they'll have your confidence. And there'll be mini-Russ's—broad shoulders and all.

They'll all have his eyes, of course. I have dibs on being their godmother, too, so take notes.'

Kassandra's mouth dropped. 'What's wrong with *my* ey—no, Wren! No babies.'

'So many babies.'

'You're impossible.'

'And you're attached!'

Kassandra sighed, dropping her gaze. Wren knew when teasing had to stop, and this was one of those times. 'I mean, I guess it had to happen sometime, right?' Kassandra said solemnly.

'It's not that bad,' Wren said. 'Sometimes it just kind of … sneaks up on you. The whole, you don't know what it's really like until it happens, kind of thing.'

'Like you and Nate?'

It was Wren's turn to have her mouth drop open. Like her and Nate? Was it? She'd never had sex as good as she'd had with Nate, sure. And he had a habit of showing up in her dreams and making her smile at the thought of him. He'd made her feel like she'd known him a lot longer than the short time she had. And, she just realised, he'd somehow made her forget that he stole her job. In fact, she'd been *happy* that he got her job. When did that happen?

Was he her don't-know-until-it-happens?

'No,' Kassandra said slowly. 'You guys are more than attached. *You're* the one thinking about babies.'

'I'm not thinking about babies,' Wren scoffed.

Was she? Come to think of it, they'd look pretty cute. Two—a girl and a boy. Their girl would have golden locks when she was young that would gradually darken until it was almost brown like Nate's. Their boy would truly look like a mini-Nate, right down to the broad, gentle hands. They'd both have his eyes, maybe with just a touch of blue, but she wasn't holding her breath. Kids always got their dad's eyes. It's just the way it is. Their days would be filled with love and fun outings—to the park, the beach. Her life would be filled with love and happiness.

Kassandra wasn't the only one who was in trouble.

Shoot.

***

He was early.

Partly because he wanted to make sure Wren didn't get a chance to get to those Bloody Mary's. Mostly because he couldn't wait. His plan was going smoother than he'd expected. Easier. As in, it was *easier* for *him* than he'd expected. Sure, he wanted to do more with her. He wanted to kiss her, touch her when no one was looking. Heck, he wanted to do all of that even *if* someone was looking. And alone— he wanted to do so much more.

But even if there was no end in sight, no specific day when they might move from friends to something more, he was okay. As long as he got to see her every chance he got. As long as he knew that her office was down the hall from his. As long as he knew that she *wanted* to spend time with him. Alone.

He'd thought he'd have to keep reminding himself of why he was going through with this tactic, but it wasn't the case. Because he knew that he cared about her. He didn't have to remind himself of that. And he also knew that he'd much rather have her in his life as a friend than not at all. Even if being her friend meant making sure no other tool could get close enough to her to be serious.

It was something about her. Something that he hadn't known existed until now. Until he'd seen it in her. And realised he couldn't live without it. And if he had to wait until she noticed it too, then so be it.

He couldn't help but smile when he saw her walking towards him, a little bit of a bounce in her step and looking slightly frazzled. If she was his girlfriend, he'd rise and give her a hug, a kiss. He'd pull her chair closer to his, so she didn't have to sit opposite him. Instead, he still rose, only to pull her chair out for her—the gentlemanly part of him coming out. Friends could do that, right?

'Morning,' he said, his hand on the back of her chair.

'Morning,' she said—nervously, if he noticed correctly. She eased herself into the chair, her cheeks tinging. 'Thank you.'

'Welcome,' he said, easing back into his own chair opposite hers. 'I already ordered coffee for us. I hope that's okay.'

'Oh, you are amazing,' she said. She let out a sigh

as if trying to relax into her chair. 'Sorry I'm late.'

'Nah, I was early,' he said with a wave of his hand. He felt silly, like the action wasn't normal for him. The way her eyebrow lifted made him realise she must have noticed, too. He grinned. 'Busy morning? You look frazzled.'

Her hand instinctively smoothed over her hair. 'Do I?' she said, her cheeks darkening again. 'Kass showed up as I was about to leave. She was having a bit of a crisis.'

His brow furrowed. 'Is she okay?'

'Yeah,' she said, sighing again, fiddling with the napkin in front of her, 'I mean, it was about Russ. She just needed some reassurance, I guess.'

He felt his eyebrow lift. 'What about Russ?' Russ hadn't said or done anything out of the ordinary as far as he could tell. Then again, the fact that he'd slept with Kassandra more than once *was* out of the ordinary.

'Ahh,' she said hesitantly, shifting in her seat so that she was leaning closer. She looked up at him through her eyelashes, making his heart pound against his chest. 'Don't tell her I said anything. Or Russ. Promise?'

He nodded, leaning closer to make it easier for her to tell him this ... secret. She sighed, dropping her gaze back to the napkin she'd started to tear up with her delicate fingertips.

'I think she likes him.'

'Are we back in high school, are we?' His teasing prompted a mischievous smirk, and another look up at him through those eyelashes.

'What I mean is that she doesn't *like* anyone she sleeps with,' she started. 'Apparently she comes up with excuses not to see them again or something like that.' She shook her head. 'Anyway, so her and Russ have this *thing* it seems, some no-strings-attached thing. And she doesn't want to stop seeing him or something.'

She let out a deep breath and leaned back in her chair. He continued leaning his elbows on the table. 'So, you're saying that she's falling for him?'

She nodded slowly. 'I think so. She didn't exactly admit it, but it seems that way to me.'

He tapped his fingers to his chin, then rested his chin in the palm of his hand. 'Well, Russ is going to have fun getting around that one.'

Her eyes shot up towards him. 'What do you mean?'

He shrugged, leaning back, and folding his arms across his chest. 'He's never done well with people getting attached to him. It's just his thing.'

She opened her mouth to respond, but before she could, the waitress brought the coffees over. She placed the first coffee in front of Nate, batting her eyelids at him.

'Extra chocolates for you,' she said with a wink, making sure she leaned over a bit more towards him.

'Thanks, Trixie,' he said, smiling. He did like chocolate.

She smiled back, fluttering her eyelids again, her cheeks tinging pink. Then, reached for the other coffee and slid it towards Wren. Wren got no such treatment, only a bored look as though Trixie was sizing her up. Once the cup was settled near Wren, Trixie turned back towards him.

'Anything else I can get you, Nate?'

'Give us a few?'

'Sure, honey,' she said, touching her hand gently to his arm. Then, she turned and swayed her way back to the counter.

He grabbed a chocolate and popped it in his mouth, glancing up at Wren. She had her arms folded across her chest, one eyebrow lifted, her lips pressed together in amusement. 'What?' he said, the word muffled from the chocolate.

'What was that?' she said, her eyebrow lifting higher.

'What was what?'

'*That*,' she said. 'With *Trixie*.'

He shrugged. 'She likes me.'

He thought he saw a twitch near her eye, but her expression mostly remained the same. 'Well, that much is obvious,' she said, her voice a little more strained than it had been before. 'Did you sleep with her or something?'

He felt his own eyebrow lift. 'Oh, I wouldn't *dare*,' he said, feigning shock. 'We have a good thing going.'

'Which is what?' she said. There was the twitch again.

He shrugged, his lips curving at the thought she didn't like seeing another girl flirting with him. Step one, complete. 'She makes my coffee,' he said simply. He lifted another chocolate and eased it towards his mouth. 'And gives me extra chocolates.'

Wren squinted at him. 'She didn't spit in my coffee, did she?'

He dropped his gaze to her coffee and studied it emphatically. 'Hmm, maybe,' he mumbled. Then, he slid his coffee across the table and brought hers towards him. 'There,' he added. 'Now you're safe.'

Her lips curved up in a smile and she relaxed a little, picking up one of his extra chocolates he'd purposefully given her in the exchange, and popping it in her mouth. 'Mmm,' she hummed. 'I see what you mean about the chocolates.'

'Good, right?' he said, lifting the cup to his lips.

Her eyebrow lifted again. 'She gave you the coffee with the heart on it,' she said, pointing to the pattern in the froth.

So she had. He pulled the cup that was given to Wren and studied the simple squiggle patterned onto the froth. He hoped Trixie wasn't holding her breath for him.

'Huh, we might need to have brunch somewhere else next time,' he said, taking a sip of the coffee. 'Mmm, Trixie spit.'

He thought he saw a smile when he mentioned a next time, but she recovered quickly. Though, maybe the smile was about the Trixie spit. She sighed. 'You have to talk to Russ.'

He lowered the cup to the table, tracing his fingertip up and down the handle. 'Why do I have to talk to Russ?'

'So he doesn't mess it up with Kass.'

'Why?'

'Because I would have to hurt him if he hurts her,' she said, taking a sip of her coffee.

He laughed. 'I'd like to see you try.'

'I'm serious!' she said.

'So am I,' he said. 'Don't hurt Russ without me there. I want to see it.'

'You're horrible,' she said, her eyes flashing with amusement, her lips curved high.

He winked at her, eating the last chocolate resting on the saucer. 'All right,' he said, rolling the chocolate around in his mouth. 'If he looks like running, I'll kick him in the ass. Deal?' He reached his hand out towards her.

She glanced down at his hand, as if hesitant for a moment, then reached for it. 'Deal.'

As if Trixie had her hawk eyes trained in on them, she popped up next to them and stared at their joined hands. Wren released his hand, sitting up straighter, her lips pressed together as though trying not to laugh.

'Decided what you want yet?' Trixie said, tilting her hip in a way he assumed she thought was seductive.

He glanced towards Wren to see if she knew what she wanted. She cleared her throat. 'Oh, you know what, Trixie, *honey*,' she started.

Trixie licked her teeth, making a bulge under her lips that were pressed together and turned slowly towards Wren. He smirked. He could see Wren's intentions. He could see it wasn't just *helping him out*. Heck, it wasn't that at all. He saw the challenge in her eyes for Trixie. And he'd be lying if he said he didn't find the jealous Wren a little bit … exciting. Trixie lifted an eyebrow, waiting for Wren to continue.

'We need a bit more time,' Wren continued, smiling sweetly. 'Why don't you go along and clean that table there? The smell of that burger is *really* not helping with the morning sickness.' She pressed her hand to her stomach and nodded, smiling up at Trixie.

The colour drained from Trixie's face. 'Oh, of course, I'm sorry,' she said, seeming to recover quickly. 'I didn't … I'll just … excuse me.'

She turned away nervously, gathering up the plates and quickly taking them to the kitchen. It was then that Wren's words caught up to him. *Morning sickness*?

Hell.

Chapter 16

Wren watched the hussy scamper back to the kitchen with the dirty plates and smiled in triumph. She didn't know why Trixie's flirting with Nate agitated her so much. Well, she did know. She liked Nate. But she was also desperately trying to keep a friendship with him because any more than that was a no-go zone. And being friends meant he could flirt with whomever he wanted. Still, he could do *so* much better than that fake-blonde, fake-boobed barbie.

And what better way to throttle her than throw the pregnancy card in the mix? Sure, it might be a total lie. And it might mean that Nate doesn't get all his extra chocolates or special treatment. But it also stopped the poor girl from being too attached to someone she clearly didn't have a chance with.

She sighed, returning her gaze back to Nate, only to see him staring at her, his eyes wide, his mouth open.

His face was white.

All colour had drained from his face.

And she was pretty sure he'd stopped breathing.

'Nate?' she prompted. 'You okay?'

He blinked, but he was still pale. He lifted his hand slowly to rub the stubble on his chin. 'You're not … umm … you … are you?'

Her brow furrowed. What was he on about? Then, she realised. 'Oh, God,' she started, trying to reassure him. 'No, Nate, I'm not.'

'You're sure?'

'I'm sure.'

He started breathing again. 'There's … no chance?'

'No, there isn't,' she said awkwardly. He didn't look convinced. She sighed. 'If you *must* know, I'm on my … you know.'

His brow furrowed, and for a second, she thought he didn't know. Then, his nose scrunched up. 'Oh, gross,' he said. 'I didn't need to know that.' And she hadn't wanted to tell him.

'Well, you didn't believe me,' she said.

'I just wanted to make sure.'

'Oh yeah?' she said, lifting her eyebrow in a challenge. 'And what would you have done if I was?'

'I don't know,' he mumbled, sipping his coffee.

'You looked about two seconds away from

running,' she said softly. She'd be lying if she said it didn't hurt a bit.

He took a long slow breath and held her gaze. The moment seemed to go for a lot longer than it probably was. She could almost see the wheels turning in his head. Well, at least the colour had returned to his face. But she was still worried about the fact he looked like he was going to make a break for it when he thought she was pregnant.

'I wouldn't run,' he said decidedly.

'But you looked like you were going to.'

'I wouldn't run. Not from you.'

Not from you. What did he mean by that? She realised then that he hadn't said he wouldn't *have* run. He wasn't talking about just in *that* moment. He was talking about in general. About any time. Now, in the future. Unless she was looking too far into it … which she was convinced she wasn't. Not when he looked at her with those eyes.

He straightened, picked up a menu from the side of the table and handed it to her. He picked up another for himself. 'Since that stunt has cost me my coffee spot,' he teased. 'We better decide what we want before we make Trixie any more pissed off.'

She smirked. 'You have to admit, though,' she said, smiling, even though her heart felt heavy for some reason. 'It was a good tactic.'

'Oh, yes,' he agreed, glimpsing up at her over the top of the menu. 'Very convincing.'

'What are the bets she'll spit in our food?' she said, keeping her eyes on him.

His eyes paused from scanning the menu and he looked up at her, squinting. 'Mmm, pretty high,' he said, closing the menu, and placing it flat on the table. He pulled his wallet out and dropped a bank note on the table—enough to cover the coffees and a bit of a tip. 'I vote we find somewhere else. You?' He rose to his feet and held a hand out towards her while he tucked his wallet and phone into his back pocket.

She glanced at his hand, hesitant for a moment. Sure, it was a perfectly friendly gesture. A gentlemanly one at that—consistent with him pulling her chair out for her. But it still somehow seemed … intimate. That little bit more. He wiggled his fingers.

'Come on, Wren,' he said, his eyes flashing. 'Unless you want to explain to her *how* it happened, too.'

She smiled and took his hand, letting him help her to her feet. Once standing, his hand briefly lingered on hers—only slightly longer than what would be considered normal—and he held her gaze with a mischievous look in his eyes. She felt his thumb brush over the tops of her fingers and could have sworn he'd given her hand a squeeze before letting go. She fought the urge to pout when her hand missed his touch. It had felt nice. A perfect fit, even. Natural.

He nodded his head towards the door and started walking towards it. She hooked the thin strap of her bag over her shoulder and felt her body start breathing again. How long had she held her breath for, exactly? And did it suddenly get a whole lot hotter?

***

He'd felt the warmth her hand in his sent through his body. He'd noticed how right it felt. And if he read her correctly, she had, too. He didn't exactly have a plan for what they would do instead of eating brunch at his regular coffee spot. Well, his ex-regular coffee spot. He'd have to find a new one now. Both of them would, since she probably felt awkward going into the café where Kade worked. Perhaps they could find one together.

He squinted when they left the café, the sun having a bite to it today. He slowed down, waiting for Wren to catch up to him. She was smiling that beautiful smile and still looked that little bit frazzled. It made him smile. Uncontrollably. God, he would be in trouble if his plan didn't work.

'So, where were you thinking?' she said, shaking her shirt a little to allow for better airflow. She shaded her eyes with one hand.

'I didn't really have anywhere in mind,' he said, falling into step beside her. 'Do you have anywhere you go?'

Her nose scrunched up as she stared at the path in front of them. 'I used to go to *HotSpot*. I never went anywhere else.' She tilted her head to the side and sighed. 'But ...'

'I know,' he said, so she didn't have to. He

nudged his finger over his shoulder in the direction they were walking from. 'I've got the same problem.'

She glanced up at him, a cheeky grin on her face and her eyes flashing. 'Yeah, sorry about that.'

'No, you're not,' he teased, bumping his shoulder against hers. He saw her cheeks tinge a little, and her smile widen. If only her mind was easier to read than her face.

'The poor girl was crushing on you,' she said, her voice hitting a pitch higher than her normal talking voice and laced with amusement.

'And I was benefiting from it,' he said. 'You have to agree—the chocolates are good.'

She glanced up at him sideways. 'So, tell me,' she started.

'Hmm?'

'Who's the player? You, or Russ?'

He opened his mouth wide, amused. 'I resent that comment!'

Her mouth dropped open, equally amused, her eyes dancing. She shoved him on the arm. 'You were leading her on!'

'Oh, please,' he scoffed. 'I know when there's a line that shouldn't be crossed.'

She stopped walking, and he turned to face her, surprised at how close she was. 'Is that so?' she said, unconvinced. Her arms were folded across her chest, but not defensively. More like waiting for him to explain.

She stepped closer as someone nudged past them on the footpath. She was close enough to kiss.

His eyes dropped to her lips—soft and supple. Inviting. And he could still taste her, even though it had been too long since he'd kissed her properly.

'Hmm?' she prompted, lifting her chin.

He could hear the noises around them—the cars, people talking, the dinging of bicycles. The normal bustle of the Gold Coast. But none of it mattered. Not when she was standing so close to him.

He lifted an eyebrow. 'Well,' he said, slowly bringing his gaze back up to her challenging eyes. 'Mostly.'

He snaked his hand around her waist, revelling in the feel of her body under his hand, wishing there was no clothing between them. No rules. He registered her sharp intake of breath and wondered if she felt the same. No, *knew* she felt the same. She had to. He was sure of it. Certain, in the way she looked at him, the way she stirred up Trixie. The challenge in her eyes. One of her hands crept up and rested on his chest, the look in her eyes darkening, as though letting him look deep into her soul.

Then, he tugged her to his side, out of the way of the passing asshole of a cyclist that felt his right was to ride on the footpath and over anyone who was in his way.

'Get a room!' the cyclist yelled in passing.

'Get a life!' he yelled back, annoyed that the only close contact he could have with Wren was because he was pulling her out of some asshole's path.

He reluctantly released his hold around her waist and glanced towards her. She'd dropped her hand the moment she must have noticed the cyclist. And damn it if it didn't make him more pissed. She folded her arms across her chest again—this time, defensively, protectively—and checked the path behind them to make sure no one else was going to run over them.

'So, I ... umm,' she stammered, starting to walk next to him again. 'I'd say Russ is more of a player, but still.'

He didn't reply. Only walked beside her, his hands balled beside him, trying his damnedest to not chase down the cyclist and give him hell for wrecking what could have been a near perfect moment. They walked in silence for a few minutes. Neither knowing where they were headed, he figured, just forward. The only way they could go.

Because they couldn't go back to the past. The past had awesome, carefree sex. And he'd give anything to go back to that. Go back to the before he started working at her work. Back to that first night and just stay there. But he couldn't. Now, he could only work on *winning* her, making her realise that he was the air she needed to breathe as much as she was for him. But he couldn't control that, either. He could only hope that the attraction they clearly had for each other would be enough. That she'd come to like the guy he is—the spur of the moment, determined, persevering, focussed, caring, and apparently sulky guy he is.

'So, I hate to be a buzzkill,' she said sarcastically, hesitantly. 'But I actually haven't eaten today, and I am running out of energy.'

He glanced at her and smiled. It started out a little forced, but seeing her face made it real. He couldn't help but smile around the woman. 'What do you feel like?'

The corners of her lips flicked up a little. 'I suppose it's too early for a drink, huh?' she said, nudging her shoulder against him.

His brow furrowed and he studied her, trying to determine whether she was serious or not. 'You don't have a … problem … do you, Wren?'

She scrunched her nose up, turning slightly to face him better. 'No,' she said, shrugging. 'But you do.'

'I don't have a problem,' he said, frowning.

'Oh yeah?' she said, her eyebrow lifting. 'Then what's with the cranky pants?'

'*Cranky pants*?' he repeated, half amused, half still annoyed.

Her face grew serious and she dropped her gaze. 'Did I make you mad?' she said cautiously. 'I'm sorry. I didn't mean to piss off Trixie, I just—'

'*Wren*,' he said, turning towards her, resting his hands on her shoulders, urging her to look at him.

They'd stopped walking again, and he realised how silly he was being. Why should he have his *cranky pants* on when he was hanging out with the most incredible woman he'd ever known? Sure, the cyclist annoyed him. But he was still with Wren. Whatever they were going to define *this* as, they were on talking terms. And if he had to define it, he'd say they were getting there. Possibly quicker than he'd planned for. And he had to remember that. He couldn't let something irrelevant get in the way of that.

Her ocean blue eyes shimmered like sunlight on the water, and he felt the tug on his chest. 'I'm not mad at you,' he said.

'I mean, I get it if you are,' she said. 'I probably ruined whatever you and … Trixie … might have had … or could have.' She dropped her gaze.

Ahh. *That's* why she thought he was cranky? The saucy minx was jealous. And *damn*, jealousy looked good on her. He nudged her chin up with the knuckle of his index finger. Slowly, her eyes flickered up to meet his.

'There's nothing with Trixie,' he said, his lips curving up at the side.

He wiped a speck of chocolate powder off the tip of her nose with his thumb. Her lips parted, and he felt that pull again. The urge to say screw it to the rules, the plans, and just have her, and this moment.

The rest of it could go get—

***

His touch.

God, his touch!

How could a single touch—a stroke of his thumb across the tip of her nose—have her melting in front of him? She blamed it on the lack of food, the lack of sustenance and nutrition, that made her knees weak.

It couldn't just be from his touch. Surely not.

But even *that* didn't have her convinced.

She already knew how good his touch felt, how good his kisses were. How impossibly *right* it had felt with him. But there was so much in the way. So much that made him off limits. Made the whole thing impossible. But how could she expect to be friends with him without falling for him? Especially if he touched her like this.

His touch still lingered on her waist from before, and she felt like she was missing it more than she should. She'd reciprocated. *She'd* put her hand on his chest and waited for him to kiss her. God, she'd wanted it. And it wasn't until he'd pulled her out of the way that she realised what a fool she was, that he wasn't touching her the way she *wanted* to be touched. All because of a damn cyclist.

The rules.

Screw the rules!

Her brain could remind her of the damn rules all the damn time, but she hadn't regretted anything more than driving that damn wedge between them. Maybe they would have become friends naturally. Maybe they wouldn't have that awkwardness they had whenever something happened. Like Kade. Or Trixie. *Damn it*! When had she started being the jealous type?

His thumb rubbed over the tip of her nose again, then, he tapped his finger against it and winked. 'You've got nothing to worry about.'

She felt her heart skip a beat. And when had she

become like *this*? So obviously jealous over something so simple and silly, *pining* after a man she'd kept at arm's length. And he'd … he'd *noticed*. He'd picked up on her jealousy. *Oh, God*.

'Oh, I'm not … umm … *worried* … or anything,' she stammered, trying to cover up what he so clearly saw. Though, she *was* worried she'd only made her jealousy more obvious.

His nose crinkled, and his lips curved. He dropped his hands from her and started walking again. 'Sure,' he said. But his smile showed that he didn't believe her.

She almost had to jog to keep up with him. 'Not *every* girl is falling at your feet, you know.' Just her. And just about every woman who had the pleasure of laying eyes on him, she'd bet.

He pressed his hand to his chest, facing her. 'That hurts, Wren,' he said. But the bastard didn't look hurt. In fact, the smug look on his face was almost one of triumph. He knew what she was doing. *Damn him*.

'Truth hurts, Nate,' she said, desperately trying to cover her tracks. Even if he'd already seen through her. 'You're not … *all that*.'

'Wow,' he said, his eyebrows lifting. The smugness was still there. She squinted at him. 'You're pretty vicious when you're hangry,' he added.

He opened the door to another café on the street. She hadn't been to it, but she assumed he must have. On the plus side, it had neither Kade or Trixie working at it. She stared him down.

'Vicious?' she repeated. Her mouth fell open. '*Hangry*?'

He placed his hand on her back and guided her through the door, still smirking smugly. 'Can we *please* get this woman some food before she bites my head off?' he yelled out.

The café workers all smiled at them, and she felt her cheeks heating up. Oh, he was about to see how much she could bite off—

He pushed down on her shoulders until she was sitting in the chair, then called out for some cake and some menus, before taking the seat opposite her. That smug smile still on his face, his eyes dancing with amusement. Her body still feeling weak. It wasn't because she was lacking sustenance. It was him. All him.

Damn him.

Chapter 17

'I have a question for you,' Wren said, bending over to pick up a leaf from the ground. She started shredding it slowly.

'Another?' Nate said, his eyebrow lifting.

She smiled up at him. She had to admit, she was feeling a lot better now that she'd actually eaten. Though, perhaps she'd eaten *too* much. They walked slowly, aimlessly, through a nearby park that should lead them back to the general vicinity of their cars. It was a lot nicer than the footpath, and the shade of the trees provided a nice relief from the blistering of the sun. Summer was almost over, but it had been a hot one. And it seemed that, this year, the sun wanted to get at least one last kick in before letting the weather cool down a little. Though, being the

Gold Coast, the temperature didn't vary *that* much.

'What made you want to plan the camping trip with me?'

Something flickered in his eyes before it disappeared—too quick for her to discern what it was. His lips curved up higher on one side. 'Figured you'd be a fountain of knowledge,' he said, nudging against her shoulder.

She laughed. 'I know *nothing* about camping. But you still want me to help you plan it?'

His nose scrunched, teasingly. 'All right, you caught me,' he said. 'I don't *really* like people. And you're the only person I knew there, so I figured that even though you hated me, it would be much more tolerable than picking someone who *looks* interesting but ends up making me bored out of my brains. At least it would be interesting with you.'

She felt her eyebrows pull together. 'I don't *hate* you, Nate,' she muttered.

'Maybe not now,' he said. 'But when you found out I got your job?'

She shrugged lightly, focussing back on the shredded leaf in her hands. 'I didn't hate you.'

'But you were annoyed.'

'Of course I was annoyed,' she said, looking up at him. His eyes held a look of sorrow, and she wondered if it was reflective of how she looked. 'I worked hard for that job, thinking it was mine. Then, Durgan hired out. Who wouldn't be annoyed?'

He pressed his lips together. 'You deserved the job.'

'Apparently I didn't,' she said, biting the inside of her cheek. Why did her eyes burn? 'But there's nothing we—I—can do about it. And it wasn't so much … *at* you. Really more in general.'

'So, I was just imagining that I was the last person you wanted to see?'

He stopped walking, and she slowly turned towards him, dropping her arms to her side, the stem of the bedraggled leaf still in her hand. 'It's not *that*,' she muttered.

'What is it then, Wren? Because it's been slowly killing me inside.'

She blinked her eyes—once, twice, too many times to count—trying to work through the burn. 'I wasn't *supposed* to see you again, Nate.'

There. She'd said it. He straightened, as though he'd just been shocked, and studied her. She recognised the hurt flicker across his face. It was the same hurt she felt in her chest the moment she said it.

'You … *planned* it?' he said slowly.

'I didn't *plan* it,' she said, dropping the remains of the leaf to the ground. She folded her arms across her chest—a protective measure she'd grown used to lately. 'I was *grieving*, Nate. I was supposed to leave alone. I didn't … we weren't supposed to—'

'You have a very odd way of expressing your grief, Wren.' His eyes clouded over, his lips set.

'I—I don't think we should talk about this,' she muttered, dropping her gaze. Her throat was tightening, her eyes burning, her stomach clenching.

'I think we should—'

'Hey, Tank!'

Her eyes shot up towards him. *Tank*? Where had she heard that before? And the voice … it somehow sounded familiar. His jaw set, his body stiffening. So much that she wondered if he would break if she knocked him over.

'Nate, sorry, I keep forgetting,' the voice said again.

Closer this time. She felt a wet nose press against her leg and looked down at the terrier looking at them. Her eyes followed up the lead to see a dark-haired woman. Shorter than her, but she was pretty. The woman looked at Wren and smiled.

'And girl,' she said, her eyes warm. 'Good to see you've recovered from last week.'

Last week? Her mind wandered back to the bar. Of course! This woman was the bartender. She remembered that now. But why did she call Nate *Tank*? Did she know him from university or something?

The woman laughed, glancing nervously back up at Nate, nudging her head towards Wren. 'I mean, she already knows your stripper name now anyway, right?'

Stripper name? Wren shot her gaze towards Nate and that came back to her too. She didn't remember much about that night, but the phrase *Nate the Tank* was sounding a hell of a lot more familiar than it should. Nate gave her a worried look, a look that said he'd explain. But it wasn't just the stripper part that had her freaking out. He'd said nothing happened.

How much more of that night *didn't happen*?

'Tell me, did you end up finding Russ?'

'Ahh, yeah,' he said, shifting his gaze slowly towards the other woman. 'He's been found.'

'Oh good,' she said, relieved. 'Well, next time you see him, tell him he owes me a shift. The bastard didn't show up last night and *I* was supposed to be having a date instead of working.'

Nate's brow furrowed. 'Russ skipped work?' His voice almost sounded ... shocked. Much like the state she was in right now. She could feel her blood boiling slowly inside of her. 'He never skips work.'

'He did last night. So, now he owes me.'

'I'll let him know.'

'All right, thanks.'

There was silence for a little longer, but Wren had already started staring at the ground, wondering how much longer it would take before she either exploded or fell apart. Or both. Her mind was slowly sorting out what was likely a dream and what had really happened.

Dancing? Real.

Nate having been a stripper? Real.

Excessively drunk? Real.

'Jess?' Nate said slowly.

'Hmm?' the woman hummed.

Wren sighed. She was still here? The terrier nudged against her leg again, as if picking up on her mood.

Inability to keep herself upright? Real.

Nate *holding* her upright? Real.

'We were kind of in the middle of something,' Nate said, dismissing her.

'Oh, right! Of course,' she said nervously. 'Silly me. Sorry. I'm told I have no awareness of things like this. Or a filter. Apparently, I have no filter. Like I just say things without thinking about it—'

Unfiltered bartender? Real.

Blurting out that she'd *banged Nate the Tank* to said unfiltered bartender? Likely.

'*Jess*,' Nate said again, firmer, this time.

Staying the night at Nate's? Obvious.

Sleeping in his bed? Definite.

Alone? Unsure.

'Going!' she said, throwing one hand up in surrender and tugging on the lead until the terrier followed her.

Throwing herself at him—naked? Unsure.

Kissing him—naked? Being *rejected* by him? *Sleeping* with him?

Wren took a deep breath, gathering up as much courage as she could, and slowly looked up at Nate. Her mind was chaos. And she felt like she'd been too quick to trust him, too quick to let her guard down. Too quick to let him in.

'Wren,' he started.

But she cut him off. She felt the sting on her palm as it met with his cheek, surprising herself more than it seemed to surprise him. Her eyes burned, and she fought the urge to slap him again when he looked back at her, his eyes wild.

'You *lied* to me,' she forced out, fully aware that her voice was shaking.

'*Wren*,' he said, reaching towards her.

She took a step back, registering the hurt on his face when she did so, ignoring the ache in her chest. Then, she took another, shaking her head.

'I *asked* you if anything happened, Nate, and you *lied* to me.'

'Nothing did happen!' he said, exasperated.

She laughed, though she wasn't finding it amusing. No, it was as though her body laughed instead of letting the tears fall. Crying showed weakness, right? And he sure as hell didn't deserve to see that side of her.

'You're still sticking with that?' she said sarcastically. 'I *believed* you, Nate. God, I'm a fool. And an idiot! An idiot who can't tell when she's being *played*.'

'No, you're not,' he said, grabbing onto her shoulders, urging her to look at him. She shook his hands off her, even though it felt like it was only quickening her breaking process. 'I didn't lie,' he added. 'Nothing happened.'

'So, you're telling me that there wasn't any touching?'

'You were drunk,' he said. 'The only touching was me acting as your bloody crutch to make sure you got home instead of sleeping in the bushes.'

'*Your* home,' she pointed out.

'Well, I could hardly take you back to *your* home, could I? I don't even *know* where you live.' He sighed, rubbing his forehead. 'That was it, Wren. I swear, *nothing happened*.'

'So, we didn't kiss?'

He faltered.

God, she wished he hadn't.

'That was not—'

'Kissing is *not* nothing, Nate! Not for me, damn it!' She stomped her foot in frustration, mentally marking kissing off as real.

'*You* threw yourself at *me*, Wren!' Real.

She blinked, trying to breathe, but finding it a struggle. 'You didn't stop me!' she yelled back.

'*What*?'

'You took advantage of me, Nate,' she said, swiping at her eyes. 'I *trusted* you.'

She saw a muscle twitch near his jaw. 'Is that the kind of man you think I am? Someone who takes advantage of an insanely drunk and *lost* woman?'

'I know you are!'

'Well, you're wrong!' he yelled, straightening, taking a step backwards. Then, another. There was fire in his eyes, matching the fire burning inside of her. 'I didn't take advantage of you, Wren,' he continued. 'And I think, deep down, you know that.'

She spread her arms out. 'How do I know what to believe, Nate?'

He shook his head, running a hand through his hair, this time, taking a step forward instead of backwards. Then another, until he was so close, she could feel the heat from his body reaching hers.

'What else do you remember from that night,

huh?' he said, his voice a growl, the look in his eyes so fierce it took her breath away. 'Do you remember feeling rejected because I didn't kiss you back? Do you remember sulking because I gave you clothes to wear instead of letting you keep prancing around in your *nothings*?'

'Nate,' she said. It was more of a breath.

'Or that you got *cut* that I wouldn't sleep with you because I wanted to do things *right*?' he continued.

His teeth clenched together, his eyes searching hers, making her feel a lot smaller than she was. How much of what he was saying was true? He was raw. Everything he was saying was raw, real. And it shocked her to her core. She opened her mouth to say something, but nothing came out.

'What about how you *felt*,' he growled. 'When I told you I *fucking loved* you?' She felt the wind get knocked out of her. *What*? He held her gaze, almost like she was physically being held captive. Only, he wasn't touching her. 'What about then, Wren?' he took a step back, his hands stretched out to the side.

There was no taking it back. None of it. What she'd said was out there. What he'd said was real. She hadn't trusted him, and now, there was no taking back the hurt that caused. Even when she knew the only mistake she'd ever made was pushing him away.

'When I've fought against every cell in my body to follow *your* stupid rules and make sure *you* didn't do anything you'd regret. When I put my *heart* on the line, for *what*?'

'Nate,' she whispered, trying to find something to say, but coming up empty. It was like she was in shock, unable to move. Unable to speak. Barely able to breathe.

He shook his head, backing up even more. 'You win, Wren,' he said. 'I give up.'

'What?' He wouldn't have heard her. She barely heard herself.

'I didn't tell you what happened last week because I didn't want you to be embarrassed,' he said. 'But you know what? It shouldn't have even got to that. I should have left you alone at that bar drinking your whisky. I should've ignored the pull towards you.' She shook her head, trying desperately to clear her head enough to *think*. 'Congratulations, Wren,' he said, pausing only briefly, staring at her—*through* her. 'You wanted me to forget that night. Consider it done.'

Then, he was gone. Not even a single glance back at her.

What the hell just happened?

***

Nate slammed the car door closed, swearing again as he did. The drive home had done nothing for trying to calm himself. He was sure that by the time he'd got home he'd probably regret everything he said and call her to apologise.

But there was no such inclination.

His blood was still boiling, his head still burning.

She thought he was that kind of guy? The guy to take advantage of a drunk woman? There was nothing that infuriated him more. He could look past many things. He could put up with a lot, but that—*that*—was something that he couldn't look past. Insults he could deal with. Comments about how he looked he could deal with. But questioning his *character*? His morals?

People who did that were not worth his time.

He just wished it wasn't Wren.

Damn it!

Wren, the girl he'd been so *sure* about. That he was willing to jump through hoops and *wait* for. The one he was willing to bet would trump anything he'd ever feel with anyone else. The one he said he loved—twice—without thinking about it when he'd never said it to anyone else before.

He swore again, kicking the post out front of his house—the very post she'd leaned against in her totally drunken state. *Damn it.* He rubbed his forehead and lifted his hand to unlock the door, only to pause before the key reached the lock. The light was on.

He hadn't seen it when he was getting out of his car, or when he'd walked towards his house. But he saw it now. The lounge room light was shining through the crack in the curtains. Of course, it would be hard to see to someone who didn't know, considering it was still light outside. But he knew it was dark in that room when the curtains were closed. And light *shouldn't* be coming from *inside* the room.

He stretched his arm up above him, feeling for his spare key on the top of the door frame, relieved to find it still there, still caked with a layer of undisturbed dust from disuse. Was it possible he'd simply forgotten to turn the light off? Unlike him, but it was *possible*. He was excited to be going to brunch with Wren, after all. So much for that ordeal.

He moved his key into the lock and turned. But it didn't click. He turned the doorknob. It was already open. What the hell?

He might have forgotten to turn the light off. But there was no way he'd forgotten to lock the door. Heck, he even *remembered* locking the door, even if his mind was currently in a state of frenzy and chaos from what just happened with Wren. He took a deep breath, readying himself to confront anyone that might be in his house, and turned the doorknob, only to have the door yanked open in front of him.

'*Damn it*, Russ! What the hell are you doing here?'

He started breathing again. He really needed to do something about Russ having a key. In fact, it was just occurring to him that he already *had* a spare key—above the door. Why did he give Russ a key, again? Something about if that one went missing?

Russ shrugged, shoving the remains of a bread roll—Nate's bread roll—into his mouth. 'Looking for you,' he said, his words muffled by the roll. He followed the mouthful with a sip of coffee. Nate's coffee.

'Well, you found me,' he said sarcastically, dropping his keys and wallet on the hall table, then turned back towards Russ. 'By the way … I bumped into Jess at the park. She said you didn't show up to work last night.'

Russ shrugged again, as though the answer was simple. 'I was with Kass.'

He should have known. Wren had already said that Kassandra showed up at her place that morning freaking out. 'Yeah, well, she's pissed she had to cover for you.'

'She'll get over it,' Russ said, his brow furrowing. 'What were you doing in the park?'

'Doesn't matter,' he mumbled, kicking his shoes off, and shoving them under the hall table. A benefit of living alone—all of his very limited selection of shoes could fit under the hall table.

'You were with Wren, weren't you?' Russ teased, following him as he headed towards the kitchen for some coffee for himself.

He felt his jaw clench at the mention of her name. So much for wanting to wallow in peace. Maybe he needed something stronger than coffee. 'We are not talking about Wren,' he said flatly.

'Something happen?' Russ said inquisitively, then sped up to walk closer to him. 'Oh, before you go in there, there's someone here to see you.'

He froze, directing his gaze to his friend. '*What*?' Who the hell would be here to see *him*? Russ was the only one that visited, the only real friend he had who knew where he lived. Unless—

'Some guy,' Russ said, shrugging confusedly. 'He was hanging around out front when I got here. Said he was looking for you. Claimed he was your brother, though, to be honest, I couldn't see the resemblance.'

He felt his eyes widen. His *brother*? Surely, not. He picked up his pace and halted when he got to the kitchen and saw him standing near the table.

Leo.

Chapter 18

'Hi, Nate.'

'Leo.'

What was he doing here?

'Oh, now I see the resemblance,' Russ said slowly. 'I'll just … ahh … leave you to it.'

He heard Russ leaving the house, but he still stared at his brother. His brother who he hadn't spoken to since he announced he was moving to the Gold Coast. Since he'd said he wasn't going to take on the farm. Who hadn't answered his calls, his messages, his letters. Who'd made it clear he didn't want anything to do with him again.

'Nice place you've got here,' Leo said in a tone that sounded bored. Leo looked around them, and Nate's eyes followed his gaze.

His place was fairly average, he'd thought, even though it was pretty different to the old farmhouse he'd grown up in. He thought there was something else in Leo's tone and wondered if he was still sore about not having a choice with staying at the farm.

'What are you doing here, Leo?'

Leo turned slowly to face him, spreading his arms out to the side. 'Is that how you greet your little brother?'

What he wanted to do was pull him into a hug—his brother who he hadn't seen in years had reached out to him. But deep down, he also knew that there had to be a reason why his brother was here. Something must have happened. Leo picked up a glass from the table and took a sip. Nate registered the amber-coloured liquid swishing in the glass. His eyes shot towards the bottle still sitting on the kitchen bench. Again.

'Good quality whisky,' Leo said, holding the glass up as if examining the liquid. 'Good choice.'

He felt a muscle twitch in his jaw. Even if things were over with Wren before they could properly start, it still didn't feel right that someone else was drinking their whisky. He urged his feet to move him towards the kitchen in search of coffee.

'How'd you find me, Leo?'

His brother shrugged, placing the glass back on the table. 'Thought I'd have to dig a little deeper to find your address, but nope. There it was in the last letter you sent. That was some time ago, Nate.'

He found a cup and turned towards him, pouring

the coffee that Russ had clearly made in the cup. 'Well, I stopped writing when I realised I wasn't going to get a reply.'

Leo shifted his gaze as if avoiding eye contact. God, his little brother looked the same as he always did. A little older, a little stronger, a little more worn. But mostly, the same. Then, he sighed, and reached into his worn leather jacket—a jacket he was sure he'd grown used to wearing even when it was hot— and pulled out a pile of envelopes. Leo walked towards the kitchen bench and dropped the pile in front of him. The envelopes looked worn, tied together with a rubber band. Torn in some corners, stained in other spots. Addressed. Stamped. Unsent.

'Ma never stopped writing,' Leo said.

'Why do you have these?' Nate said, looking up at his brother. *Why weren't they sent?*

'Because,' Leo said, sighing again. He rubbed at his forehead. 'Because I never sent them for her.'

The anger he was feeling from before had started to boil up again, simmering to the surface. He suppressed it as much as he could. If Leo had been the reason he never heard from his parents, why was he here now? He clenched his jaw in an attempt to stop himself from saying something he shouldn't say. Like he probably should've done with Wren. He felt a stab of guilt in his chest and reminded himself that she'd judged his character. He couldn't go there again …

'As far as she knew, you were getting her letters and couldn't care less,' Leo continued, dropping his gaze to the pile of letters, his hands pressed firmly on the bench. 'And she didn't want to call in case Pa found out. He changed all our numbers when he did.'

So, *that* was why she'd stopped answering. As he'd suspected. He sipped his coffee. 'Why are you telling me this?'

'Because I screwed up, man.'

Nate lifted an eyebrow. Who was really at fault in this situation? His family shouldn't have disowned him like that, cut off all communications. Leo should've sent those letters when he'd said he had. He shouldn't have been pressured to take over the farm. Then again, they *were* his family, and maybe he wasn't so right in leaving them.

'Ma's been depressed since you left,' Leo said. 'And now, with Dad ...' He trailed off, diverting his gaze towards the bottle at the end of the bench. Nate was sure he saw Leo swallow, saw the weariness in his eyes, the sorrow.

'What's wrong with Dad?' Nate prompted, feeling his chest tighten.

Leo paused for a moment, then looked back at him. 'He had a heart attack, Nate.'

Nate felt his breath catch in his throat, the blood draining from his face. He hadn't been in touch with his father, hadn't been on the best terms, but he was still his *father*. 'Is he okay?' *Don't tell me he's dead*.

'He's ... recovering,' Leo said. 'Still relatively housebound. But recovering.'

'How long ago?'

Leo shrugged. 'A month. Six weeks, maybe.'

He swallowed the lump in his throat. 'And you didn't *tell me*?'

'You left us!' Leo yelled. '*You* shirked all your responsibilities onto me!'

'*You're* the one that didn't send those letters!' he yelled back. 'Or is that acceptable in your books?'

Leo lifted his chin and rubbed his forehead again. 'I didn't come here to fight, Nate,' he said. 'I already admitted I screwed up. It's your turn to do the same.'

'And why should I?' he said. 'I tried to keep in contact. How did I screw up?'

'Because *you* made Ma like this,' Leo growled, his voice shaky. 'I'm not here because of Dad. Ma's the one I'm worried about.'

'Leo,' Nate said, his jaw set. 'What's wrong with Ma?'

Leo held his gaze for a moment and swallowed. 'It's time for you to come home, Nate.'

***

Wren waited for the elevator doors to open, gathering up as much sleepless energy as she could. She'd practically layered on the makeup that morning to cover the bags under her eyes that were a result of two horrible, sleepless nights. Not even spending all of Sunday with her dad helped distract her mind. She still hadn't worked out what to do with Nate or how she was going to keep working with the guy after he'd said what he said. After she'd assumed the worst of him.

She didn't blame him for losing it at her.

Heck, *she* would have, if she was in his shoes.

But it was *what* he said that got to her. He said he'd loved her? God, she'd thought it was a dream— her mind playing stupid tricks on her, making her believe that *she* was the one that loved him. It was too soon, it had to be. She didn't believe in fairy tales. She didn't believe in love at first sight. She didn't really believe that there was anyone out there for her, or that everything happens for a reason.

She once had.

She'd believed it all—with Griffin. And look how that turned out for her.

Once he'd said those words on Saturday, she'd had mixed feelings. First, she'd been relieved that he'd actually said it, that her mind wasn't playing tricks on her. Then, she'd freaked out, reminding herself that it was too soon. He shouldn't be feeling like that. *She* shouldn't be feeling like that. Then again, she'd felt the pain of losing someone she'd actually cared about, the specifics of that he'd said he *loved* her—past tense—and not that he still did, catching up to her. The fact that he'd told her he'd forget that night.

Like she'd wanted him to.

Except, now she wished she'd never told him to forget that night. Because forgetting that night, it seemed, meant that he'd forget *her*. And she wasn't sure she was ready to let him go. Not really. And it would be impossible when she saw him every day, worked closely with him. And couldn't even be friends.

And she'd dug that hole for herself.

She was the only one to blame.

Because she'd pushed him away when she should have been finding a way to hold onto him. And now? She had no chance.

The elevator dinged and the doors opened. She blinked, trying to focus on the day, and caught his eyes. His grey eyes that had grown cold, empty. Sorrowful? The warmth she'd once seen was no longer there. His hands were in his pockets, his shoulders slightly slumped. And though he was dressed neatly, he wasn't wearing his usual business attire. He, too, looked like he'd had some sleepless nights. Though, he wasn't wearing makeup to cover it up.

She stepped out of the elevator, and he stepped in. She felt the brush of his shoulder past hers, even though it hadn't touched. The wind of him moving past her was enough to send a shiver down her spine, make her body ache for his touch again. The touch she wouldn't have.

She turned back to face him, just as the elevator dinged again. She caught his eyes again and could have sworn she'd seen the slightest nod of his head. But there was no emotion in the way he looked at her. The doors closed.

'Nate,' she whispered.

But it was too late.

'Wren, a word?'

She swallowed the lump in her throat, blinked

back the tears that burned at the back of her eyes, and turned towards her boss, following him into his office.

'Have a seat,' Durgan said as he lowered himself into the oversized chair behind his desk. She eased herself into the seat opposite him and tried to bring her mind into the same room as her body. It seemed stuck in the elevator. 'Big weekend?'

'Hmm?' she said, blinking again to try her best to focus on him. 'Oh, just a terrible sleep.'

Durgan leaned back in his chair, rubbing his clean-shaven chin. Wren swallowed again, thinking only about how Nate's stubble had felt against the palm of her hand that first night. 'Everything okay?' he said.

She nodded, trying to convince herself as well as her boss. 'It's the heat, I think,' she lied. 'Makes it hard to sleep.' Yes, it had been a hot couple of nights. But she did have a fan in the bedroom. And she knew it wasn't *really* the heat keeping her up at night. In fact, the thing that did just left in that elevator.

'You should invest in a good cooler,' he said, folding his hands in front of him.

She nodded. 'I'll look into it.' He held her gaze for a moment. She shifted in her seat. 'Is that all?'

He shook his head and sighed. She swallowed again. Why *had* Nate been leaving in the elevator at the start of the workday? He should've been coming in, not going out. And why would Durgan wish to talk to her now? Unless he knew about what happened with her and Nate …

'I was just talking with Nate,' he started. 'Mr Hoffman—though I'm sure you're on a first name basis by now.'

She froze. This *was* about Nate. Likely, *her* and Nate. *Shoot*.

'Wren, I like to think of us as … family,' he continued. 'Our little management team, in particular. But also, everyone else that works here. Just one, big, happy … family.'

She lifted an eyebrow and quickly straightened her expression. Her boss might think of them as family, but the thought had never once crossed her mind. Except when it came to Kassandra—her best friend and the only one here who she would even remotely consider as family.

'And when something happens with one member of that family,' he continued, bringing the weight of his upper body over his elbows that rested on the desk. 'It effects everyone else in that family.'

God, how much of the her-and-Nate debacle did he know?

'Is everything … okay … in this … *family*?' Wren said, acting as oblivious as she could when her mind was chaos.

'No, it is not,' he said, leaning back in his chair again. 'Nate's just informed me that he needs to take some time off—personal reasons,' he said, waving his hand. 'Being so soon into starting work here, it does have me concerned. But his references were respectable and immaculate, so I'm giving him the benefit of the doubt.'

'Is he … okay?' Wren said, genuinely concerned. Surely it wasn't just because of her … was it?

'He assured me he'll be back and will carry on with as much as he can by correspondence,' he said. 'He simply said that there were some … family matters … he had to attend to.'

Wren's brow creased. *Family matters*? He might expect Durgan to believe that, but he'd told *her* he hadn't spoken to his family in years, that they'd practically disowned him. It was because of her. There was no other excuse. But, if Durgan didn't know about their involvement, it would be better if she played along, right?

'I see,' she said, shifting in her seat. Kassandra always told her she was a bad liar. She hoped that Durgan didn't know that. 'And you're telling me this because?' she prompted.

'Because someone needs to do the parts of his job that he can't do by correspondence.'

Ah. There it was. Again. She was good enough and valued enough to fill in for that role but wasn't good enough to *get* that role. 'I don't know …' she started.

Durgan held a hand up between them. 'It won't be the same as before he joined us,' he said. 'Like I said, he'll still be doing some things. I'll just need you to pick up on the few things he can't attend to.'

'I—' she started. She what? She barely had the energy to do her own work, let alone someone else's? That she'd practically driven herself to a breakdown from working so hard? That she can't fill in for those *few things* because that meant she'd have to keep in contact with him? 'Can't,' she finished.

Durgan frowned. 'Nate said you might be hesitant to help, considering the … misunderstanding … with the position recently.' What else had he said? 'Which is why you'll only have to pick up a few things.' He pushed a folder across the desk towards her. 'Everything you need to know is in here. If you have any questions, just come to me. And, of course, while you're filling in for him as the face of the position, you'll be paid that rate.'

She was about to refuse when the extra pay repeated itself in her mind. Sure, it wasn't *that* much extra on top of her already new pay rate—thanks to Nate. But it was still extra. And, well, if she was saving for whatever she was saving for now, every bit counts. Unlike when she was taking on all the responsibilities of that position before and not getting a cent more than her contracted wage.

'Will I … umm … need to keep him updated?' she asked warily, as though it was the determining factor. Maybe it was.

Durgan shook his head and tapped the folder. 'Like I said,' he said. 'It's all in there. And it's only for a short time. A couple weeks or so. Maybe longer.'

A couple weeks? Did he need to be away from her that long? She tried to ignore her heart dropping to her stomach. She couldn't even imagine not seeing him that long …

'What about the camping trip?' she said. 'That was supposed to be this weekend.'

'Nate will continue planning it while he's away,' he said. 'But I've decided it's for the better if we push it out until after he gets back. It *is* his baby, after all.'

Wren nodded. 'When will he be back?'

'Undetermined, at this stage,' he said. 'But he promised to keep me in the loop.' He waved his hand again. 'That will be all. I'm sure you'll want to read through the folder before the day officially starts.'

She nodded again, picking up the folder and heading towards the door. How should she feel? Elated at the temporary pay rise? Thankful that she was still Durgan's go to for things like this? Relieved that she won't have to deal with the awkwardness with Nate for an *undetermined* amount of time? She wasn't sure how she *should* feel, but she sure as hell knew it wasn't what she *did*. She turned to face her boss before leaving through the door.

'Mr Durgan?' He looked up at her. 'Why me?' If she sounded hesitant to ask it, it's because she was.

'Because you're the only one I can really trust to get the job done.'

Chapter 19

Nate rolled his car to a stop as he neared his childhood home. He pulled the key out of the ignition and stared at the farmhouse. The old weatherboards were starting to wear, the metal roof faded, the veranda railing broken in parts. Apart from looking a little more worn, it looked the same as he remembered it.

The farm had been in his family for generations, but his Grandad had built that house when they were expecting Nate's uncle. Out of four boys, Nate's dad was the youngest, and the only one still alive. The rest had been a heartbreaking tale—and all, coincidentally, from farming incidents.

The old tyre still hung from the huge oak tree near the house, though he wouldn't trust the rope to hold him now. He took a shaky breath, his body still not recovered from seeing Wren that morning. There'd been a reason he went to work earlier than usual—to talk with Durgan before anyone else was there. What were the odds that Wren would show up early, too? But maybe that's what she did. How was he to know? He'd always been on time, and she'd always been there. He should have figured that day wouldn't be any different.

So why did it disappoint him that it wasn't?

Perhaps it was the fact that she seemed to be carrying on as usual after their fight. Hadn't it affected her the same way it affected him? Or maybe she simply didn't give a damn about him. Even in her drunken state, she'd had a go at him for *stealing her job*. And when she was sober, she questioned his morals. He was probably better off without her.

But he still had to convince himself of that. He didn't even know when he'd see her again.

He'd told Durgan he'd keep him in the loop, continue doing some work from the farm. But in all honesty, he had no idea when he would be going back. *If* he went back. It seemed that would be determined from how this went.

He'd spent all of Saturday night reading through his Ma's letters that he never received. He'd spent all of Sunday tying up loose ends so that he wouldn't have to rush back to the Gold Coast. He'd spent all of Sunday night thinking about her. He'd had Wren three times—only once in his bed. Twice, if he counted the time that nothing happened. And somehow, his bed missed her. He missed her. But he couldn't let himself go down that path. That path was dangerous. She'd said it herself—they were written in the sand. They wouldn't last. He might hate it now, but he would thank himself, one day. Maybe.

He dragged himself to the house, his duffle bag by his side, and froze at the door. Did he knock? Did he let himself in? Was he still family, or a guest? Years ago, he wouldn't have thought twice about letting himself in. But now? He lifted his hand to knock, but before his fist connected with the wood, the door swung open and he came face to face with a set of round brown eyes he hadn't seen in years.

'Well, I'll be,' the woman muttered, swiping at a strand of thick hair that stuck to her forehead from sweat and dirt.

Winifred. The girl next door who'd been his best friend for as long as he could remember. They'd been inseparable—a pair, as most seemed to think. Bets were taken that they'd be forever, and he'd once thought they were right. She was his first, and he was hers. She, too, had stopped talking to him when he left.

'Hey, Fred,' he said, resting against the doorframe.

He saw something flicker across her face. A memory. Pain. Then, she recovered, straightening, her expression growing firm. 'I don't go by that name anymore, Nate.' She diverted her gaze. 'It's Win, or Winifred, now.'

He lifted an eyebrow. 'You hated your name.'

She lifted her chin, her lips set in a thin line. 'Well, I got used to it.'

He smiled, amused. She might be trying to act like she'd changed. But he'd bet she hadn't really. He briefly wondered if they could go back to how they were before he left. Then, he felt a pang of guilt for even *thinking* of having anything with anyone except Wren. *Damn her*. Maybe time would help.

She shifted the basket in her arms as if trying to hide something. But he'd seen it. A single gold band on her left ring finger. He hated that it saddened him.

'Y—you're married?' he blurted before he could stop himself.

He saw that look flicker across her face again and she diverted her gaze. 'I am.'

Damn. Even if he *had* really wanted them to go back to how they were, they couldn't. She was already spoken for.

'Who's the lucky guy?'

She looked up at him—almost apologetically— then glanced behind him. Only then did he hear the footsteps behind him, taking the steps up onto the veranda.

'I am,' Leo said.

He felt his body stiffen. He had no claim on Winifred. He'd given up any right to that. But to have married his *brother*? He wasn't sure which hurt most. The fact that she'd married his brother, or the fact that his family didn't bother to tell him? He turned towards Leo, still leaning against the doorframe to keep him from launching himself towards him.

'You didn't tell me you got married, Leo,' he said through gritted teeth, even though he'd tried to relax his jaw.

Leo shrugged, shifting his gaze. 'It was a short ceremony,' he said. 'All happened very quickly. You understand.'

Did he? What he understood was that his brother dealt a low blow. Even with all that was going on between them, wouldn't he have wanted Nate to know he was getting married? *Who* he was marrying? He knew that if it was him getting married, he still would have wanted his family to be there. Even if they weren't talking.

'Yeah,' he said roughly. 'I understand.'

Leo nodded. 'Well, we're expecting, too.' He nodded his head towards Winifred. Nate followed his gaze.

Her cheeks darkened, and she gave him that apologetic look again. He realised that she shouldn't. She wasn't the one that should be apologising. He was. He'd left them all. Of course, life would go on, they'd form new connections. Winifred had basically been a part of the family from the get-go. It made sense she'd fall for Leo.

'I'll go tell Ma he's here, then,' she said, lowering the basket to the floor.

'All good, Winnie,' Leo said, nudging past Nate, and pecking her on the cheek. Her cheeks darkened further. 'I'll take him myself. She in the craft room?'

Winifred nodded, picking the basket up again. Nate moved to the side to let her out the door, noticing the bump on her belly was larger than he could see in the dimmer lighting of inside. The thought occurred to him that perhaps *that* was what she was trying to hide when she shifted her basket, not the ring. He followed Leo inside, the house looking familiar but still a little different. He could tell what Winifred's touches on the place were.

'A few things have changed since you were here last, Nate,' Leo said, glancing back at him as he led the way through the hallway where the bedrooms were. It looked different, larger. 'We added some extra rooms when Winnie moved in. Ma's been focussing on her craft some more. A lot.'

He halted in front of the room on the left at the end of the extended hallway and turned to the door on the right. 'This is Dad's new office.'

'Is he in there?'

Leo shook his head, smiling. 'He's made it down to the shed to plod with his woodwork. But he's spent most of his time in his office since ...'

Nate nodded. Leo didn't need to finish the sentence. Heck, Nate could barely say the words. His father had almost died, and no one bothered to tell him. He wondered if he would have been invited to the funeral.

'Ma doesn't know you were coming,' Leo said, turning back to the first door.

'You didn't tell her?'

'I didn't want to get her hopes up if you didn't

come.'

Nate wondered how Leo had grown into the man he was. As he studied the lines on his face that he was too young to have, he figured Leo had only done what he thought was best for his family. He hadn't sent the letters in case Nate didn't respond. Heck, he wondered if he'd even been ignoring Nate in hopes it would bring him home. He couldn't say the same for his dad—he'd changed their numbers so that Nate *couldn't* contact them. But there was nothing stopping him from ever coming home, not really.

Leo tapped on the door and opened it, nudging into the craft room. Nate scanned the room. Leo had done good, making a room like this for Ma. It was something she'd always deserved and never had. She'd always put everyone else first. It was time she was looked after in the same way she looked after everyone else all those years. His eyes rested on the greyed head sitting on top of a frail-looking body. She was thin—a vast difference to the roundness she'd had before he left. His heart ached for her and the guilt hit him like a wave. Was Leo right? Had he done this to her? Made her age quicker than she should? Made her grow frail?

'Hey, Ma,' Leo said, resting a hand carefully on her shoulder. 'Someone's here to see you.'

She looked up at Leo, thin glasses perched on the end of her nose. Leo pointed towards Nate. She shifted in her seat to look at Nate, her eyes growing wide. They started to glisten. She held a hand over her mouth and tugged on Leo's arm.

'Oh, Leo, he looks just like my boy, doesn't he?'

Nate felt the stab in his chest. 'Ma, it's me,' he said, taking a step towards her, and halting when Leo shook his head. Her eyes had widened again, and she looked taken aback. What the hell was going on? 'You don't … remember me?'

She shook her head slowly. 'You seem sweet, dear, but you're not my boy.'

'*What?*'

'Nate,' Leo warned.

'Oh, you even have the same name.' She dabbed at her eyes with a handkerchief. 'But you're not my boy,' she repeated, lifting her chin. 'My Nathaniel is dead.'

What?

'Ma,' Leo said soothingly, rubbing his hand on her back.

'Leave me, please,' she said, turning her back towards him. 'You've upset me.'

Leo sighed and, doing as he was told, walked towards the door. Nate kept his gaze on his mother. She didn't know who he was? He couldn't even begin to describe the way it made him feel. His own mother thought he was dead. And he'd made her think that. Somehow.

'Nate,' Leo said softly.

He turned to his brother, not sure if he was going to break or burst out in anger. Leo nodded towards the door. He followed him, waiting until the door was closed between him and his mother, waiting until they would be out of ear shot.

'Why does she think I'm dead, Leo?' he said, his voice shaky.

He waved a hand over his shoulder as he headed towards the kitchen—another room that seemed to have been renovated. It looked modernised, the worn cupboards from his memory non-existent. The old wooden benchtop replaced.

'It's the medication,' he said dismissively.

'Medication?' Nate said, running a hand along the marble benchtop.

'Yes, Nate, the medication.'

Leo grabbed two glasses and reached for a bottle of whisky at the back of the top shelf. He wouldn't have known it was there and couldn't help but notice it was too high for his parents to reach. He placed the glasses between them and sloshed a couple fingers in each one. He returned the bottle to the shelf.

'She started losing her mind when Dad changed the numbers,' Leo started explaining. 'She'd been sad before then, but things went downhill after that. She tried to ... to...'

Leo took a sip of his drink, and Nate did the same. He suspected he knew what Leo was trying to say. Clearly, it was difficult for him to talk about. And it was difficult for him to hear. Leo studied the liquid in the glass like he had when he showed up at Nate's place.

'She's been on medication since,' Leo said. 'She wasn't quite ... all there, I suppose. But she'd been acting better once she started. Her mood got better when Winnie moved in, and we got married. But it was short-lived.'

'Why didn't you come get me sooner?' Nate said, sipping his whisky.

He rolled the mouthful around in his mouth and swallowed, his mind drifting back to the night he met Wren. The way she'd studied the liquid. The way her eyes shone when he spoke to her. *Damn.* A five hour drive away and she was still stuck in his mind. He lowered his glass to the bench. Maybe it was whisky in general that reminded him of her.

'Because it's only recent that she's gone *this* bad,' Leo stated, rubbing his forehead. 'After we renovated, she started hallucinating. She couldn't tell what had really happened and what wasn't real. We went to Winnie's uncle Nathan's funeral. She was convinced it was yours.'

'That's why she thinks I'm dead,' he said flatly.

Leo smirked. 'She hated that they kept calling you Nathan. She kept correcting people, saying it's Nathaniel. She confused a lot of people that day.'

'It's not funny, Leo,' Nate growled, his body feeling like it was vibrating.

Leo pressed his hands against the bench, staring him straight in the eye. 'No, it's *not,* Nate,' he growled back. 'But we've had to get used to finding the funny in everything because it's the only way the rest of us have stayed sane.'

Nate shook his head. 'You can't blame me for that,' he said. '*You* didn't send the letters.'

'I was mad, okay?' Leo said, throwing his hands in

the air. 'I was *furious* at you for leaving me! We were mates, and you ditched. You left me to clean up *your* mess.'

'Well, it looks like it ended up better for you anyway.' He took another sip of his whisky.

If eyes could smirk, he was sure Leo's eyes were doing just that. 'You're not sore about Winnie, are you?'

Nate shook his head slowly. Was he? Maybe he was sore that he wasn't the one that was married and expecting by now. Maybe he was a bit annoyed that his little brother married the only woman he really cared for before he left. But it didn't seem to bother him as much as he thought it should. Sure, it might be weird. He had to wrap his head around the fact that a lot had changed since he left and that no one even bothered to tell him about said changes. But to be honest, he'd always suspected Leo had been crushing on Winifred even when they were kids. Maybe it took Nate leaving for her to realise she was meant to be with the younger of the brothers.

'So, you've got yourself a woman, then?' Leo said, clearly trying to change the subject from their mother. Perhaps it was for the better. Maybe it's just how he coped. Especially since he'd had to deal with it on a daily basis.

Nate considered his brother a moment and dropped his gaze to the small amount of whisky left in his glass. He shook his head, barely. But it was still enough to make his chest tighten. Wren wasn't his. She never really was.

'Your friend—Russ?' Leo continued. Nate nodded. 'I heard him mention someone when you got home.' He tapped his chin thoughtfully. 'It was a bird name … Lark? Sparrow?'

Nate sighed, his eyebrow lifting. 'Wren.'

'Yeah, Wren,' Leo said, leaning on his elbows. 'That someone special?'

'She's someone I thought might've been special,' Nate admitted, turning the glass in his hand.

He heard a cupboard door open and soon, his glass was being refilled. He glanced up at his brother, who had genuine concern on his face. He'd missed hanging out with Leo. They were as close as brothers could get. Talking about life. Plans. Girls—though, that had been a more sensitive topic, he now realised.

Leo smiled, as though remembering the same fun times that Nate was remembering. 'Want to talk about it, cowboy?' he said, the drawl from years of farming showing.

Nate smiled at his brother's crooked grin and took another sip of his whisky. Did he? At the very least, the whisky was going to help take the edge off seeing his dad again after so many years. And for *that* conversation, he'd need as much liquid courage as he could get.

Chapter 20

Wren took a sip of her glass of wine, staring at her phone. She wasn't sure what she expected to see or even hoped to see. But she knew it had to do with Nate. And, whatever it was, wasn't there. She dropped her phone on the couch next to her and reached for a slice of pizza.

'Everything okay, Sweet?'

Wren leaned back in the sofa and glanced at her dad. Ever since she was a child, her dad had called her *Sweet*. She half suspected he couldn't call her by her name because it reminded him too much of her mother. Then again, most parents had pet names for the kids. Perhaps that was just his. She took a bite of the pizza and propped her feet up on the edge of the coffee table.

'Mhmm,' she muttered. 'Everything's peachy.'

Her dad's eyebrow lifted. Joe Kingsley was a man of few words. Mostly. Which meant that when he had advice to offer, Wren really considered it. She wondered if this was going to be one of those times.

'What?' she muttered, swallowing her mouthful.

He shook his head. 'I'm not sure I've ever heard you say *peachy* before.'

She felt her lips pull to the side. 'No better time to start than the present, right?' She took another bite and rolled it around in her mouth.

She made a habit of having dinner with her dad at least once a week. Pizza seemed to be the go-to, but they sometimes felt daring and would order Indian or Thai. They opted for their usual this time.

'Why do you ask?' she said, finishing off her slice.

Joe shrugged and reached forward to turn the television down. He focussed on her, leaning his elbows on his knees. 'You've been a bit … off … the last couple of weeks,' he said, hesitantly. 'Is it about Griffin?'

'Uhh,' she said, swallowing her last mouthful. 'No. I don't know. I guess there wasn't as much to get over as I thought.'

'You're still at work?' he said, lifting a slice from the pizza box. 'Or are you taking some time off.'

She shook her head, having another slow sip of her wine. 'Still at work,' she muttered. 'Keeps me busy.'

He nodded. 'Hear about the promotion, yet?'

She pressed her tongue to her cheek and stared

down at her phone sitting next to her on the couch, wondering if there was any change from a few moments ago. She resisted the urge to check. 'Yeah, I heard,' she said, shifting into a slightly more comfortable position. 'I ... umm ... I didn't get it.'

She saw something twitch in his jaw. 'But you worked hard for it.' He should know. She'd missed some of their dinners lately because of it. And on the days that she'd made it, she'd probably been poor company anyway.

'Maybe too hard,' she said, forcing a smile onto her face, and picking at a loose thread at the hem of her shorts. She wondered if it was more to convince her dad, or herself. 'Apparently Durgan can't afford to lose me in my current position, so he hired out.'

'They nice?'

'Hmm?' She glanced up at him.

'The person he hired,' Joe said. 'Are they nice?'

'Oh,' she said, focussing back on the thread. 'Yeah, he's nice.' The heat involuntarily flushed to her cheeks as she remembered how *nice* he could be.

'*He*, huh?' Joe said, his eyebrow lifting. 'Bet you gave him an earful.'

She smiled, flicking her gaze back up to her dad. 'You know me well,' she said.

'Well, it runs in the family.' He leaned forward slightly more. 'So, what is it about this guy that's got you so worked up?'

She felt her cheeks flush again. 'What do you mean?' she said, trying to seem naïve. He wasn't fooled.

'You're distant. Always checking your phone,' he said, indicating towards the phone next to her. 'Acting like you'd rather be somewhere else. *With* someone else. And I know it's not Kass since she's joined us for almost more pizza nights than you've come alone. And it's certainly not Griffin.'

She stared at her dad and the way the man of few words had managed to delve right to the heart of her issue. She should have known her observant father would see right through her. She bit the corner of her bottom lip and stared at the coffee table.

'Well,' she started slowly. 'We met before I found out I was going to be working with him and we kind of … hit it off.'

'You mean, you slept with him?'

'Dad!' she said, her eyes shooting towards him, her mouth open in shock. Her skin was prickling from the embarrassment.

He sat back in his chair, his arms stretched out. 'We're both adults here.' He waved his hand. 'So, you slept with him. Continue.'

She pressed her lips together, not wanting to admit it, but also knowing that she didn't have to. She dropped her gaze to the wine glass in her hand, watching the red liquid swish back and forth as she swirled it.

'Well, I didn't think I'd see him again,' she admitted. 'And then he showed up at my work and got the job I'd been working for. And Durgan has this … aversion … to relationships in the work place, so we figured we could try being friends.'

'His idea, or yours?'

She shrugged one shoulder lazily, easing further into the couch and resting her head on the back, staring up at the ceiling. 'Mine.'

'And he went for that?'

'Well, I thought he did. And we gave it a go, but some … things … happened, and we fought. And now, I—I think he's avoiding me.'

Joe's eyebrow lifted. 'Well, that explains the phone checking. But what makes you think he's avoiding you? It'd be hard to do at work, wouldn't it?'

She tilted her head to the side and sighed. 'He's not there,' she said. 'He's taken some time off, apparently.'

'After working how long?'

'Two weeks,' she said hesitantly.

'And Durgan let him?'

She shrugged again, sipping her wine. 'He gave Durgan some crap about needing time off to deal with some *family matters*.'

'Well, that sounds like a legitimate excuse if you ask me.'

'Yeah,' she said, looking back up at him. 'Except he told *me* that he hadn't spoken to his family in years.'

Joe nodded, his lips pursed. 'I see why you think that, then.'

She nodded, and they both sat in silence for a few moments, both staring at the television. Nate had to be avoiding her. There wasn't any other reason she could think of. There was so much … energy … between them, that she wouldn't be surprised if he needed to distance himself from it. Especially after their fight. Especially when she'd assumed the worst of him. And after he said that he'd loved her.

Joe cleared his throat and she glanced up at him. 'So, this guy—'

'Nate,' she offered.

He seemed to consider the name for a moment, then nodded slowly. 'You've known him how long?'

She sunk a little further into the couch—like she could go any further. 'Two weeks,' she said. 'And two days.'

'And he's in your head *that* much?'

She nodded. What was he getting at?

Joe reached for the remote again. 'Well, he must be a decent guy, then.'

She frowned. 'What do you mean?' Hadn't she just finished telling him that the guy was avoiding her?

Joe shrugged. 'He's, what, the only spontaneous thing you've ever done?'

'I can be spontaneous!' His eyebrow shot upwards. She scrunched her nose. 'Sometimes.'

'My point is, Sweet,' he continued. 'You spend a lot of time weighing up the pros and cons of things.'

'It helps to be prepared,' she muttered.

'Griffin? Remember how long you spent trying to decide if you wanted to be *friends* with the guy? And how long it took for you to agree to go out with him?

Then—'

'And look how that turned out,' she said instinctively.

'*It didn't*,' he said flatly, staring at her. 'That's my point, Wren. You really thought him out, and it didn't work. This ... Nate ... could be the spontaneous, not-so-thought-out thing you need.' He tapped his nose. 'It could work.'

'N—no, it couldn't,' she stammered, dropping her feet to the ground, and sitting up straight. 'I could lose my job. Durgan could *fire* me if he found out.'

'So, sue him for unfair dismissal,' he said, shrugging. 'He can't fire you for getting involved with a co-worker, Wren. He might not be happy about it. But he won't fire you. A man who runs a company that big knows better than to set himself up for a law suit.'

She shook her head. 'It doesn't matter, anyway,' she said, realising that her dad was right. What *could* Durgan do about it, really? 'Nate's avoiding me, remember?'

'Have you tried contacting him?' Joe said. She shook her head. 'No texts, calls? Visit him, even?' She shook her head again. 'Well, how do you know he's avoiding you?'

'Because he hasn't spoken to his family in years,' she said. 'His excuse is bull.'

'What if it's not?'

What *if* it's not? What if Nate's excuse was true? Just because he hadn't heard from his family in a long time didn't mean that he hadn't heard from them since their fight. Or really, even, since he'd told her he hadn't spoken to them. It's not like he was obligated to tell her if he heard from them, or if he reached out to them.

'And what if he *is* avoiding me?' she said, blinking back the threatening tears.

Joe shrugged, turning the sound on the television up again. 'He'll come around, Wren,' he said. 'Just give him time. But a few attempts at contacting him won't go astray. He might just need that *nudge*.'

***

'What are we having?'

'Nuhuh, old man. None for you—doc's orders.'

Nate had just closed the door to the spare room after putting his bag in there—or rather, his old room that had been wiped clear of any essence of him and replaced with a double bed, two bedside tables, a couple lamps, and an empty wardrobe. The room had been repainted from the flaky blue he remembered it being. It was like he'd never been there. It wasn't far from the kitchen, and he could hear his dad's voice. He sighed. It had been way, *way* too long since he'd heard his voice. And he was sure that this was going to be the only glimpse of that natural voice he'd have. Once his father realised he was there, he was sure it wouldn't be a warm welcome. Danny Hoffman wasn't much of a forgiving type. He walked slowly, quietly, towards the kitchen, towards his father's back.

'Well, I know you're not drinking with your pregnant wife,' Danny said. 'So, whose is it?'

Leo had a look on his face that was almost a grimace. He supposed he knew what was coming, too. He glanced towards Nate. He stopped walking. 'Dad, you remember Nate, right?' Leo said casually. 'Your son?'

Even from near the edge of the room, he could see his father's back stiffen. Danny turned to face him, and he could tell that he wasn't happy to see him. *Damn*. Talk about a warm welcome home.

'Hey, Dad,' Nate said warily.

Danny straightened. 'What are you doing here, Nate?' Definitely not welcome.

'I asked him to come,' Leo said. 'Figured he could help.'

'We don't need his help,' Danny snapped.

'You're still a long way off from getting back out there,' Leo said firmly. '*I* could use his help. And think about Ma—it could be good for her recovery.'

'She's only like this *because* of him!'

'*You're* the one who pushed her over that line!'

'*Guys!*' Nate yelled, moving towards them.

They both glared at him. Did they always argue like this? Or was it only because he was there? Either way, it didn't matter. Whether or not it was because of him, he was going to fix it. He *had* to fix it. Because he couldn't leave again until it was.

He steadied his voice. 'What are we doing, here?'

'*You're* leaving,' Danny said gruffly.

'Dad!' Leo scolded.

'No,' Nate said, shaking his head. 'I'm not. Whether you like it or not, I'm here. And I came because I care. I never stopped caring, even when I wasn't welcome here.' Danny opened his mouth to say something, but Nate threw his hand up between them. 'I'm not here to play the blame game. I'm here to help fix things.'

'Ma's not a problem that can be fixed,' Danny growled.

'You're right, she's not,' Nate said, narrowing his eyes. He circled his finger between the three of them. '*This* is the problem.' He pointed to his dad. 'You are—' then, to Leo. '—you are—' and finally, to himself. '—and I am. Do you want to know why she's like this? *Because of us*. There's no point blaming each other for it, because we're all at fault.'

'You didn't have to leave,' Danny said.

'Sure,' he said, shrugging. 'But I did. And you didn't have to change your numbers and cut off all communication, but you did. And Leo didn't have to hoard the letters Ma tried to send to me, but he did.'

Danny and Leo shared a look that made Nate suspect that Leo wasn't alone on the letter-hoarding issue. He shook the thought from his mind. No more blame games. No more living in the past. Just the here and now. Planning for the future. That's what he did best, right? Doing things now to better the future. That's why he worked hard to get to where he is now. Why he didn't give up easily.

He felt the niggle in his chest, the back of his mind. The same niggle that he felt whenever he thought of Wren. Had he done that with her? Sure, he didn't like to give up. And every man had a limit. Wren had hit his. But he couldn't help the what ifs getting at him. What if he'd let it slide? Would it have worked out for better, or for worse? What if he'd held on, and never given up on her? Would they still be together, twenty years from now? Or would he have only been delaying the inevitable?

He shook his head, bringing his thoughts back to the issue at hand. 'My point is,' he said. 'We have an opportunity to fix this. And I'm sure as hell going to try. We just have to put the past behind us.'

For a moment, it looked like they were considering it. He was sure Leo was all for it—he was the one to reach out to Nate, after all. But he figured his dad would be a tougher nut to crack.

Danny's lips pressed together, and he lifted his chin. 'It's not that easy, Nate,' he said.

Nate shrugged. 'It's not that hard, either.'

Chapter 21

It wasn't that easy, as it turned out.

But it was a start.

Nate rested his elbows on the railing of the porch, cradling his cup of tea in his hands, looking out at the stars.

Dinner had been no surprise. Ma refused to eat with them—which apparently wasn't uncommon. According to Leo, she'd mostly only been eating gherkins and other pickled delights. Occasionally she'd accept one of Winifred's sandwiches, but not much else. The four of them—Nate, Danny, Leo, and Winifred—had eaten in near silence. He wondered if it was because no one had anything to say, or if no one had anything *nice* to say.

Once dinner had finished, his dad had gone to

bed mumbling something about the doctor wanting him to rest. He suspected it was, in part, because he was there. Leo refused his help in cleaning up after dinner. Which he was grateful for tonight. He needed time to think. Time to sort out his thoughts into two categories—things he had to deal with now, and things to deal with later. Somehow, Wren sat somewhere in the middle.

He heard Winifred's footsteps approaching but didn't turn. She'd once liked to sneak up on him. He suspected it was harder now that she was carrying more weight than she was used to. She came to a stop next to him, resting her hands on the railing. He glanced at her, but her eyes were glued to the stars.

'Bet you don't see this in the city,' she said, sighing.

He lifted his gaze back up to the stars. 'Not like this,' he admitted. 'But there's a spot I like to go to along one of the beaches at night when I need a breather. Reminds me of home.'

He heard her take in a shaky breath. 'I'm not sure I'd like to be on the beach so late.'

He shrugged. 'It is a bit shady,' he admitted. 'But the view is worth it.'

'So, things are … umm … going well … for you, then?'

He sipped his tea, shifting his gaze to her. She'd dropped her gaze from the stars, but she still wasn't looking at him. 'Yeah,' he said. 'I got my degree, a good job.'

'A girl,' she muttered. He shifted his body to face

her better, leaning only one elbow on the railing. Her tired gaze slowly flickered up towards him. 'Leo,' she added.

'Ahh,' he said. He should have known that the information Leo extracted from him would make it to Winifred the second Leo had the chance. 'How much did Leo tell you?'

'Most of it,' she admitted. 'That you're not on good terms.'

He groaned, leaning both arms back on the railing and staring at the dark tea in his cup. 'It wasn't really ...' he started. Wasn't what? 'It was a fling, really,' he corrected. 'I guess. We don't have to talk about it.'

He could see her watching him from the corner of his eye. 'We used to,' she said quietly. 'You used to talk to me about everything. Dreams. *Girls*.' She nudged her shoulder against his arm.

He chuckled. 'Easy to do when you were the girl I talked about,' he said, his tone quieter. For a moment, he wondered if she'd even heard him. But when he glanced at her, she was still watching him, her lips pressed in a fine line, her eyes darker than he remembered.

'Things change,' she whispered. 'I married your brother.' The darkness in her eyes lightened. 'I'm happy, Nate. And I want you to be, too.'

He felt his nose crinkle, and he stared back at his cup again. 'I don't know how to be happy,' he mumbled, realising, for the first time, the truth in those words. He'd kept busy, sure. He'd made a life for himself. He was content, satisfied. But had he really been happy? Had he ever? The only time he could think of where he *was* truly happy, was with Wren in his bed, in his arms.

They stood in silence for a moment, then, Winifred sighed, standing up straight to face him. 'I'm going to give you some sisterly advice,' she said. He focussed on her. She smiled. 'Since I'm now your sister-in-law.'

'And what would your advice be?' he prompted.

'I think you overreacted,' she said. His brow furrowed. 'With the girl.'

'She questioned my morals, Fred—' she opened her mouth. 'Win,' he corrected. She nodded. 'She questioned *me*.'

She tilted her head slightly, sighing long and slow, as though approaching a delicate subject. She probably was. 'A woman's mind is a very complex thing,' she said, pressing a fingertip to her temple. 'Trust me—I have one, and I still can't work it out.'

He chuckled, and she smiled the same smile he'd been used to before he left for the city. Only now, it was weary, burdened. He nudged his shoulder against hers. 'So, what's your advice?'

'You have to give her a chance, Nate,' she said, turning to face him, her face serious. 'I can guarantee you she was only freaking out. Things with you two started a bit … unconventionally. And to end up working together? I know *my* mind would be muddled. She was probably just shocked at how amazing you are, and her reflex was to push you away.' She leaned in a little closer, looking up at him.

'Like you're doing with her.'

He pressed his tongue to his cheek, contemplating Winifred's theory. Honestly? It made sense, what she was saying. But at the same time, *he* was hesitant to try to fix things between them. What if Winifred's theory was simply that—a theory? Wren had been pushing him away from the start. What's to say that will change?

'And what if she meant every word she said?' he said, looking up at his old friend, a challenge in his eyes. 'What if she was pushing me away because she doesn't *want* me?'

Winifred laughed as though the thought was inconceivable. 'All right,' she said, her face growing serious. 'Let's look at it from a different angle.' He lifted an eyebrow, waiting for her to go on. She turned her back to the railing and leaned against it, resting her hands on her round belly. 'What are *you* going to do about it?'

He frowned. 'What do you mean?'

'Well, you obviously like the girl,' she said teasingly. 'Maybe *love*, even?'

He pressed his lips together. He hadn't told Leo *that* part, which only meant that Winifred was either fishing, or she'd derived it from what *he* had said. He cleared his throat, trying to sound as neutral as he could. 'What makes you think that?'

'Oh, please,' she said, obviously seeing through his act. 'I know—knew—you, Nate. You're a calculated guy. You look at what your actions are going to lead to, and then you weigh up your options to see if it's worth it. I know it didn't *seem* like that when you left here, but I can see it now, even if no one else can. You can't expect me to believe that she was only supposed to be a one-night stand, or a fling, or whatever you want to call it. You *calculated* her, and it didn't play out how you wanted it to, so you ran. Admit it.'

His lips parted to defend himself, but, how could he? If anyone knew that he was a calculated guy, it was Winifred. And maybe—just maybe—she was right. Had he calculated Wren? He certainly hadn't spent hours mulling over the idea of talking to her in the bar—it was barely even minutes. But maybe he didn't need as long to mull it over with her, because he *knew*. In his gut, he knew that he wanted to know that woman. Wanted to know her story, her life. Wanted her in *his* life. He hadn't expected things to take a turn the way they did. And he honestly didn't know that he was starting at her workplace. *That* was a pure coincidence.

Or was it fate?

Did he believe in fate?

He blinked back the thoughts, trying to urge himself to breathe again. He'd never thought about fate, never really believed in it. Never had a reason to. But he also didn't think that coincidences like *that* really existed either. So, what was it? The haze cleared from his vision to see the smug look on Winifred's face, her arms folded across her chest.

'I *knew* it,' she said triumphantly.

'I didn't calculate her,' he said quietly. 'I didn't

have to.'

'So,' Winifred said, still smiling like she'd just solved the biggest mystery in the world. 'I repeat— what are you going to do about it?'

What could he do? He couldn't exactly hightail it out of there—he'd just got there, and his family *needed* him. Even if they didn't realise it yet. And then what? Once he'd fixed whatever needed to be fixed here, what was his plan then? Would his family hate him again if he went back to the city? Did he want to risk that?

But simply the thought of staying there didn't sit right. It might have been the place he grew up in, and he had missed it throughout the years. But it also didn't feel like *home*. Not anymore. What felt like home was when he was near Wren, seeing her smile, hoping that things would work out. Like his subconscious had calculated.

He shrugged, finishing off his cup of tea. 'I have no idea,' he said.

Because, for once, he didn't.

***

'Why are we here?' Kassandra whispered.

Wren sighed, shifting her gaze from Nate's front door to her best friend. She wasn't sure why Kassandra was whispering. Maybe she thought it was some kind of covert operation and if she spoke any louder that any bystanders would hear them. Even though they were in the car.

'The light's on,' Wren said, pointing to the bit of light coming through the slit in the lounge room curtain.

Now that she thought about it, perhaps it did look a bit odd that they were parked out front of his place spying on him. Although, the whole situation didn't sit right in her stomach, especially since his car wasn't sitting in the driveway.

'And nobody's home,' Kassandra pointed out, indicating towards the driveway.

Wren shrugged. 'Maybe he parked in the garage?'

'Oh, please,' Kassandra scoffed. 'Everyone knows that no single guy actually *parks* in his garage. He's probably got some kick-ass gym setup in there. Have you seen his body?' Kassandra waggled her eyebrows.

Oh, *had* she? She bit her lip as her mind drifted back to that first night, and any time she'd had his body against hers. She felt her stomach roll over, an ache for his touch again. She shook her head, reminding herself that he was avoiding her. And that she had to know where they stood. Especially after what her dad said. She glanced at the time on her phone, then quickly turned off the screen to shut off the glow. It was almost midnight. And maybe it was the wine, but she was sure that she'd just seen a shadow—a man's shadow—pass the slit in the curtain.

'Did you see that?' Wren said, grabbing onto Kassandra's arm.

'See what?' she said, looking towards the house.

'He's in there. I saw his shadow.'

'He's not home, Wren. His car's not here.'

'Well, maybe he parked up the street a bit,' she said, glancing up and down the street. Nope. No car. 'Or maybe he was out drinking and walked home?'

Kassandra scoffed. 'You know that he would have *walked* to the bar if he was going drinking. Heck, *I* know that.'

The shadow passed again. 'I'm telling you, Kass. He's in there.'

'Listen to yourself, Wren,' Kassandra said, turning to face her. She was frowning. 'You know I'm all for random stake-outs in the middle of the night and stalking hot guys but *come on*. You're obsessing.'

'I'm not obsessing,' Wren said, her eyes wide. 'He's avoiding me, and I want to know why.'

'Oh, I don't know,' Kassandra said. Even through her whisper, the sarcasm was still dripping from it. 'Probably because you tore him a new one.'

'I didn't tear …' she drifted off as the light in the lounge room flicked off. 'See? I told you he's home!'

Kassandra shook her head, looking back at the house. 'Okay, so he's home. He's lying. You caught him. What are you going to do now? Tell him you've been watching his movements for the last half hour?'

'No, now I'm going to give him an earful,' she said, opening the door.

'Are you sure you're not drunk, Wren?'

'I only had one glass,' she said, climbing out of the car. 'You coming?'

Kassandra shook her head. 'I think I'd rather stay here. Don't want to be caught in the crossfire.'

'Suit yourself,' Wren muttered, closing the door. She stormed towards the front door, her footsteps slowing the closer she got.

This wasn't crazy, right?

Maybe it *was* the bit of wine that she had and her dad's suggestions that put this in her mind. But she had to know if he was avoiding her. His excuse about family matters just wasn't convincing. She didn't believe it. He *had* to be avoiding her. And it was childish.

She stopped at the door and took a big breath. Then, she banged her fist on the door. Once, twice. Then, she banged it again. And she didn't stop until the door swung open.

'Wren? What are you doing here?'

'Where is he?' she said, pushing past the hugeness of man that stood between her and Nate.

'Who?' Russ said, turning to watch her storm down the hallway, glancing in the rooms that she passed.

'*Nate*. Where is he?' she said, turning to face him.

'He's not here.'

'Like I believe that,' she mumbled. 'Nate!' That time, she yelled.

'You can look all you want, but you won't find him,' Russ called after her.

'Why not?' She turned back towards Russ, folding her arms across her chest.

Russ shrugged as if it was obvious. 'Because he's

not *here*. He's gone home.'

'*This* is his home,' she said, her voice shaky.

Her eyes drifted back to the lounge room. It was obviously Russ's shadow that she saw. And now that she thought about it, she should have known it wasn't Nate. Russ was a fair bit bigger than Nate. But then, shadows can be pretty deceiving.

'I mean he's gone *home*, Wren. Back to his family.'

Her mouth dropped open. It was true? Or was Russ just playing along with Nate's avoiding-Wren plan? 'Forever?' she whispered.

'What? No,' Russ said, his brow creasing. 'I don't think so.'

'W—why has he gone home? I thought he hadn't heard from his family in years.'

'He hadn't,' Russ said, eyeing her, as though trying to decide how much to give out. 'But his brother showed up on the weekend. All Nate said was something happened, and he had to deal with it.'

She slowly stepped back towards the door, staring at the floor. So, he'd been telling the truth. It wasn't a lie. It wasn't an excuse that he made up to avoid seeing her. The sadness in his eyes that she'd seen earlier that morning hadn't been because he saw her. It's because something had happened. She wondered what it was that happened—what made his brother reach out to him. Why it was so important that he had to go back home so quickly. She felt an uneasiness in her stomach, and she wondered if it was the wine and pizza backfiring on her or the realisation that she might have made a terrible mistake.

What if he didn't come back?

What if he decided he liked it better back home and felt he had nothing to return to here?

'I don't suppose you know where … *home* … is, do you?' she said. She had no address, all she knew was it was this side of Armidale, and that wasn't enough to go off.

Russ shook his head. 'Wish I could help, Wren, but I don't know.' His brow furrowed. 'Is everything okay? You're not … in trouble … are you? Are you by yourself?'

He started turning slowly back towards the door. She glanced towards the car in time to see the passenger seat drop backwards and Kassandra's head ducking out of sight before Russ could see. She lifted an eyebrow. Who's avoiding who, now?

'Umm, no!' she said, moving faster so Russ couldn't see Kassandra in the car. 'No trouble! I'm alone. Just wanted to … talk.' She slid past Russ and ran her hand along the front door as she eased out. 'He wasn't at work today,' she continued. 'Wanted to make sure he was okay.'

Russ's eyebrow shot up as though he didn't believe a single word. It wouldn't surprise her if he didn't. She froze before moving too far away from the door, a simple fact suddenly dawning on her.

'What are *you* doing here?' she said. 'I mean, you knew he wasn't home.'

Russ shrugged. 'I have a key.' He said nothing else.

'Huh,' she said, easing back again. She wondered if it was something he did regularly and if Nate was aware of it. Maybe Nate asked him to keep an eye on the place. Who was she to question it? 'Goodnight, Russ.'

'Night, Wren,' he said, nodding his head.

He closed the door between them, and she moved back to the car, sliding into the driver's seat. She sighed, turning the key in the ignition to start the car. Now what? Nate's excuse checked out. And it had to be serious. It just seemed a bit excessive that he'd return home where he'd thought he wasn't welcome, just to avoid her. Before she started moving the car, she shifted her gaze to the passenger seat to see Kassandra laying as flat as she could in the seat. Wren lifted an eyebrow.

'What?' Kassandra said, as though it was normal behaviour.

'Nothing,' she said, shaking her head. She shoved the car into drive and started rolling forward. 'You're avoiding Russ.'

'I'm not avoid—' Kassandra scoffed. She straightened the seat. 'Why? Did he say something? Did he see me?'

Wren smirked. It looked like Kassandra was in deeper than she'd originally thought after all.

Chapter 22

Nate took off the broad-brimmed hat and wiped at the sweat on his forehead as he took the steps onto the porch and pushed through the front door. Working on the farm was a lot harder than he remembered, and he was dying for a drink of water. Especially in this heat. And the morning had barely started! Unlike Leo, he hadn't been prepared with a drink bottle. He made a mental note to pick one up from the shop when he went into town to pick up the grain.

A week had passed since he'd come back to the farm. And every day had been a little less tense. Though it seemed his father was still hesitant to let him in, and his mother still didn't know who he was, there was healing happening. He could feel it. He

was working the farm with Leo—things were almost
the same as they used to be between them—and it
wasn't as awkward as he'd first thought with having
Winifred as his sister-in-law.

He couldn't say the same for things with Wren.

He'd been too busy on the farm and keeping up
with the work he promised Durgan he'd do, too
focussed on his family, to work out a way to make
things right with her—*if* he could make things right.

He moved to the kitchen and filled a tall glass
with water. He finished it without taking a breath.
Then, he filled it again, heading back towards the
lounge where he knew it would be cooler—it always
was. He froze once he saw his mother looking
through an old metal case—one he knew contained
photographs. But that's not what surprised him
most. What surprised him was the fact that his
mother was out of her craft room. A cup of tea and
small platter with two biscuits sat on the coffee table
next to the metal case.

What was he supposed to do? He'd been hesitant
to call her *Ma* in case it upset her, but he also
couldn't bring himself to use her name. So, he
avoided *that* part of the conversation, which wasn't
usually difficult since there hadn't been much
conversation with her at all. And as far as he knew,
she'd been like that with everyone, never leaving her
craft room except to sleep or use the bathroom.

So, what was she doing in the lounge room,
looking through photographs? And was it a good
sign, or bad?

Carefully, he cleared his throat. Her eyes shot up towards him like he'd just startled her, and she smiled. Her eyes twinkled with something that he hadn't seen there the whole time he'd been back. Something that reminded her of the twinkle he remembered her having when he was a kid.

'Oh, Nate,' she said, focussing back on the photographs in her hand. 'I was just looking at some pictures. Want to see?' She shuffled over slightly on the couch and patted the empty spot next to her.

He glanced towards the door. He had told Leo he would be quick, but he also hadn't expected to see his mother out of her room. Leo would understand, he was sure of it. Ma was the reason he had come, after all.

'You're busy,' she said flatly, the twinkle in her eyes clouding over. 'I understand.' Watching that twinkle disappear made his heart ache.

'No,' he said, closing the distance between them. 'I have a minute.'

The smile returned to her face as he lowered himself into the seat next to her. She squeezed his arm. 'You're a strong man, aren't you?' she said. 'Stronger than my Nathaniel was, but he was solid. See?'

She held a photograph out to him, and he felt his chest tighten. He knew the picture. He knew it well. It was taken only a few weeks before he left—on Leo's birthday—of him, Leo, and Winifred, their arms wrapped around each other. The three were close. Always had been. He didn't look much different from the guy on the left, did he? His eyes drifted to Leo, who was in the middle and then to Winifred on the right. Their heads were slightly inclined towards each other, their bodies pressed a little closer together than he'd first thought. Heck, even then they'd been meant for each other. It just took Nate leaving for them all to realise it.

His throat tightened and his eyes burned at the back, but he refused to let his emotions take hold. God, he hadn't shed a tear in as long as he could remember, he wasn't about to start now. He cleared his throat again, steadying his voice.

'That's a … a nice picture,' he said.

'It's my favourite,' she said wistfully, studying the picture again. She was smiling, and the smile looked good on her. It only made his heart ache more. 'I miss my boy every day, you know?' Her eyes clouded over again. She didn't hold back the tears. 'He was taken too soon.'

He shifted in the seat, reaching for her hand. She retracted it, swiping at her eyes. 'Ma, don't you recognise me?' he said, not caring that his voice was shaky now. He was hurting. And every second that she didn't connect the dots and accept that he was her son only hurt him more. He took the photograph from her and held it up next to his face, his finger pressed to the younger him. 'Don't you see it?'

She blinked a few times, another tear rolling down her cheek, her mouth open, her brow creased. Worried. Saddened. 'I said the resemblance is uncanny …' she whispered, drifting off.

'It's *me*, Ma!' he said, not caring that his voice was louder now. He was desperate. Desperate for his mother to know who he was. Her eyes widened. '*I* am your son! *I* am Nathaniel! That's *me* in that damn picture.' He jabbed at his chest to make his point. 'Don't you see it?'

She shifted in the seat, shifting away from him. Pushing him away. It would have hurt less if she'd actually shoved him. 'N—no,' she said, shaking her head, sobbing. The twinkle in her eye was long gone. And he'd taken it from her. 'We buried my son. I went to the funeral.'

'No, you went to *Nathan*'s funeral—Winifred's uncle.' He rose to his feet and started pacing. '*I* didn't die, Ma. I'm *here*.' He heard the front door open behind him, but he didn't turn to look. He needed his mother to understand. He *needed* it.

She kept shaking her head and pressed her hands to the sides of her face. 'No, n—no,' she stammered. 'They kept calling him that. It's *Nathaniel*—I told them. I *told* them, they didn't listen.'

'Because it wasn't *my* funeral!'

'Nate.' *Winifred*.

It was spoken softly, a warning. He tried to control his breathing, tried to steady his voice, steady himself. But he felt like he was breaking apart, being ripped open from the inside out. His *mother* had no idea who he was—refused to believe he was her son.

'Don't you *remember*?' he said, the frustration and anger bubbling over.

'*Nate.*'

'I don't … I don't—' she stammered, her eyes darting to somewhere behind him. To Winifred, he assumed. Someone familiar, someone she recognised. 'Winnie, I don't—'

Her hands shaking, she dropped the photograph into the case like it was on fire and slammed the case shut, shifting it along the coffee table, knocking the teacup and saucer to the floor. They shattered. But it was nothing compared to how he was feeling inside. She fell to her knees, fumbling with the broken pieces.

Winifred shoved past him, her shoulder hitting his as she passed, and knelt beside his mother. 'It's okay, Ma,' she said sweetly. Always sweet. *Damn it.* Damn it all!

'Winnie, I'm s—I'm sorry. I don't … remember.'

Winifred shushed her, rubbing her hand over her back. 'You go rest, Ma. I'll clean this up.' She pried the broken pieces from the fragile woman's hands.

He swallowed, then swallowed again. But the lump was still in his throat. He still felt like he was combusting inside, but seeing his mother like that— fragile, when she'd been so strong, and not remembering—he didn't know what to do.

'Win—' he started, taking a step towards them.

Her eyes shot up towards him, full of fire and fury. Anger. 'Go, Nate,' she hissed. 'You've done enough.'

'Let me help—'

'*Go.*'

He backed up slowly until his back hit the door, his eyes on the mess in front of him. The mess *he'd* caused. Fighting the battle inside him, he pushed through the door and stormed down the porch steps, throwing his hat as hard as he could. It didn't help. He needed something more, something to *really* take the edge off. He could count on one hand the number of times he'd been this angry. And each time, he'd done the same thing to let it out.

He left the hat where it landed, turning towards Storm—the horse he'd been riding all morning—and swung himself up into the saddle as Leo slid off his. He heard his brother call out to him as he dug his heels into the horse's sides, but he couldn't make out the words. His mind was buzzing, blinded by the frustration and anger—at the situation, at his dad, his brother. Himself. God, he was angry at himself. Storm could sense the frustration, he knew it. But he'd grown used to Nate riding him this past week, and like the well-trained horse he was who acted like he had frustrations of his own, he knew what to do.

The horse ran fast—faster than Nate had ever been on horseback. But he didn't stop him. He bent low, embracing the speed. He needed this. He needed to feel the wind pushing against him. He needed to feel like he'd be thrown off the horse if he dared sit up straighter or loosen his hold on the reins. He needed to feel *one* with the horse, feel like he was flying. Unstoppable, invincible, like he'd once thought he was. He needed to feel every damn thought and trouble fly from his mind until his head was clear, and he could *think*. Really *think*.

He tugged on the reins to direct Storm up the hill that gave him a good view of the farm, the hills around them. The horse didn't hesitate to go there. Didn't hesitate to jump over the fallen trees that blocked the once-clear path or take the rough road where the path no longer existed. All through the ride, his thoughts slowly drifted, his mind slowly cleared, but his heart only weighed heavier in his chest. He was at a crossroads, and he didn't know which way to go.

He pulled the horse to a stop at the top of the hill, and instead of panting wildly, Storm stood still. Proud. Tall. And as Nate scanned the view around him, and let out a yell—a loud, carnal, uncontrollable, let-everything-out yell—the horse didn't flinch. He was firm. The strength that Nate needed beneath him. The reminder that he had this. He just had to keep pushing through.

A lot could be learned from a horse.

***

'What the hell is *this*?'

Wren stared at the pile of paperwork that had just been dropped in front of her. It didn't take her long to realise what it was, or rather *whose* it was. Nate's. Nate's work. That *he* was supposed to be doing. *Damn it*.

'Nate's commitments are more than he expected,' Durgan said, folding his arms across his chest. 'He's put in for a proper leave of absence.'

Wren's eyes widened. 'And you expect *me* to do it all?'

'It's different to last time, Wren.'

She shook her head and pointed to the pile in front of her. 'I'm not seeing it.'

'Well, *this time*, there'll be someone else doing *your* work, while you do Nate's.'

Her eyebrow lifted. Someone else coming in and messing with her carefully constructed and organised work? The very thought of it had her shuddering. But, admittedly, it did make taking over Nate's work a bit more appealing, since she wouldn't be doubling up again.

'For how long?' she said, attempting to remain neutral about it all.

But truth be told, she was dying a little inside. She still hadn't heard from Nate since their fight, and even though she'd found the guts to go to his place, she still hadn't found the courage to try contacting him. Sure, a text message was simple. An email, a phone call—all simple things. But there was also that niggling thought at the back of her mind that made her stomach churn. What if he didn't reply? What if he didn't pick up? His excuse about family matters might check out, but it didn't mean he wasn't avoiding her as well. And she wasn't sure she could handle rejection like that.

'For as long as it takes,' Durgan said. He sighed, dropping his hands to his side. 'I know, it's not ideal, Wren. But it's the only option. You're the only one here who knows how to do the job properly.'

She leaned back in her chair. 'I'm the only one who knows how to do *this* job, too.'

He shifted his head from side to side, as though mulling over what she'd said. 'Well, maybe it's time to train someone else in social media marketing.'

She squinted. What was he saying? 'You don't think Nate will be back?'

Durgan shrugged. 'I don't know what will happen, Wren,' he said, picking a thread at the hem of his sleeve. 'But if he doesn't, you should take his place.'

Wren swallowed. She should be happy about that. It's what she wanted, wasn't it? She'd always wanted to be the marketing manager, ever since she knew the position existed. So, why did it only make her heart sink to her stomach? Why did it make her feel like she'd never see Nate again?

'Nothing's set in stone yet, of course,' Durgan said, holding his palms out towards her. 'For now, I'm holding his position. But if he doesn't come back, it's yours.' He cleared his throat. 'Now, since we're not sure when or if he'll be back, I wanted to talk to you about that camping trip.'

Her eyebrow lifted again, and she felt her spine prickle. Camping was definitely not on her agenda. It might have been for Nate, but she knew next to nothing about it. 'What about it?' she said cautiously.

'We're going to go ahead with it,' he said. 'This weekend. Everyone was expecting it to be the weekend just gone, so this weekend will be fine. You're in charge of it.' He winked, turning to leave, but still watching her. 'Impress me.'

She wasn't sure how long after he left that she felt her body start breathing again. He wanted *her* in charge of the camping trip? *Hell*. There would certainly be no impressing happening. She felt her stomach twist into a knot. Damn Nate for suggesting it in the first place! Damn him for pulling her into it. And *damn him* for not being here. She covered her face with her hands. She couldn't do this without his help.

Damn him.

Chapter 23

Nate slid off the heaving horse and led him to the water trough, patting his neck, and pulled his phone from his pocket. He frowned at the screen. Two missed calls and a message. From Wren. He hesitated. After the episode with his mother earlier and his outburst at the top of the hill, he wasn't sure he had it in him to deal with whatever Wren had to say. He hadn't heard from her all week. Why now?

He suspected it had something to do with him telling Durgan he couldn't keep up with the work. Sure, he'd been meaning to message her, call her even. See if he could fix things between them. But he still didn't know what to say, what he needed. It was painful to admit it, but he had to prioritise. And right now, his family was his priority. Even if he'd worked hard for his job. Even if it meant keeping Wren at arm's length for a little longer. He sighed, tucking his phone into his pocket and leading Storm towards the stable.

If Wren *had* heard that he couldn't keep up with his work, it probably meant that she had to cover for him. And no doubt, she wouldn't be happy about it. But she could do it—he knew she could. And he was sure that Durgan wouldn't overwork her again. Not after their discussion about recognition. Still, Wren wouldn't be happy, and he *knew* he couldn't deal with that now. Besides, dinner would be almost ready, and he had to get Storm settled. He clipped the horse to the grooming lead and found the brush. From head to toe, he brushed the horse's hair, hoping that with every stroke, the horse would know his appreciation.

He had missed it if he was being honest. Moving away from the city meant moving away from the animals. The horses. Leo had told him that his old horse had passed away. It didn't surprise him—he was an old horse. But it would have been nice to know. Storm, however, was a descendant from his old horse. And he was just as strong and trusting— perhaps more so. He'd just finished brushing Storm and had put some grain in a bucket for him when Leo came into the stable looking for him.

'All over your little hissy fit?' Leo said, leaning against the wall.

Nate glared at his brother, closing the gate to Storm's stall behind him. He hung the harness on the hook. 'It wasn't a hissy fit.'

'Oh yeah?' Leo said, his eyebrow lifted. 'I heard a yell earlier. Funny how it really *carries* across the valley. Don't suppose you know who it was?'

He said nothing, busying himself with setting everything back to where it belonged. He hadn't thought that his yell would've been heard. And, at the time, he didn't care. But now? Knowing that his family had heard it? Well, he wasn't sure what to think.

'Thought so,' Leo said, staring at his boots as he scraped the toe along the floor. 'Ma's fine if you're wondering. Went straight back to how she usually is. Like it never happened.'

It should make him feel better, but it didn't. It wasn't his proudest moment, but what else could he do? His own mother didn't even *know* him. Maybe it would be better for everyone if he just disappeared back to the city again. And this time, not come back.

'Nate.'

He lifted his eyes to his brother. Any resentment that he thought he might have seen wasn't there. He looked weary and concerned. For him.

'I get it,' Leo continued. 'She wouldn't even talk to me for a while. Only Winnie. She'll come around, hopefully. It might just need time.'

'What if that's something we don't have?' he said.

He hadn't let himself think that until now. But there it was. The woman inside wasn't the same as the woman who he'd known growing up. The woman who'd clothed and fed him. The one inside was only a shell. And he didn't know how long they'd even have that for.

Leo nodded as though he understood. As though it was something he'd already thought about before. Then, he sighed, straightening. 'Winnie wanted me to let you know that dinner's in ten. You might want to clean up a bit.'

He felt his phone vibrating in his pocket and nodded his acknowledgement. A quick shower might make him feel a little better. At the least, a hearty meal and a good sleep would. If, of course, sleep came easy for him tonight.

'You might want to get that,' Leo said, leaving the stable.

He sighed, plucking the phone out of his pocket as it stopped calling. Wren. Again. He moved to leave the stable and head for that shower when he got a message. This time, he looked at it, seeing the first message she'd sent first.

Call me back, please.

His eyes drifted to the most recent message.

PICK UP THE DAMN PHONE!!!!

He smiled, then frowned, stopping in the shade of the huge tree near the house as his phone rang again. It must be important, he figured, if she was persistent. Still, he wasn't sure how much he could deal with. Like the sucker for punishment he was, he picked it up.

'What's up, Wren?'

'*You* are the biggest *asshole* I've ever met, you

know that?' Yep. She wasn't happy. He opened his mouth to say something, but she didn't give him the chance. 'First you don't say anything to me, then I hear from Durgan that you're dealing with *family matters*, then you bail on all your work altogether? Well, guess who has to pick up the slack, Nate? *Me*. Where the hell are you, anyway?'

'I'm at the farm.'

'What do you mean you're at the farm?' Her voice hit a pitch that was a little shrill, even for her.

'I mean I'm at the farm,' he said. 'My *parent's* farm.'

'Thought you said you weren't in touch,' she said flatly.

'I'm not,' he said. Then, corrected. 'I *wasn't*. My brother visited, needed some help with my parents—' he paused, frowning. 'Did you call just to give me a grilling, Wren, or do you actually have a point?'

There was silence at the other end, only briefly, then he heard her sigh. 'Durgan wants me to cover your work while you're away, and I wondered if—if you … planned … on coming back.'

He leaned against the tree for support, staring at the farmhouse in front of him. 'I don't know, Wren,' he said softly.

There was another pause, and when she spoke, he could have sworn it sounded a little shaky. 'I see,' she muttered. 'Well, you should probably know that Durgan's lined me up to take your job if you don't.'

He nodded but realised she couldn't see. 'You deserve it,' he said, feeling something stick in his throat.

'I know, but,' she whispered. He heard her sniff. 'Maybe I ... maybe I don't want it.'

He bit his cheek, reading between the lines. He knew she wanted his job. She'd made it clear when he started. And even told him she'd worked hard for it that first night they were together. There was no way in hell that she didn't want it now. Unless it was the fact that her having the job meant he wasn't going to be there. Somehow, he couldn't believe that either.

'Of course you want it,' he said, noticing the flatness in his tone. 'You worked hard for it.'

'But it's not the same,' she whispered.

He nodded again. He understood. Of course he understood. Priorities change. And they can change quickly. His did. Perhaps hers had, too.

'Durgan ... umm ... he wants to go ahead with the camping trip,' she said hesitantly. He felt his brow pull together. 'He postponed it to start with since it's your thing, but he wants to do it this weekend.'

So, that's why she was calling. She thought he should know since it was his project. But in all honesty, *that* was just a ploy to spend more time with her. The facts he'd presented to Durgan were true. The facts being his intention was not.

'I'm not going to be pissed about it, if that's what you're checking, Wren.'

She scoffed. 'I don't give a damn about how you feel about it, Nate. *I'm* freaking out.'

He frowned. 'Why?'

'Because he wants *me* to take over. I don't know anything about camping! How am I supposed to organise it?' She paused, her voice sounding stronger when she spoke again. 'I blame you, Nate. I told you it wasn't a good idea. But *nooo*, you didn't listen to me, did you?'

His lips pulled to the side. 'You'll be fine,' he said. 'Everything's already sorted. It's all in the top drawer of my desk. You don't need anything else. It's all there.' He paused to hear her sigh. It sent a pulse through his body, but he had to ignore it. 'You've got this, Wren.'

'You're sure?' she said softly.

'It's broken down enough that an eight-year-old will understand. You'll be fine.'

She sighed. 'Thanks, Nate.' Even through the phone, he heard her shaky breath. 'Are you … umm—'

He half-expected her to ask him again if he was coming back. And he'd readied himself with the same response as before. But that's not what she asked.

'—is everything okay? With your parents, I mean.'

He snapped his mouth closed and waved to Leo standing in the front doorway. He wouldn't have time for a shower, now, it seemed. But he'd almost give anything to hear her voice a minute longer. But at the same time, he knew it would near on kill him.

'I don't—' he started, sighing. 'No, not really. But I can't talk right now, Wren. Dinner's ready.'

'Oh.' She sounded disappointed. And he wasn't

sure it was because of the first part he'd said. When she spoke again, she spoke so quietly he'd almost missed it. 'And with … us?'

He felt his chest clench, the lump in his throat growing bigger. 'I don't know, Wren. I—I've got a lot going on at the moment—'

She sniffed again. *Damn it*. 'Nah, I get it,' she muttered.

He sighed, feeling the burn in his throat as he spoke. *Priorities*. He had to remember that. Right now, his mother needed him most. His family. He hadn't been there for them for years, and he wasn't going to neglect them now. Even if it tore his heart right out of his chest.

'I need time, Wren,' he managed, lifting his eyes upwards to look at the fading sunlight between the leaves. He felt a chill through his bones, and he refused to think it was from the breeze that had picked up.

'I get it,' she repeated, her voice changing. She was shutting him out, he could feel it. But he was the only one to blame for that.

'Wren—'

'No, you need time,' she repeated, her voice shaky, distant. 'Enjoy your dinner, Nate.'

He wished he could take the words back, tell her that he wanted to jump in the car and hightail it back to see her. But he couldn't. He was at the point where he had to choose between his family, or a maybe. He couldn't have both. And he was already at his family's place.

Either way, she didn't give him the chance to say anything, because the second after she'd said his name, she was gone.

He pinched the bridge of his nose between his thumb and forefinger and took a deep breath. Then, he headed for the outside tap and splashed some cool water on his face. Although it made his body feel more refreshed, it did nothing for his insides. He went inside, seating himself at the table and bowed his head while Leo said grace. When he lifted his head, muttering an *amen*, and everyone else did the same, he hadn't expected to see his mother standing near the table, her hands twisted together.

No one had.

'Ma?' Leo prompted. 'Everything okay?'

Her eyes flicked towards Winifred, then to Leo, to Danny, then finally, to Nate. Then, down at the roast in the middle of the table. 'I was hungry,' she said hesitantly, swiping at a loose hair falling over her eye. 'And the roast … smelled good.'

'Do you want some, Ma?' Winifred said, easing out of her seat, her hand resting on her lower back for support.

Nate wondered how much Winifred really did for this family, how much she sacrificed. She should be enjoying her pregnancy, not carrying the weight of the world on her shoulders.

'Please,' Ma said, resting her hand on Winifred's shoulder, easing her back into the seat. 'I can get my own plate.'

'You sure, Ma?' Winifred said, her brows pulled

together. Something was different, even Nate could see it.

Ma nodded, grabbing a plate from the cupboard, and coming back to the table. All eyes were on her, waiting, watching.

'Help yourself, Ma,' Leo said, waving his hand towards the roast.

Ma's eyes flickered across the table again, back to Nate. He didn't dare to speak. There was a look in her eyes as she looked at him. The kind of look a mother might give a child she wanted to hold, crossed with an apology, hesitant, like she, herself, was stuck at a crossroads.

'Ma?' Leo prompted.

Her eyes drifted around the table again. 'I was thinking maybe … maybe I could … eat here … tonight.'

'You want to … to join us?' Winifred said, her eyes glistening.

Ma nodded. 'I wanted to eat with my son,' she said, looking at Leo. Then, she smiled at Nate. 'Both of them.'

He couldn't describe the feeling, the wave that washed over him. It was as though he couldn't hold the tears back anymore, except there were none. But instead, it came out as a smile. He pulled out the empty seat next to him and waited for his mother to sit down.

'What changed?' he said as she loaded some roast onto her plate.

'I skipped those horrid meds,' she said.

'Ma,' Leo said, shaking his head. He didn't look surprised.

'Oh, they tasted terrible anyway,' she said, waving her hand. 'But I started to think. And it didn't make sense that my boy was dead. And I thought of you.' She turned to Nate and cupped his cheek with her hand. 'And I wondered how I couldn't see it before. You're my son. *Of course* you're my son!' Her eyes welled up.

He felt the back of his eyes burn, his throat tightening. 'Ma,' he said, putting his arm around her.

She leaned into him, and the first time in as many years, he held his mother. And he didn't have to worry about her not recognising him, not knowing him. Because somehow—by some *miracle*—she did. And the moment might have been perfect. It almost was. But he couldn't help but think that the only way it could *truly* be perfect, was if Wren was sitting at that table as well. But he might have messed up any chance of that happening.

Chapter 24

'You look like you're having fun.'

Wren rolled her eyes at her best friend and tried poking the tent pole through the loops. 'Have I mentioned how much I hate Nate?'

Kassandra's eyes glinted. 'Mmm,' she hummed. 'Many times in the last week.' She leaned closer and winked. 'But I know you don't mean it.'

Wren sighed. Of course, she didn't *really* mean it. But this whole thing would have been a hell of a lot easier if he was there. She squatted down to slot the pole onto the pin, only to have the other end of the pole spring free on the other side. She groaned, dropping onto the ground, and folding her legs in front of her.

'Well, I really mean it now.' She waved her hand

towards the impossible tent that she'd managed to borrow off her dad specifically for this stupid camping trip. 'He's the one that suggested this trip and he's not even here. I don't even know how to set up a stupid tent.'

'You've never been camping before?' Kassandra said.

She frowned at her friend. 'You have?'

'Uhh, yeah,' Kassandra said, as though it was obvious. 'Pretty sure everyone's been camping at least once in their life.'

'Not me,' Wren muttered, picking up a dry leaf from the ground next to her.

'Seriously?' Kassandra said, propping her hands on her hips. 'How did you manage to avoid it?'

Wren shrugged, shredding the leaf until all that was left was the mangled stem. She sighed, dropping the stem to the ground, and glanced up at her friend again. 'Help me?'

Kassandra laughed, nodding. She lifted up the other end of the pole and indicated for Wren to grab her end. 'You know, this is probably the easiest tent design to set up. *Ever*.'

Wren scoffed. 'Well, then, I'm screwed.'

'Eww,' Kassandra said, pulling a disgusted face.

Wren rolled her eyes. Miraculously, it didn't take long for them to set the tent up together. And though she was still worried that the blasted thing might fall apart on top of her, it was certainly a whole lot better than she could have done on her own.

She realised now that she hadn't been so worried about the trip before because she knew Nate would have been there. It was *his* project, after all. He'd planned everything and had it all written down in a way that even a kid would understand. It was almost like he'd ... expected ... that he wouldn't be there. She took a shaky breath, pushing the thought aside. Nate hadn't expected not to be at the camping trip. He couldn't have. She had been convinced that he'd originally planned it to try to force them to spend time together. And the thing with his family? He wouldn't have lied about that, right?

But deep down, as much as she wanted to believe him and trust that his intentions were sincere, she still found it hard to trust it was real. That his intentions with *her* were real. And now, he said he needed *time*. Time! Sure, even if the things going on with his family were real—which, surely, he wouldn't have lied about—how much *time* would he need? They'd barely started anything. They *hadn't* started anything. Not really. And he needed *time*? For what, exactly? To work out what they didn't have? To decide whether he was still even remotely interested in her?

And what, exactly, was she hoping for?

She kicked a log as she walked, trying to decide if it would make good firewood and if it would be light enough for her to carry back. It rolled to the side and she smiled in satisfaction. It'd be light enough to carry. Perhaps this camping thing wasn't going to be so difficult after all. She bent down and picked up the log, realising she'd underestimated its weight. She could still carry it, but she was just about certain that even a leaf more would make her topple over. She turned back and took some slow steady steps towards the campsite, smiling when Kassandra started bouncing towards her.

'Need a han—' Kassandra started. Then, her eyes widened and her face paled. 'Wren, don't move!'

She frowned, stopping with one foot in the air. 'Why?' She felt herself wobble.

'*Don't move*,' Kassandra repeated, her eyes dropping to something on the ground. She wobbled again. 'Stay perfectly *still*.'

'I'm trying!' she yelled, wondering what the hell was going on.

Was this some kind of joke of Kassandra's? Seeing how long she could balance on one foot with a heavy log in her arms? She felt herself tipping off balance and planted her foot on the ground. She felt something slam against her leg and figured she must have whacked it directly on a stick. She was starting to wish she'd worn jeans—surely that wouldn't have hurt as much if her legs were covered. The look on Kassandra's face told her there was something else.

'*Snake*, Wren!' she said. 'Stay still.'

She felt her heart racing. Stay *still*? When there was a *snake* at her feet? Like hell she was going to do that! In what seemed like a self defence reaction, she dropped the log and jumped backwards in time to see the snake strike at the log. Then, once the log hit the ground, the snake turned and slithered away. It wasn't until the snake was out of sight that she realised she'd stopped breathing. She took in a deep breath, relieved that she was no longer in danger, and started walking towards Kassandra.

'Why would you tell me to stay still when there's a *snake*?' she said, frustrated, her chest heaving with her deep breaths.

'That's what you're supposed to do,' Kassandra said, her eyes dropping to Wren's leg. 'Wren, you're bleeding.'

Wren glanced down at her leg that had started to pulse. Sure enough, there was blood. 'Stupid stick,' she groaned, reaching down to wipe the blood away. 'I hit my leg when I put my foot down.'

Kassandra grabbed Wren's hand before she could wipe the blood away and she crouched to look at the wound. She swore under her breath and Wren's heart started pounding again. 'It's not a stick, Wren,' she said. 'It's a bite.'

'A—as in a—a *snake* bite?' She started feeling light headed. God, was she mad at Nate right now. Who even *suggests* going camping for a work trip? If he hadn't, she wouldn't be *here* getting bitten by a *snake*!

'*Yes,* a snake bite,' Kassandra said, standing upright. 'Just stay calm.'

'How can I stay calm?' she shrieked.

'You *have* to,' Kassandra scolded. She called out to one of their colleagues nearby to get the medical kit, but Wren wasn't sure what else was being said. All she could hear was her pulse pounding in her ear and she was becoming increasingly aware of the bite on her leg.

'What was it?' she whispered.

'A snake,' Kassandra said, her brow furrowed as she focussed back on her.

'What *kind*?'

'A brown, I think.'

'Are they … venomous?'

Wren focussed on the concerned look on her friend's face. Kassandra nodded. Yes, that was a yes. She'd been bitten by a *venomous snake* and it was all Nate's fault! Damn him for making her do this alone.

Damn him.

***

Nate smiled as his mother waved to him from the porch. She took her hat off and went inside. Things had been going well the past week. His mother was improving—slowly, but surely. At least she knew who he was now. And that he wasn't dead. She still had a lot of strength to rebuild, but she'd started helping Winifred around the house. She'd even requested that Nate build her a garden bed not far from the house—she wanted to grow vegetables again. It was all a start.

And things weren't so bad with his father, either. Since Ma started joining them for meals again and started looking like she was improving, it was as though something softened in Danny. He'd started to smile. Something he was sure he hadn't done for a long time, judging by the look on Leo's face when he saw it. They'd started talking more. They were on the mend. He was sure there were still some hard feelings there—those would take time. But they would have that.

He plucked his phone from his pocket and saw five missed calls from Wren. He sighed. Wasn't she supposed to be at that camping trip? Maybe Durgan postponed it again. Wouldn't be so bad, really. He liked camping, and it would be a shame if he missed that trip. Still, he hadn't heard from Wren since he'd asked her for time. *Time*. And why the hell did he do that? Perhaps because he hadn't quite worked out what he was going to do. The obvious thing would be to go back home where his life was. But there was that part of him that wondered if the same thing would happen if he left again—that his mother's health would deteriorate, he'd lose contact. Just because things were looking up with his family for now, that didn't mean it would stay that way if he left again.

But it wasn't just his life back home. Wren was there.

And he had feelings for her. Feelings he hadn't had for anyone—not even for Winifred. And he hadn't managed to stop thinking about Wren, despite their fight, despite what she'd said. Despite him asking for time. And how could he ignore something that was impossible to ignore?

And while that space in his heart that had been empty for years slowly filled the more time he spent with his family, another part of it emptied. A part that he suspected only Wren could fill. But he had to be sure. He had to regain the strength to resume chasing her if he was going to do that. Because he was also sure that she wasn't going to make it any easier on him.

What Winifred had said made sense—that Wren might have lashed out because she was scared. But he also suspected that if that were the case, then she was unlikely to change her mind over the course of a couple weeks. Especially with how they left things.

He wiped the sweat from his brow with the back of his hand and sipped some water from his drink bottle—it was, as he'd thought, easier to work around the farm since he bought it. He stabbed the shovel into the ground and rested his elbow on it, looking at the freshly dug garden bed with pride. It was good that Ma wanted to grow things again. It was progress. From what Leo and Winifred had told him, she hadn't touched the garden bed that she'd once immaculately kept since he left for the Gold Coast. The thought that she'd been on a downward spiral since then …

Nate took a shaky breath and tipped some of his water onto his head, enjoying the temporary cool relief it provided. He might not have been there for her then, but he was here now. And he wasn't going to leave until he knew everything was going to be okay. Until he was absolutely certain that Ma wouldn't go downhill again and that his father wouldn't cut off all communication again. He wanted to see his niece when she's born.

A niece. He wasn't supposed to know the gender—no one was. But Leo—the sappy sod—couldn't stand Winifred's desire for it to be a surprise and secretly asked the sonographer to tell him. He hadn't told anyone—until Nate, when he accidentally let it slip. He imagined a little dark-haired, brown-eyed girl like Winifred had been. No doubt, she would look just like her mother had. He smiled. He'd always thought he'd make a good uncle. When he was cut off from his family, he never thought he'd get the chance. And now, he could.

His phone started ringing again and he glanced at the name on the screen, wondering if Wren was still trying to call him and why she would be trying to call him so much on a weekend. Surely, she couldn't have thought of something else to bite his ear off about. He breathed a sigh of relief to see his best friend's name instead of hers, but at the same time, he felt a little … disappointed. He wasn't *trying* to avoid her like it would be coming across as. But at the same time, he worried that if he heard her voice again, he'd be jumping into his car and speeding back to see her.

Damn.

This trip did nothing for sorting out *that* part of his life. He answered the call.

'What's up, man?'

'Where the hell are you?'

He frowned, wiping the droplets of water from his forehead before they mixed with his sweat and he had a waterfall coming down his face. 'You're joking, right? I'm at my parents' place, you know that.'

Russ swore, and Nate's frown deepened. He heard a woman's voice—Kassandra's, if he guessed correctly—say something to Russ and heard Russ's muffled reply. Russ sighed. 'Dude, Kass is pissed you didn't answer her calls.'

He lifted his gaze up towards the house, waving a hand as Leo paused to look at him. 'Kass didn't call me.' In fact, he was sure she didn't even have his number. Why would she need to?

He heard Kassandra's voice again. 'Ahh, she called from Wren's phone,' Russ said slowly.

She called from … 'What's going on, Russ?' he said, feeling his chest tighten. The calls from Wren— they weren't from her. So, why were they from her phone? Unless … 'Is Wren okay?'

'Not … particularly,' Russ said slowly.

Nate felt his pulse quicken, and the farmhouse started to seem a whole lot further away than it did before. 'What do you mean?' he said, his voice growing a little louder with each word. '*Damn it,* Russ! What the *hell* happened?'

'Wren got … bitten. By a snake.'

He heard Russ continue telling him something about the camping trip and Kassandra trying to call him to let him know—he couldn't quite be sure. He felt the blood drain from his face. They went through with the camping trip. And Wren got bitten by a snake. And it was his damn fault. *Damn it!* If he'd been there ... He felt the fist in his chest again, wrapping around his heart and squeezing it hard.

'Where is she?' He was well aware it sounded more like a demand than a question, but he knew Russ would understand.

'In hospital—'

'Which *one*?'

Russ told him while he yanked the shovel from the ground and walked quickly towards the shed to put it away. God, if anything happened to Wren, he wasn't sure he could forgive himself. *Something already had*. He pushed the thought aside. If he'd been there, on the trip, with her, she wouldn't have been bitten, he knew it in his heart.

He knew where snakes would likely be hiding. He knew to scan the surroundings consistently. If he'd been there, she would have been safe, damn it! And now, she was laying in a hospital bed, venom coursing through her body, and he wasn't *there*. He swore. He knew he couldn't have everything—he'd always known it. But God, why did this have to be his fault, too?

'I'll be there as soon as I can.'

He hung up his phone and closed the shed door behind him, racing towards the house. His bag wouldn't take long to pack—a few minutes, tops. Then, he'd be on his way home. He sped through the hallway until he came to his room and shoved everything he could into his duffel bag. He'd go straight there—straight to the hospital to see her. To hold her. If anything happened before then, he didn't know what he'd do. But he couldn't think of that possibility. He just had to trust that she was strong—strong enough to fight the venom, to survive. To hold on, for him. He wouldn't stop driving until he was there, holding her in his arms, making sure she was safe.

He paused, glancing down at his clothes. He couldn't go to the hospital like this—covered in dirt, his shirt soaked with sweat. He grabbed a fresh shirt from the stash of clothes he'd just shoved into his duffel bag and swapped it with the one he was wearing. His thoughts drifted to Ma and his family. How could he just leave them behind again? So suddenly, when things were going well. When things were improving. That was just it—they were *improving*. They were on the road to being good again, but they weren't there *yet*.

He zipped up the bag and rested his hand on it, squeezing his eyes shut. He couldn't leave yet. Not, when they were so close.

But, Wren.

Wren.

She needed him. Heck, even if she didn't, he needed *her*. He needed to know she was okay. He needed to see for himself.

'Leaving so soon?'

Nate slung the bag over his shoulder, his decision made and turned towards his brother. His father was standing behind Leo, and Nate knew that look. It was the same look he'd given him when he first left.

'I have to,' he said, feeling the fist tighten around

his heart, squeezing it to a pulp. 'Wren needs me.'

Danny scoffed, turning back down the hallway, shaking his head. 'A *girl*. You'll leave your family for years but you're happy to go running back to some girl—'

'She's not *some girl*, Dad,' he said, pushing into the hallway to face his father. 'She's *my* girl.'

Danny scoffed again. 'And how serious can it be, huh? It's not like you've spent your whole trip here with your phone glued to your ear.'

He waved his finger between them, his other hand gripping the straps of the duffel bag. 'No, we're not doing this. I came back to fix things, to make sure Ma was all right. I *have* to go back now. Wren's in hospital, and I—I ... I don't want the last words I ever said to her to be asking her for *time*.'

He felt a hand rest on his other shoulder. 'Why's she in hospital?' Leo said.

He gave a quick run down of what happened— well, basically everything he could remember Russ telling him while his head had felt like it was going to explode. And he was sure that his father's expression had softened—ever so slightly—as he explained. But he didn't want to get his hopes up. He wasn't sure he could really trust any of his observations in this state.

'You have to go.' He turned towards the soft voice to see Ma and Winifred standing behind him, listening to the whole story.

'Ma,' he said apologetically. 'I'm sorry.'

She shook her head. 'No, don't apologise. Of course you have to go!' She turned her focus to her husband. 'And shame on you for making him feel guilty.' Danny's mouth dropped open, but he said nothing. Ma lifted her hands to cup Nate's face. 'Go to your girl, Nate. And make sure you bring her home to us. Because a girl who manages to capture my son's heart must be a special kind of lady.'

He felt the backs of his eyes prickle and pulled his mother in for a hug. Then, he said his farewells—for now, not forever—and headed towards the car, his mind and heart set on one thing.

Wren.

He tossed his bag onto the back seat and opened the front door, pausing with one foot in the car when he heard his dad's voice.

'Son.'

He turned towards Danny, his foot still in the car.

Danny folded his arms across his chest and took a deep breath. 'I should apologise.'

He waited a moment, in case Danny had anything else to say, then nodded when nothing else was said. He always knew his dad had an odd way of apologising. 'Me too,' he said simply.

Danny pressed his lips together in a look that was halfway between stopping himself from crying and ... pride? Unless that was simply Nate's imagination again.

'Come home soon, eh?' Danny said, relaxing his arms beside him, his fists clenching and unclenching—a habit Nate had grown used to when he was young. It was what Danny did when he wasn't quite sure what to do with his hands. It was also something Nate had caught himself doing in similar situations. 'And next time,' Danny added. 'Bring her, won't you? Otherwise, Ma will have my hide.'

Nate nodded again, smiling. 'I will.'

He wasn't going to settle for less.

Chapter 25

'What do you mean she won't see me?'

'I mean exactly that,' the nurse said, flicking through some paperwork, looking like he was taking up her precious time. 'She has specifically requested that no *Nate Hoffman* should be allowed in. But I assure you, she's on the mend.'

Damn it. He knew he shouldn't have told her his name. The damned wench had thought ahead— *clearly,* she hadn't taken well to him asking for time. He pushed off the reception bench and turned back towards the door. She must have been in the biggest hospital he'd ever seen—one he didn't know his way around. Even if he wanted to, he wouldn't be able to find her.

So, this was it.

There was nothing he could do except wait.

And he'd rushed home to see her, pushing himself to get to the hospital before the end of visiting hours.

And she won't see him.

Bloody stubborn woman.

At least he knew she was okay. And if she'd told the nurses she didn't want to see him, that meant he had no chance of getting in through Kassandra. *Damn it*. He'd have to find another way.

And he wasn't going to give up until he did.

***

Wren walked slowly along the beach, feeling the sand between her toes, the water lapping at her feet, her sandals dangling from one hand. A week had passed since she was bitten by a snake. Who knew that some snakes lash out with a warning bite first before they attacked with venom? The bite was barely visible anymore, but she still felt weary. Or perhaps that was all the work she'd been doing catching up to her. She hadn't had time off work in … well, ever. And because of this incident, Durgan made her take the week off work.

The nurses had told her that Nate came to visit her in hospital. She didn't know what to think. Kassandra had already given her a heads up that they'd let him know. She was mad, at first, that's why she told the nurses not to let him in if he came. She didn't expect that he would. And when they told her he had come, she was almost ready to retract her statement. Except that she suddenly felt … embarrassed. She didn't want him to see her in a groggy state, not after the way they'd left things. Not after only being able to think about one thing between being bitten and knowing she was going to be okay.

Nate.

And how she wished she could see him again. That she didn't want things to end the way they'd left it. The very thought of dying before feeling his touch, his kiss, again almost killed her.

But when she found out he'd come back to see her, her mind filled with questions and what ifs, and she'd grown totally confused with it all.

On one hand, she was grateful that Durgan made her take the week off. It gave *her* time to think. But on the other hand, the time didn't help. Not when her thoughts got her nowhere. He tried calling her a couple times that first day after he'd tried to visit her. But then? Nothing. And she was really starting to worry she'd never see him again.

Perhaps it would be better that way, even if her ego was bruised, and her heart ached for the foreseeable future.

She sighed, glancing around her as the sun started to set. It was a beautiful sight, watching the orange and yellows of the sunset stretching across the water. She saw a figure up ahead—a man—bent over. He looked like he was drawing something in the sand, though he might have been picking something up. Her gaze didn't linger, and she continued scanning the beach. Where the hell was Kassandra? She was supposed to be meeting her somewhere here and, once again, she was late.

Her being bitten had somehow pulled Kassandra and Russ back together, even though Kassandra had been avoiding him. At least someone got some benefit out of her near-death experience. She wished it had provided at least some clarification for herself.

Her gaze drifted back to the man as she neared him. She could now see a stick in his hand as he dragged it through the dirt. She wondered what he was drawing, whether he was an artist playing with a new medium, or just someone who was bored. Did he have a purpose in what he was doing?

She watched as a wave came in and washed away half of his drawing. It didn't seem to faze him. He watched the wave go back into the sea and went straight back into fixing up his drawing. She wondered what the point was. If it was her drawing, she would have given up once the wave washed it away. But not this man. He was determined to keep going with it regardless of how damaged it got. It was as though he wanted it to stay there, and he was going to keep drawing it until it did.

He'd be there a long time.

He finished off another stroke with the stick and straightened. The lighting wasn't that great, now that the sun had dropped further, but she saw it. The broad shoulders, the way his hair was tussled by the wind, the same length as …

He turned towards her and felt her breath catch when she saw his smile.

Nate.

She felt her heart quicken and her breath catch, but though she told herself to stop, her body didn't listen until she was standing only a few feet away from him.

'Wren,' he said simply, lightly. 'I'm glad you came.'

Her brow furrowed and she tucked her hair behind her ear as the wind picked up. 'How did you—' she started. Then, she realised. 'Kass,' she whispered.

Of course, it was Kassandra! She was the only person who *really* knew how Wren felt about Nate. Now Kassandra's evasive messages made sense. She'd helped Nate set up a chance to talk to her— and after she'd said she didn't want to see him! And here she thought it was because she was back with Russ, taking things *slow*—or their version of it.

She saw him squint. 'You're not mad, are you?'

She probably should be. But she wasn't sure if it was the sea breeze, or the ambience, or the reflection of the sunset in his kind grey eyes that soothed her. She shook her head slowly. Another wave lapped at their feet and he glanced briefly at the ground behind him, then back at her, lifting the stick. He gave her a look that she couldn't interpret. Then, he turned, dropped to the ground, and dragged the stick through the sand.

'What are you doing?' she said, not taking her

eyes off the back of his head. How she longed to dive her fingers through his hair and see if it felt the same way she remembered it.

'You know, I came to a realisation while I was away,' he said, continuing to drag the stick through the sand. All she could see was part of a curve, his body blocked the rest. 'I had a lot of time to think.'

About what to draw in the sand? 'Oh yeah?' she said, craning her neck to peer over his shoulder.

He rose before she could see anything and faced her again, lifting his eyebrow at their closeness. Funny, she didn't recall moving closer to him. Though, now that she thought about it, she must have.

'Mhmm,' he hummed, clearly amused. She folded her arms across her chest, pulling her light poncho tighter around her to keep her warm. 'I'm glad you're okay.'

She nodded. 'Me too,' she whispered, then, cleared her throat. 'What did you … umm … realise?' She rose to stand on her toes, hoping to get a glimpse of what he was doing, but he moved his body so she couldn't see. His eyes were dancing. The bastard found this whole thing amusing when all she wanted to know was what he was doing for so long.

'I realised that I missed you,' he admitted, shrugging one shoulder. 'A lot. I would have been back sooner, but Ma wasn't well.'

She felt her brow furrow and her heart skip a beat at the same time. 'Is everything okay?'

He nodded. 'It is now. And we all cleared the air.

So, I guess you could say I'm part of the family again.'

'That's good, though, right?' He nodded. 'I'm happy it's worked out,' she added, dropping her gaze to his chin. She swallowed, remembering the feel of his bristles rubbing against the palm of her hand. Against her cheek. And elsewhere. She felt her cheeks heat and brought her gaze back to his eyes. He was studying her with an intensity that made her stomach flip.

'What I realised was that I was missing something all along.'

His family—of course, it was his family. 'And now you have it?'

He shook his head slowly. 'Not quite.'

Another gust of wind dishevelled her hair again, but this time, his hand beat hers. His thumb lingered against her cheek and she closed her eyes, memorising his touch, her heart aching for more, knowing they were probably too far gone. His hand dropped and he cleared his throat.

'I was looking up at the stars back home and thought about what you said last time we were here,' he continued, sighing. *Oh, no*. She remembered clearly what she'd said—that it wasn't going to happen, and she wanted him to forget that night. She'd wished she could have taken it all back. 'When you said we were … *written in the sand*. Remember that?'

She nodded, feeling her eyes burn. She wanted to take it back, she wanted him to forget she'd ever said that. She didn't want him to forget their night together. Heck, she couldn't forget it herself. No matter how hard she tried. And, believe her, she'd tried.

'You weren't at work,' he said pointedly.

She felt her eyebrows pull together. 'N—no, I— Durgan gave me the week off.' What the hell was going on with him? He was jumping all over the place. And she wasn't sure if he realised it or not. His eyes flickered with that amusement again, and something else she didn't quite catch, though she'd seen it there before. It sent something rolling in her belly.

'Good,' he said, watching as another wave rolled in. This time, it reached her ankles. She wobbled a little as the wave receded and shifted her weight to regain her footing. 'You deserve it, you know,' he continued, dropping back to redraw whatever it was he was drawing in the sand. 'Time off work. You work too hard. Shame it was forced upon you, though.'

She shifted her gaze towards the sea, watching as the sunlight on the water started to dim. There was something that sunsets at a beach offered— something healing for the soul. She shifted her gaze back to him only to find him standing up again, studying her. His brow was creased.

'I should have been there,' he said, holding her gaze.

She told herself to look away, but she couldn't. His eyes were holding hers captive. She swallowed. There were worse fates, no doubt. Especially since this one was quite … enchanting. 'At work?' she said, a little behind in the conversation, it seemed.

'At the camping trip.' He lifted a hand and brushed his thumb against her cheek again, tracing a fiery path. 'If I'd been there ... if I'd ... you might not have been bitten.'

She swallowed again, the lump in her throat growing. 'Someone else might have.'

He shrugged. 'But *you* would be safe.'

'You can't promise that.'

'I can.'

She blinked a few times and felt her body take in a deep shaky breath. Heck, all of her felt like she was vibrating, and her cheeks had grown hot. She finally managed to break her gaze free and looked somewhere behind him. 'What were you ... umm ... what were you doing? With the sand. And the stick.'

His hand dropped from her cheek. 'I was ... ahh ... making a point.'

Her eyes shot back towards him, involuntarily, quizzically. 'I don't ... understand.'

His lips tilted upwards on one side and it made her breath catch. 'So, I was looking at the stars, right?' he started.

She frowned. Again, with the all over the place! He didn't seem to notice the change in her expression.

'And I thought about what you said,' he continued. '*Written in the sand.* And I wondered what the opposite of that would be.' He spread his arms out as though it were obvious. 'Written in the stars, of course. Which is really beside the point.'

She squinted at him. *Where*, exactly, was he going with this?

'Because, you know, it's really impossible to write something in the stars.'

She shook her head, closing her eyes for a moment. 'It's a figure of speech,' she whispered. 'Things written in the stars means it's fate. In the sand means it's temporary. It wa—'

'Washes away with the next tide,' he said. 'I know. You told me.' He sighed, steadying his thoughts, it seemed, and lifted her hand, silently demanding that she look at him. She did. How could she not? 'But what if it wasn't? Temporary, I mean.'

She shook her head, not following. He sighed, his eyes drifting towards the sea. Then, he shifted, so she could see what he'd drawn. A simple heart. And four letters, paired in twos—*WK* and *NH*—separated by a plus sign. She felt the sharp inhale when she realised it was their initials.

'You said we're written in the sand,' he repeated. 'And that that meant we wouldn't work out.' He tugged on her hand until she looked up at him again. 'I refuse to believe that.'

'Nate,' she whispered, not sure what to say. Not sure what he was getting at, exactly.

'I can't write our names in the stars, Wren,' he said. 'Even if I think it was a hell of a lot more than a coincidence meeting you. But I *can* write our names here, in the sand.'

She dropped her gaze back to the heart in the sand and watched as it washed away with the next tide, dashing her dreams, proving her point. Her eyes prickled with threatening tears. 'And when that happens?' she said, her voice shaking. 'When it washes away?'

Chapter 26

He lifted the stick, his lips flicking up into a mischievous grin, and he bent down, dragging the stick through the sand until the picture was there again. Then, he rose, holding her gaze, standing a little closer than before.

'Then, I'll write it again,' he said, his voice low, resonating through her. 'And again. And I'll keep writing it until it stays.'

'It'll never stay,' she said, a tear spilling from her eye.

He shrugged, wiping the tear away with one of his knuckles. 'Then, I'll never stop writing it.'

Before she could protest any more, his hand slid to the back of her head and his lips were on hers. Tender, at first, in a moment that seemed to make time stop. His lips were exactly as she'd remembered them, only there was something else there, too. Something that made her heart ache, made her want to press her body against his, but at the same time, she felt like she couldn't move. Every thought, all the confusion that was in her mind, the battle going on between her head and her heart—it all settled. It was as though her mind got wiped clean the more his lips moved against hers. Everything she'd worried about, everything that didn't make sense before, suddenly made sense now.

After what seemed like both an eternity and only a few seconds, he broke the kiss, pulling back only enough to let the last of the sunlight shine on her face. And on his. She could see the certainty in his eyes, no hesitation, no fear. No worries. And it both terrified her and excited her.

'I love you, Wren,' he whispered, his words washing over her as though they'd been shouted. 'And I fell for you the second I looked into those two incredible oceans you call eyes.' She felt her lips part, and for the life of her, she couldn't say anything. 'You don't have to say it back if you're not ready,' he added, rolling his thumb across her cheek in a manner that sent a spark shooting to her core. 'But I want you to know that I do. Love you.'

She willed herself to speak. The words were right there—*I love you, too*. She just had to somehow join up the broken wires between her head and her heart and her mouth. It was simple. *I love*—

'What about Durgan?' *Damn it.* Wrong wires.

He frowned. 'What about him?'

'Our jobs, if … if he found out about … us.'

His lips curved higher, more mischievous than before. 'So, you admit there's an us?'

'I don—our jobs are at stake.'

'No. No, they're not.'

'You can't be sure.'

'I can.'

'How?' She felt her heart quickening. Nate had just confessed he *loved* her—that he *still* loved her—and she was rambling about Durgan?

'Because he knows what's good for him.'

'But—'

His lips were on hers again, silencing her with another tantalising kiss. Just as well, she was going down the one path that would ruin the most romantic gesture she'd ever seen. When his lips left hers again, she was well and truly dazed, intoxicated by him—his taste, his smell. Him. Nate. Her Nate. And suddenly, it wasn't so hard.

'I—I love you, too,' she whispered, watching as his smile reached his kind, mischievous, promising eyes. So promising. And she knew what some of those promises entailed.

***

Nate dropped his keys on the hall table and kicked off his shoes, Wren doing the same. They hadn't said a word since they'd reached his house, but, in a way, he didn't feel like they needed to. Her eyes said it all.

The way she looked at him, her eyes darkening to a tempting shade of blue. If she was nervous, he could understand why.

The last time she was in his place, she'd drunkenly thrown herself at him. The time before that, they'd drunkenly slept together. Tonight, they were totally and completely sober.

He glanced towards her and saw the blush creep onto her face. He smiled. A movie—that's what they'd planned to do. Watch a movie. Take things slow. Starting again. Now they were here, he didn't feel much like a movie. He moved to the kitchen and went to flick the kettle on, his eyes drifting to the bottle of whisky that had managed to make its way back to his bench. He lifted it, wiggling it a little to get Wren's attention.

'Whisky?' he said.

She hesitated—only briefly, he noticed—then, she sighed. Relief? 'Please,' she said, moving to rest her hands on the kitchen bench.

He grabbed two glasses from the cupboard and poured a couple fingers in each. He made his way around the bench until he was next to her, handed one glass to her, and raised his. 'To new beginnings,' he said.

They tapped their glasses together and both took a sip. Wren took another sip. He smiled again. God, this woman … How his life had changed since that first night. He placed his glass down on the bench and tucked a lock of her hair behind her ear, his fingertips tingling from the feel of the soft skin of her cheek. He could tell her breath caught from the way her lips parted, the way her chest heaved once. He heard the clink of her glass on the bench and felt her hand rest on the crook of his arm.

He searched her eyes, those two oceans that promised a whole world different to the one he'd ever imagined possible. They were dark, alluring. Wanting. Filled with one thing he *did* recognise, and it matched his—pure and utter desire. His fingers trailed her jawline and nudged her chin upwards. She swallowed, and he felt it shoot to below the belt. This woman …

'Do you really want to take things slow?' he said, his voice somewhere between a rumble and a growl.

'Hell no.'

He wasn't sure if he pulled her close, or if she met him, but their bodies slammed together in a tangle of arms. He felt the rumble at the base of his throat, and by the way she smiled against his lips, she felt it, too. He kissed her thoroughly, deeply, desperately. He needed her, needed to feel her body against his. Nothing between them. He felt her hands sliding beneath his shirt, lifting it higher. He obliged, releasing her only to pull the shirt over his head. Her hands pressed against his chest, sending that warmth shooting through him again.

He slid his hands around her waist, under her shirt, and made quick work of sweeping it over her head until they were facing each other, their chests heaving. Nothing but their pants and her bra between them.

'You're sure?' he said, surprising himself in the fact he was *panting*. But God, it was the only way he could control himself right now with this ... beautiful specimen ... right in front of him. Willing.

'Damn it, Nate,' she said, frustrated. '*Make love* with me. *Now*.'

His eyebrow lifted, his lips curving, and he took a step towards her. Then, another, until his body was pressed against hers. 'The lady asks,' he said, lowering his hands to cup her ass. 'And she shall receive.'

In one swift movement, he lifted her until she was straddling his hips and carried her to his room, lowering her to the bed. She reached for the button on his shorts, and he stilled her hands. 'You wanted *slow*,' he said.

She propped herself on her elbows. 'Didn't you hear me? I said *hell no* to slow.'

His smile deepened, and he looked into her eyes, those eyes that captured his heart the second he'd first looked into them. 'Trust me, sweetheart. For *this*, you want slow.'

She squinted, and he wondered if she knew what he was talking about. He flicked the button of her shorts undone and shimmied them—her panties, too—down her legs until they fell at the end of his bed and she was bare to him, completely naked, except for the delicate white bra she still had on. *In time*, he thought. For now ...

He leaned towards her, nudging himself between her legs, pressing his palms against her thighs until she was open to him.

'Nate—' He closed the distance. 'Ohhh …'

She flopped back against the bed, clutching the sheets with one hand, gripping onto his hair with the other as he gave her the attention they didn't have time for those first times. Licking. Sucking. Nipping. He felt her arching her body against him, pressing closer. And he felt her body tightening beneath his roaming hand as he slipped a finger inside her, moving it rhythmically. He felt the way his body responded when she cried out his name as he tipped her over the edge.

But it wasn't over.

Not by a long shot.

He helped her ride out her wave and shifted his attention to the rest of her body, bringing himself higher—kissing a trail from her center to her lips. And once again, he loved her with his mouth, kissing her, touching her, until her body was once again arching against him, wanting more. Hell, he wasn't sure he could take much longer.

'Now, please, Nate,' she whispered when his kisses trailed to her neck. '*Now*.'

If the lady asks …

He stripped his pants off, and in barely a moment, he was poised above her, willing and ready to, for the first time, *make love*—sweet, sweet love, not just sex—to the woman who changed him forever. She wrapped her legs around his hips, nudging him closer, giving her answer. He obliged, pressing his body against hers until he was where he belonged.

It was different, somehow, to the last times.

It was so much more.

And while he held her gaze as they both launched over the edge together and fell in a pile of sweat and total and utter bliss, he realised why.

It wasn't because it was slow.

Or because it was the start of something new.

It was because it was Wren—*his* Wren. His beautiful, incredible, and forever, Wren. The first and only woman he ever truly loved, and ever would. And for the first time since he'd met her, he knew she would still be there in the morning. And every morning after that, if he had his say.

Because there was no reason for her not to be.

They *were* written in the sand, after all. And he'd keep writing it until the day he died.

And after that?

He'd write it in the stars.

Books by R. J. Groves

The Bridal Shop series
Save the Date
Be My Valentine
Say You'll Be Mine

Jilted Brides series
Finding a Bride
Written in the Sand

Cities of the World series
In Paris
The Irish Maiden

Set Ups series
The Set Up

Mail Order Brides series
The Calm in the Storm
The Warmth in the Winter
The Song in the Silence

Standalones
Writing You
Two Babies Too Many
Second Chance
The Boyfriend Application
Sweeter Things
Home Bound
Stay With Me
Her First Noel
When Dreams Come True
To Fall For You

Thank you for reading! I hope you enjoyed this story as much as I did writing it.

R. J. xx